THE POISONED CHALICE MURDER

THE POISONED CHALICE MURDER

Diane Janes

This first world edition published 2018
in Great Britain and the USA by
SEVERN HOUSE PUBLISHERS LTD of
Eardley House, 4 Uxbridge Street, London W8 7SY
Trade paperback edition first published
in Great Britain and the USA 2018 by
SEVERN HOUSE PUBLISHERS LTD

British Library Cataloguing in Publication Data
A CIP catalogue record for this title is available from the British Library.

ISBN-13: 978-0-7278-8819-8 (cased)
ISBN-13: 978-1-84751-942-9 (trade paper)
ISBN-13: 978-1-78010-994-7 (e-book)

All Severn House titles are printed on acid-free paper.

Severn House Publishers support the Forest Stewardship Council™ [FSC™],
the leading international forest certification organisation.
All our titles that are printed on FSC certified paper carry the FSC logo.

MIX
Paper from
responsible sources
FSC® C013056

Typeset by Palimpsest Book Production Ltd.,
Falkirk, Stirlingshire, Scotland.
Printed and bound in Great Britain by
TJ International, Padstow, Cornwall.

ONE

'So,' said Mo. 'What it comes down to is that Tom's aunt suspects there's a killer in the congregation.'

'It sounds a bit far-fetched, doesn't it?' Fran laughed and reached up to adjust her hat, which still felt unsettled by the wind that had almost blown them into the tea shop a good ten minutes earlier.

When the two friends had planned their excursion into Ulverston several days previously, they had not anticipated that the weather would turn so spectacularly against them.

'Ah, the joys of the English weather,' Mo remarked, as they were momentarily distracted by the sight of a runaway newspaper being gusted past the rain-soaked windows. 'And when are you going to meet this eccentric aunt of Tom's?' she asked, returning to the matter in hand.

'Well, we've been meaning to fix something up for ages. You know that Tom first mentioned it before we went down to Wimbledon, but somehow things keep getting in the way. Anyway, we're going to motor down there this weekend.'

'Staying overnight?'

'Tom's aunt is putting us up. It's all very respectable.'

'My dear old thing, I never suggested for a moment that it wasn't.'

There was a slight pause before Fran said, 'I see Helen Wills has won the American National Championships, as well as Wimbledon. Poor old Phoebe Watson only picked up half-a-dozen games.'

'We hardly ever do well in the American Nationals,' said Mo. 'Our men did even worse – just Bunny Austin in the quarter-finals.'

Talk of the tennis smoothed over a potentially awkward patch, and from there they moved on to the latest world speed records. 'I don't see the point of it all myself,' Mo said. 'Though I would quite like to go up in an aeroplane, just to see what it's like to fly.'

When they had finished their tea and scones, they decided to complete their errands separately and meet back at Mo's car. Fran made her call at the post office, then headed back into the storm. It was hopeless trying to keep an umbrella the right side out. She was battling down the street towards the place where Mo had parked her car, head down and one hand restraining her hat, when a sharp voice brought her to a halt.

'Mrs Black? It's Mrs Black, isn't it?'

Fran raised her head and decided that she half recognized the woman who was glaring at her through the rain. 'Yes,' she said. 'It is. I'm sorry . . .'

'You don't recognize me, do you? I'm Winnie's sister.' The woman allowed the words to hang in the air between them for a moment, before adding, 'I just wanted to tell you that I think you're a wicked, selfish woman, Mrs Black. Wicked and selfish, that's what you are,' she repeated, before Fran had a chance to gather herself and attempt a reply. 'Forcing our Winnie to bring a child into the world without the dignity of bearing its father's name, when you could easily give Michael a divorce. Wicked, that's what it is.'

'But . . . no, wait . . .' It was too late. The woman had already marched off in the opposite direction. As Fran stood staring after her down the rain-swept street, she realized that she was shaking. She made it the few remaining yards back to Mo's car, and once inside was able to extract a handkerchief from her bag and dab at her face with it, reassuring herself that any passers-by would assume she was wiping away the raindrops. She had never been verbally attacked in the street before – out of the blue and by a virtual stranger, too. It had been horribly embarrassing, even though there had been no one else there to see it. She had never been accused of wickedness either – at least not since her mother had caught her telling fibs about the fate of some leftover birthday cake, purloined from the pantry while Cook was not around. And that had been a good twenty years ago.

It was so unfair, she thought. She had not been wicked. She was not the guilty party, Michael was. Michael *and* the wretched Winnie ('the ninny', a voice in her head could not help adding). It was they, not she, who had broken marriage vows and slunk off to live in another district, affecting to be Mr and Mrs Black when they were not, leaving her, the real Mrs Michael Black, to face the social stigma of separation. It was all very well demanding that Fran should cooperate in a divorce, but divorce was such a scandal and the disgrace hung almost equally on the wronged petitioner. Why should she put herself through the mill just to make life easier for people who had behaved so badly?

Of course, she had not known that there was going to be a child. Illegitimacy was a scandal too, and the child itself was innocent of any wrongdoing. She thought of Tom, who had married his dead brother's sweetheart in order to give the child she was carrying their family name. It had been an unsurpassed act of selfless generosity, and it had averted a family scandal too, whereas divorcing Michael would set tongues wagging in completely the opposite way.

'Fouf! Goodness but this is dreadful weather!' Mo hurled herself into the driver's seat, tossing her bag into the rear of the car in the process.

'Where's your china?'

'It hasn't come in. Some sheep-headed clerk had mixed up my order with another one, so it was a wasted journey. Why, darling what's wrong? You look really shaken. Are you feeling quite well?'

'I've had a rather unpleasant experience.' Fran told her friend about the encounter in the street.

Mo was full of indignation. 'Damn cheek,' she said, as she fired the engine into life. 'A shock too, finding out that they've got an infant on the way. I say, do you need a tot of whisky or something, to perk you up? We can easily pop into the hotel.'

'No, no. I'm perfectly all right. But Mo . . . tell me honestly, do you think she's right?'

'About the baby? I don't suppose Winnie would tell her sister unless she was sure . . .'

'No. About being selfish? Wicked, even?'

'Of course not. Oh, do get out of the way, my good man, I'm trying to turn left . . . Sorry, darling, people are such idiots, the way they stand about in the road – and in this rain, too. No, of course you're not being wicked. How can any of it possibly be your fault? Though I do wonder if you mightn't divorce the wretch for your own sake.'

'The scandal would kill my mother – and anyway, what possible good would it do me?'

'You'd be free to marry again.'

'I would be damaged goods. I could never marry in church.'

'Well, what does that matter?' Mo hesitated. 'Well, yes, of course, it *does* matter.' She punctuated the sentence with a loud blast on the horn. 'Dear me, fancy trundling that handcart into the road without even looking! But you would be free to find someone else.' She paused for a second before adding, 'Tom Dod, for instance.'

'Tom isn't free.'

'He might think differently if your own circumstances were to change.'

Fran was momentarily silent. Mo did not know about the circumstances of Tom's marriage, and could not possibly have guessed that he saw himself as honour-bound to the woman who had loved his heroic soldier brother. 'Tom will never leave Veronica,' she said at last.

'Well, there are plenty more fish in the sea,' Mo responded briskly. After a sidelong glance at her passenger, she added, 'But I suppose if you really want sea trout, it's no use trying to fob you off with cod.'

The analogy of Tom with a fish – when the reality could not have been more different – made Fran laugh out loud, and the atmosphere in the car lightened considerably.

'And in the meantime,' Mo said, 'you both have your utterly respectable, strictly platonic sleuthing.'

'Precisely,' Fran said. 'Because, as I have told you repeatedly, there is nothing romantic going on between Tom and myself. We are merely friends, with some shared interests.'

'Including murder.'

'Including murder. Or in this case, not murder, but suspicious deaths.'

'Which is how it all started last time, as I recall, and you ended up almost becoming a victim yourself. I do hope you're going to be more careful this time.'

TWO

'I'll be off for my bus now, Mum,' Ada announced, as she appeared in the doorway of the sitting room, her summer coat on and her hat already in place. 'I 'spect Mr Dod will be here soon.'

'Thank you, Ada. Have a pleasant weekend.'

'You too, Mum.'

Fran turned away, giving Ada no excuse to prolong her departure. She was uncomfortably aware of the way in which Ada was over-stepping the mark by mentioning Tom's impending arrival. It was really none of Ada's business how she spent her weekend. Fran knew that her mother would have sensed impudence in that attempt at a knowing smile and slapped Ada down immediately with some suitably acid remark. Good servants were supposed to be deaf and blind when it came to one's private affairs, but even as she tried to tell herself that it did not matter what Ada thought about it, she knew it would not do to have rumours flying around. She wondered to whom Ada might be reporting that there were 'carryings-on', as she would probably have put it, between Mrs Black and a married man. At the same time – because one did not confide in one's servants – she could hardly tell Ada outright that her weekend away with Mr Dod was to be a strictly chaperoned affair at the home of his great-aunt, and that one of their primary objectives would be to attend a Sunday service at the local parish church.

With Ada gone, Fran strolled across to the basket chair where Mrs Snegglington was lying at her ease. She attempted to rub the cat's head but Mrs Snegglington pulled back, avoiding the outstretched hand.

'I'm only going to be away for two nights, and Ada will be in every day to feed you,' Fran said, as she again attempted to stroke the cat, but Mrs Snegglington had seen the suitcase in the hall and was not to be mollified. As if to make her point more clearly, she stood up, stretched, jumped down from the chair and walked haughtily from the room.

'Hey,' Fran objected. 'You are supposed to be my faithful companion.'

At that moment, she heard the distinctive murmur of Tom's Hudson approaching along the lane. She had been on the point of rushing into the hall when she remembered that she was a sensible woman of twenty-eight, not a schoolgirl being taken out on a trip, so she paused to allow Tom time to park the car, silence the engine then walk up the front path, only permitting herself to go and greet him once he had employed the heavy metal knocker in his own distinctive way – two distinct pairs of short raps, whereas most people went in for a single run of three. It was like his own private code, she thought.

'Hello. All ready to go? Let me take that case and put it in the luggage box while you get your hat and coat.' His smile warmed her like an embrace.

'Hold on,' she said. 'I must just make sure that Ada has locked up at the back. You carry on and I'll be out in a mo.'

She joined him in the car a couple of minutes later, slightly breathless, clutching her handbag and jacket and still adjusting her hat.

'There's no rush,' he said, laughing at her. 'It's a good three hours to Aunt Hetty's. Throw those things on to the back seat.'

Once they were settled and he had turned the car around in the lane and headed eastwards, she asked politely after Veronica and young William, and he in turn enquired regarding her mother's state of health and also after Mo.

'My mother is just as usual,' Fran said with a little laugh. 'Complaining of various aches and pains while giving every appearance of being as fit as a flea. Now that the business of the village war memorial is finally over and done with, she has turned her attention to the state of some cottages belonging to a local farmer, which she claims are an eyesore and a disgrace to the neighbourhood. I sometimes think my mother only exists to be outraged about something or other. As for Mo, she is extremely intrigued by the potential mystery at St Agnes Durley Dean, while warning me to be careful not to fall into the path of a homicidal maniac for the second time in the space of a few months.'

'Sound advice,' Tom said. 'Jolly sensible woman, your friend Mo.'

'I assured her that I was not at any risk whatsoever in this particular case, since the victims, if there really are any, have all met their untimely end thanks to taking some kind of stand against the new vicar of St Agnes Durley Dean – and since I am not one of his parishioners and don't entertain such strong religious convictions, I think I should be pretty safe.'

'Do you . . .' Tom hesitated. 'Do you have any religious convictions at all?'

'Oh, of course! But I don't go to church very often and I don't get het up about form, the way my mother would. I mean, if someone wants to swing a bit of incense around it's all the same by me. And isn't that part of the problem at Durley Dean?'

'So I understand.'

She noticed that Tom sounded decidedly relieved. Perhaps he had feared that she might be an atheist. It had become rather fashionable in some circles, ever since the war, which had claimed so many lives and involved such suffering and cruelty that it was perhaps hardly surprising if some people found it harder to believe in God.

'So if I have this right,' Fran said, 'your Great-Aunt Hetty suspects that there may have been three victims so far? And though fairly ancient, she still has all her marbles.'

'Oh, absolutely. And she isn't actually all that old – not much older than my mother, in fact. Mother comes from one of those vast families where there are a million and one uncles and aunts and cousins, and the different generations all get muddled up. Her grandfather outlived his first two wives and in the end he was married three times, always to younger women. Each wife produced several children and Great-Aunt Hetty was one of the youngest batch, whereas my mother's mother emanated from the older offspring of marriage number two. I believe Mother has more than three dozen cousins at the last count.'

'Goodness, how complicated! It must cost a small fortune in Christmas cards.'

'Quite.'

'Remind me, have any of these suspicious deaths been investigated by the police?'

'Apparently not. Or at least not seriously. According to Aunt Hetty – by the way, she doesn't like "Great-Aunt", she says it makes her feel ancient – they have all been classified as genuine accidents, or in one case as a fatal illness. So, rather like our first investigation, the killer will be thinking that he or she has got away with it.'

'Remind me about the three supposed victims.'

She did not really need reminding, because she had already made a careful note of the details Tom had given her over the telephone, but she loved to listen to him talk, leaning back in her seat while the Hudson raced along at an exhilarating speed, eating up the miles as they passed all the familiar landmarks on the road east.

'The first one was possibly an accident. One Mr Vardy, a long-time attender at St Agnes, was found drowned in a pond at the edge of his land. He was an elderly chap, described by Aunt Hetty as an imbiber.'

'Oh dear.' Fran giggled. 'That sounds awfully Victorian. I suppose there will be no chance of cocktails before dinner this evening?'

'I don't think my dear great-aunt has taken to the cocktail hour, but I imagine you will be offered a sherry. She isn't generally disapproving when it comes to drink, so I rather think that what she was getting at is that our Mr Vardy liked a drop too much.'

'Oh, I see. Which would make it reasonably likely that he could fall into the pond and not make it out again.'

'Precisely. Now our second candidate, a Miss Ellen Tilling, who was a personal friend of Aunt Hetty's by the way, was found dead at the bottom of her stairs.'

'Having been clunked on the head with a statue of a naked man, if I recall correctly.'

'I understand that it was Apollo.'

'What?'

'Apollo. So a statue of a god, not a man.'

Fran suppressed a smile at Tom's pedantry. 'I honestly don't see how an inquest jury can bring in a verdict of accidental death when someone has been bashed over the head with a statue – whether it's of a man or a god.'

'According to Aunt Hetty, who is of course familiar with the interior of her friend's house, it is just possible that it was an accident. Apparently there is a shelf built into the wall at the top of the stairs, where the statue and various other ornamental objects used to stand. The theory is that Miss Tilling fell from top to bottom and as she went down either collided with something on the shelf or else made a wild grab at it, trying to save herself. Whichever way round it was, she brought everything crashing down after her, including the statue, which hit her on the head. When they found her, the entire contents of the shelf were lying on and around her, including a Chinese vase, which was smashed to smithereens and was supposed to have been worth an absolute fortune, according to Aunt Hetty.'

'A freak accident,' Fran mused doubtfully. 'I suppose it's possible. Who else was in the house at the time?'

'No one. Miss Tilling had two live-in staff, plus a char who came in to do the heavy work a couple of times a week, but it was the cook's afternoon off and the maid had been sent out to post a parcel.'

'Gosh. So it was the maid who came back and found her?'

'It was the maid who found her, but not right away. According to her evidence at the inquest, the maid returned from the post office, letting herself in by the back door, and it wasn't until the cook got back at around six that it seems to have occurred to the maid that Miss Tilling hadn't rung for anything for quite some while. So after mulling it over with the cook, the maid went into the drawing room – but when she couldn't see her mistress, she didn't look any further and just reported back to the cook. The cook seems to have had a bit more about her and once she'd ascertained that Miss Tilling hadn't so much as asked for a cup of tea all afternoon, she sent the maid back to see if the mistress had gone upstairs to lie down or something, and that's when the maid walked further down the hall and spotted the body lying at the bottom of the stairs – at which point, according to the evidence of the inquest reports, she helpfully resorted to screaming the place down.'

'So it isn't really certain when Miss Tilling fell – or was pushed – down the stairs?'

'The general idea is that there must have been an almighty

crash when she came down and that it would have been noisy enough to have been heard beyond the baize door. So everyone has assumed that it must have happened in the twenty minutes to half an hour when the maid was on her errand at the post office.'

'Which could be suspicious, I suppose. I mean, how often is someone who has a couple of live-in domestic staff actually left on their own in the house? But then again, it might just have been jolly bad luck.'

'Anyway, our third sudden death was Mrs Ripley, the bank manager's wife. That happened not very long after Miss Tilling's fall down the stairs, and it didn't raise any suspicions among officialdom because the poor woman had been suffering from some mysterious ailment or other for years and her GP signed the death certificate without recourse to a post-mortem. However, according to Aunt Hetty, one or two local people were a bit shocked, because no one had realized how serious her illness actually was and therefore, so far as they were concerned, the whole thing was rather unexpected. Apparently, she became ill after hosting a luncheon and this was initially put down to a tummy upset of some kind, but then she sickened and died within a day or so.'

'And of course it could be that she *had* eaten something which genuinely disagreed with her and then became unwell and died of natural causes?'

'Absolutely. Apart from the fact that all three were known opponents of the changes introduced by the Reverend Pinder at St Agnes's, there is absolutely nothing to connect the deaths and no reason for anyone to have been particularly suspicious about any of them.'

Neither of them spoke for a moment, and then Fran said, 'Do people really murder each other over changes at their parish church?'

'Probably not.'

Tom's response hung awkwardly in the air, making Fran wish that she had not asked her question aloud. She was well aware of Mo's opinion that there was nothing in Tom's aunt's suspicions at all, and that she and Tom were merely using the visit as an excuse to prolong their friendship. What had Tom's great-aunt made of the suggestion that he bring a female friend with him? Married men did not routinely go about with female friends in tow. (She had not provided her own mother with any particulars of the trip because, separate rooms or not, her mother would have instantly fixated on the potential for scandal and made her life unbearable until she desisted from the plan.) She had been tremendously looking forward to spending the weekend in Tom's company, but now doubts of all kinds came flooding in. If Mo was right, and she and Tom were merely deluding themselves that there was a crime to solve, then what on earth was the point of it all?

Because in the end he would go home to Veronica and she would go home alone to Bee Hive Cottage, and no shared mystery, however intriguing, was ever going to alter that.

THREE

Although Tom had already explained that his great-aunt Henrietta was not in her dotage, Fran had still been expecting an elderly, dried-up old stick of a spinster, so the delicate, elegant reality – a woman whose swept-up hair retained a silvery blonde hue, whose clothes were fashionably cut, and whose voice was light and musical – came as rather a surprise.

'Tom, my dear, how are you? And you must be Mrs Black, Tom's friend from the literary society. Tom has told me all about how clever you were in helping him solve the mystery of the murder in your book club. Do sit down, both of you – you must be simply longing for a cup of tea.'

When afternoon tea had been brought in and the usual preliminaries covered – the route they had taken, the weather conditions encountered, and the health of various relatives whom Tom and his great-aunt had in common – Aunt Hetty turned to their itinerary for the weekend.

'It will be just the three of us dining at home this evening,' she said. 'I didn't want to make a party of it because I thought you might be tired after motoring all this way. Tomorrow morning I can point you in the direction of the place where Mr Vardy drowned, so that you can view the scene for yourselves. And then – a real stroke of luck – we are invited to luncheon at the home of Mr Ripley.'

'Husband of your third possible victim?'

'Yes, Mr Ripley the bank manager. At some time or other I must have told him about the nature of W.H. Dod and Sons' business and when I happened to mention that you were coming on a visit, he immediately professed an interest in the importation of exotic fruit. Such a stroke of luck! It transpires that he spent part of his childhood in the West Indies, where an uncle of his owned a banana plantation. I said at once that you are a foremost expert on the importation of bananas—'

'Good Lord!' exclaimed Tom. 'I think that might be overegging the pudding a bit.'

'My dear Tom, it was far too good a chance to miss – I hinted that an opportunity to discuss bananas with someone who had experience of living where they are actually grown would positively make your weekend, and after that he could hardly not invite us. It's a splendid chance to see where one of the deaths occurred and to meet some of the people involved. Of course,' she added after a moment's thought, 'it won't do to actually mention the death of his wife, because rumour has it that as soon as the twelve months of mourning are up Mr Ripley is likely to announce his engagement.'

'His engagement?'

'To Miss Rose, his secretary. I don't know whether she will be one of the party tomorrow or not.'

'These rumours about a romance between Mr Ripley and Miss Rose . . .' Fran said. 'How long have their names been linked?'

The older woman smiled. 'Don't think that I don't know what you are getting at, Mrs Black, because I have a considerable fondness for detective novels myself. Are you familiar with the work of Mr Richard Austin Freeman? No? Oh well, never mind. I imagine that the truth of the matter is that Mr Ripley and Miss Rose have been secretly fond of each other for some considerable time. Mrs Ripley had never been well since the birth of her son, and it must be hard on any man to have a wife who is a semi-invalid. Mr Ripley showed his wife the utmost loyalty and devotion during her lifetime, but now that she is dead he is legally and morally free to pay court to Miss Rose. And Miss Rose, who also demonstrated the utmost propriety while Mrs Ripley was alive, is free to let him see that his affection is reciprocated.'

Fran felt herself blushing for no good reason and had to give a non-committal, 'Oh, I see,' while pretending to concentrate on a toasted teacake.

'We will certainly get a good luncheon at Mr Ripley's, so I have planned only a light supper for us on Saturday evening. On Sunday morning, of course we will go to church and you will see the Reverend Pinder and the rest of the congregation – or what is left of it – for yourselves.'

'And I suppose that if the victims are all people who have been opponents of Reverend Pinder,' Tom prompted, 'then he is your prime suspect?'

'Oh, no.' His aunt looked shocked. 'I cannot believe that a man of God would be capable of such things. I admit that I cannot bring myself to like the vicar, but surely someone who has taken Holy Orders . . .'

'Dear Aunt Hetty, surely you can see that he's the most likely suspect? And if not him, then who?'

'Oh dear . . . Well, that's the difficult part, isn't it? It seems so wrong to start suspecting one's fellow parishioners. I have thought and prayed about it a great deal . . .'

'Do you have someone in mind?' Tom coaxed.

His great-aunt continued to look uncomfortable. 'It seems so wrong to name names,' she murmured.

'Suppose you tell us what's been happening at St Agnes's since Reverend Pinder arrived?' Fran suggested gently. 'That way things might emerge of their own accord, without your feeling that you are being in any way unfair to your fellow church members.'

'Good idea,' Tom said. 'Start at the beginning, and we will only interrupt to ask questions if we need to.' He helped himself to another slice of angel cake and settled back into his chair.

'Reverend Pinder was inducted into the living just over a year ago,' Aunt Hetty began. 'I'm afraid there were difficulties right from the start. He made it clear that he intended to do things in his own way, and of course there will always be parishioners who do not welcome change.'

The older woman glanced at Fran, who nodded sympathetically, thinking of her own mother and her cronies at St Winifred's.

'Reverend Pinder is an adherent of the Oxford Movement, and he had introduced bells and incense within a fortnight. There was some grumbling, as you might expect, and Mr and Mrs Barnes went over to the Methodists immediately. They were the first to leave, but since then there have been others. Later came a statue of the Virgin Mary – whom Reverend Pinder prefers the congregation to call "Our Lady", as the Roman Catholics do. He began to encourage the use of rosary beads. Now I didn't like some of these things, but I was willing to accept or ignore them. Others, however, felt very strongly. Mrs Ripley was seen to remonstrate with Reverend Pinder after one of the morning services. I was standing nearby, waiting to shake hands on the way out of church, as always, and his face was white with anger. The following week, he preached the first of a number of sermons directed against those who opposed the changes.'

'Goodness,' said Fran. 'What on earth did he say?'

'Oh, it was couched in a lot of biblical references, but the basic message was that we were either with him or against him – and that this translated into being either for or against God. It was quite horrible. As you can imagine, after that there were more departures.'

'Dear me,' said Fran, 'I've never heard of anything like it.'

'The greatest sadness is the way it has set one person against another. You see, there are some people who think that he can do no wrong. Miss Flowers, for example, has stated her conviction at the Wednesday Prayer Group that Reverend Pinder is inspired directly by God and has been sent to put our feet on the right path. Mr Cocklington says that the vicar is the captain of the ship and we must do as he says. As for Mrs Welshman, she has always been a cassock follower – to the extent that if next Sunday Reverend Pinder were to say we should all stand on our heads to take communion, she would go around assuring everyone that it was absolutely the most spiritual thing imaginable. Mrs Dulcie Smith is so convinced of the vicar's cause that after poor Mrs Ripley was taken ill and died, she said it was a form of divine justice and should be an example to us all of what happens when people stand in Reverend Pinder's way.'

'Good heavens!' said Fran. 'What an awful thing to say. The woman sounds positively deranged. Is she some sort of religious fanatic?'

Aunt Hetty hesitated. 'I've known Dulcie Smith all her life. She was the only daughter in a household that was strictly ruled by her mother, and therefore the sort of creature who never said boo to a goose. She grew into a nervous, highly strung young woman, and I think most people assumed she would never marry, but then her mother died, and Dulcie went off on a sea voyage for her health and came back with a husband. His name was Patrick Smith and he was a quiet, pleasant enough young man, who came to live in Durley Dean and got himself some work, tutoring any local dunces who looked to be in danger of failing their matriculation, or whatever it is called these days. He and Dulcie had a child – a little boy – on whom they absolutely doted, having both come rather late to parenthood. Then of course the war came. Patrick Smith took the King's shilling and was one of the men who did not return, but Dulcie seemed to take consolation in the little boy. Unfortunately both she and the child contracted influenza at the time of the great epidemic, and though Dulcie survived the child did not. It is my opinion that the double bereavement affected the state of her mind.'

'Hardly to be wondered at,' said Tom.

'Dulcie had been brought up in an intensely religious household. Her mother, old Mrs Owen, was the sort who allowed no books other than the Bible on Sundays. Dulcie herself did not grow into the kindest of women, but she had originally been so meek that a word from one of the older women in the parish soon kept her in her place. However, the influenza changed everything. After the loss of her little boy, Dulcie threw herself even more wholeheartedly into church affairs, but the other legacy was that the influenza had weakened her heart, so it was put about that everyone should be careful not to upset Dulcie, lest it bring on a bad turn which might prove fatal.

'She had always been rather swift to criticize those who failed to live up to her own ideals, but old Reverend Caswell, who preceded Reverend Pinder, knew Dulcie all too well and he made sure she did not get above herself. Like any experienced clergyman, he recognized the sort of slightly hysterical women whom it is better to keep at a kindly arm's length.'

'But Reverend Pinder is different?'

'Reverend Pinder has managed to upset so many members of the congregation since his arrival that he has been forced to turn to women like Mrs Smith in order to keep the church running. Flower arrangers, Sunday School teachers . . . all manner of roles and committee vacancies have had to be filled, and this has brought women like Dulcie Smith, Mrs Welshman and Miss Flowers to the fore. This little coterie of favourites has come to see themselves as the vicar's protectors in the face of what they imagine to be a concerted attack by other persons in the congregation who are less fond of him and therefore less godly than themselves.'

'And has the vicar encouraged them in this belief?'

'He has certainly done nothing to discourage them. We have been subjected to sermon after sermon warning us not to stand against his attempts to return us to what he calls "the Catholic fold". The worst day of all was when he stood up in the pulpit and denounced by name some parishioners who had jointly written a letter to the bishop, asking him to intervene in the disputes which were under way about the installation of various statues and pictures within the church.'

Tom leaned forward slightly in his chair. 'Did those names happen to include any of your three suspected victims?'

Aunt Hetty nodded vigorously. 'They did indeed. Mr Vardy, Mrs Ripley and dear Miss Tilling were all signatories to the letter.'

'Was there anyone else?'

Aunt Hetty thought for a moment, then said, 'Mr and Mrs Brayshaw and Mr Hargreaves were the others.'

'But nothing has happened to them?'

'Really Tom, don't sound as if you are disappointed,' said his aunt. 'When the vicar denounced the signatories to the letter – a horrible moment, I felt quite sick – Mr Brayshaw stood up and said in a loud voice, "I am not sitting here to listen to any more of this. Come, Mona". Then he took Mrs Brayshaw's arm and they made their way out of church in what I can only describe as an extremely dignified manner, and one or two other people followed them. None have returned since. Some of them have defected to the chapel and some have gone to St Bartholmew's in Heppersley, though it is rather a long way to travel.'

'And Mr Hargreaves?'

'Mr Hargreaves stayed where he was. Afterwards, he said he had been attending St Agnes's as man and boy and no one but the Lord himself was going to stop him from worshipping in his own church.'

'And what happened about the letter to the bishop?' asked Fran.

'Very little. Apparently the vicar's group of special pets wrote to the bishop in defence of their precious Reverend Pinder, saying that almost everyone was completely behind him and that the original letter had been the work of one or two troublemakers, some of whom had now left the church. Dear me, it doesn't make me sound very Christian, does it, telling you all this gossip?'

'You can't help it, Aunt Hetty. Someone has to put the facts together.'

'Nevertheless, Tom, it is terribly distressing. One occasionally hears of rows between vicars and their congregations, but I never imagined that such a situation could arise at St Agnes's. Why, we were always such a happy band under Reverend Caswell, and indeed Reverend Gascoigne before him. Anyway,' she made a visible effort to gather herself, 'let me show you up to your rooms. And after you have unpacked your things, there will still be enough warmth in the sun for you to have a stroll in the garden before dinner.'

FOUR

Fran had considerable difficulty getting off to sleep that night. The mattress was rather lumpy, and the more she tossed and turned the closer the room seemed to become in spite of the open window. Eventually she felt around on the night table for the matches, managed to light one in the dark and applied it to the wick of her candle. (Aunt Hetty's gas lighting did not extend to the upper floor of the house.)

Like any good hostess, Tom's aunt had provided a jug of water and a glass, together with a small tin of plain biscuits. A biscuit, Fran decided, would only make her feel hotter and thirstier, but a glass of water might help. The jug was covered by a little mesh circlet, weighed down at the edges by beads in order to keep the dust out, and when she removed the beaded creation in order to pour herself some water the wretched object slipped from her fingers, clattering and clicking against the polished wood of the night table and even managing to ping against the metal biscuit tin before she could restrain it. It sounded very loud in the silent house, but though she froze to listen for any indication that other sleepers had been disturbed, no sound came from beyond the bedroom door.

She knew that Tom was in the next room, separated only by a few inches of brickwork, but there was no use thinking about that, so she carefully poured herself some water and sipped it while sitting up in bed and considering what they had learned about the trio of sudden deaths in Durley Dean so far. The case of Mrs Ripley struck her as particularly interesting, for there seemed to be another aspect there. She wondered whether Mrs Ripley had been aware that Miss Rose, her husband's secretary, was waiting in the wings, ready to console him in his loss? But perhaps there had been no more than an innocent friendship between the bank manager and Miss Rose before his wife died? Maybe the attraction had only come later, when the bank manager and his secretary were both free to allow themselves to care for one another?

How convenient it would be if Veronica were to die.

A stab of horror assailed her. How had she allowed such a thought to enter her mind? It was awful, disgusting . . . But true, an evil whisper added before she could prevent it.

Thoroughly upset and angry with herself, Fran put down the glass, slipped out of bed and crept over to the window, where she parted the curtains far enough to lean her forehead against the cool glass. The water had tasted warm and stale, but here beside the open window she experienced the welcome chill of the night air as it penetrated her cotton nightgown and reached her skin. Of course she did not wish a fellow human being dead – and anyway, as Tom had once said himself, the gate was barred at both sides because she was still married to Michael. Maybe it was just her own psyche trying to tell her something about the case in hand? How long had Miss Rose and Mr Ripley been waiting? Suppose you were married to someone and you believed it to be just a matter of time until their illness carried them off and you were free to marry someone else, but then they lingered . . . and the months turned into years and you began to realize that your inconvenient spouse might cling to life indefinitely?

Fran turned away from the window and allowed the slight draught to caress her back. The candle flame at her bedside swayed as the movement of the air reached it. That's what everything is like in life, Fran thought. Things touch us and move us from a distance. The thought of Tom's wife returned unbidden. She and Veronica had never met and probably never would. That was good, she thought. It was safer. She could neither like nor dislike Veronica, neither come to admire her or to despise her. It would have been different for Mrs Ripley and Miss Rose, living in the same community and necessarily seeing one another, even if only from afar. Aunt Hetty could be completely wrong about Mrs Ripley's demise. Perhaps there were factors in play which had nothing at all to do with Reverend Pinder. Or maybe there was no mystery at all. Perhaps it was all just as Mo had intimated: a foolish exercise undertaken for her own less than noble reasons.

FIVE

F ran was awakened the next morning by a hesitant knock that presaged the arrival of Aunt Hetty's housemaid bearing a can of hot water which she placed on the washstand before opening the curtains to admit the brilliant sunshine.

By the time she reached the dining room, Tom was already munching his way through bacon and eggs, which Fran declined in favour of toast and marmalade.

'I was just explaining to Tom how to find the way to the edge of Mr Vardy's land,' Aunt Hetty said. 'It's very easy to get there, so I don't intend to accompany you. I have one or two letters to write and plenty of other things to occupy myself with. And anyway, I'm sure your sleuthing will go much better if you leave me behind.'

Just for a second, Fran wondered whether there was some hidden meaning behind Aunt Hetty's words, but then she decided that Tom's grandmother's stepsister would never have agreed to invite her if she had suspected for a moment that the friendship between herself and Tom was anything other than platonic.

By the time they set out on their walk, Fran's spirits had lifted considerably. It was impossible to be unhappy on such a bright morning, with Tom loping along, lifting his hat to passers-by and idly humming snatches of a tune.

Durley Dean was a large, somewhat sprawling village, but by following the directions they had received from Aunt Hetty, they soon found themselves out of the main built-up area and walking along an unmade lane lined with cow parsley.

'Jolly good for blackberrying in another week or so,' Tom remarked, looking at the hedgerow.

'Goodness me, do you ever stop thinking about fruit and vegetables?' Fran laughed.

'It's the jolly old fruit and veg that keeps petrol in my motor and puts a Christmas turkey on my table,' Tom said lightly. 'Luckily people will always want fruit.'

'Very useful, too, in getting us an invite to lunch with Mr Ripley.'

'Ah, yes. Banana man. Who would ever have thought that being a fruit importer would come in so handy?'

'Did it occur to you that Miss Rose, the prospective fiancée of Mr Ripley, had a motive for getting rid of the late Mrs Ripley?' Fran attempted to speak nonchalantly, not catching Tom's eye.

'Well, yes, of course it did. And Ripley himself, too. It's perfectly possible that the death of Mrs Ripley is entirely unconnected with the deaths of the other two. That's the thing, isn't it? Aunt Hetty assumes a connection because they all happen to go to the same church and have all been opponents of the new vicar – who, by the way, is just as much of a suspect as anyone else in my book – but then it could just be a series of coincidences. Any of the three deaths might be murders, and any of them might be accidents. We could have three murders all committed by the same person or we could have three complete accidents. Or we could have three separate murders committed by three separate people for entirely different reasons, or any other permutation of accidents and murders you care to mention.'

'It's still far too early in the morning for all this,' Fran protested. 'Look, is this the stile which your aunt said is the shortcut across Mr Vardy's land?'

'I think it must be. Here, let me give you a hand up.'

There was really no need for any assistance, but Fran willingly took Tom's arm as she climbed over, glad that she had brought her comfortable flat brogues as she negotiated the bar, placed her second foot on the crosspiece at the other side and then hopped nimbly on to the faintly defined path that headed across the field. 'Lucky it hasn't rained for a while,' she said.

It was a matter of a mere fifty yards to their destination. The place where Mr Vardy had met his end appeared to be a natural pool at the edge of a narrow belt of oak and ash trees. Though partly surrounded by rushes, there was an open space beside the water where cattle evidently came to drink, because the dried-up mud at the edge showed the marks of hooves.

'Hmm, visible from the lane and probably not very deep,' Tom said, looking out across the water. 'But I suppose it would be slippery here after rain. If you fell in, how hard would it be to get back out again, do you think?'

Fran considered the question for a moment, looking out over

the opaque water, its surface reflecting the clear blue sky. 'Hard to say. You might lose your bearings if it was dark, I suppose. Or panic and start thrashing about and end up getting in deeper instead of getting out.'

Tom had been casting about on the ground and quickly saw what he wanted. He walked over to a nearby oak tree, reached under the canopy and picked up a long stick which had evidently blown down some time before, then walked to the very edge of the water and, reaching as far as he could, poked his stick at arm's length into the pond, and then brought it back up and considered the end that had been immersed. 'Barely more than a couple of feet deep there,' he said. 'But by the look of things there's a lot of mud and leaf mould on the bottom that might make it difficult under foot – especially if you were the worse for drink, which would presumably have been the reason for stumbling into the water in the first place.'

'Your clothes and shoes would hamper you, too.'

'Setting the question on its head, how easy would it be to murder someone here?'

Fran .considered again. 'Jolly difficult, I should say. Firstly, you've got to either persuade the victim to come here or else wait here in the hope that they will just happen to turn up. Then you would have to take them unawares, push them into the water, and hold them under until they drowned. Your victim, in the meantime, would presumably be struggling like billy-o.'

'If they stumbled in accidentally,' Tom continued the train of thought for her, 'I suppose a reasonably fit and active person might easily manage to get out – unless they happened to be hopelessly drunk. How old was this Mr Vardy, I wonder? But then again, it's hard to imagine anyone actually holding someone under the water until they stopped breathing – it would be a terrific struggle and the killer would get soaking wet.'

'So Mr Vardy's drowning is starting to look more and more like a genuine accident.'

'I'm inclined to think so. Of course, the Ripley situation is completely different – and then there's Miss Tilling. What a pity Aunt Hetty hasn't managed to find some way of wangling us a peek into her house.'

By unspoken consent, they turned away from the pond and began to retrace their steps towards the lane.

SIX

At Aunt Hetty's suggestion they left Tom's car parked in her drive and walked to the home of Mr Ripley, as their route afforded them an opportunity to stroll along the road where Miss Tilling had lived.

'Here we are,' Aunt Hetty announced, as they approached the property in question. 'Poor Miss Tilling was found lying at the foot of the stairs, just on the other side of the front door.'

They all turned to look at the door, as if it might yield up some helpful clue, but it was just a normal sort of front door, with two panes of coloured glass set in stained oak panels, about which there appeared to be nothing out of the ordinary.

'No neighbouring houses for quite a few yards in either direction on this side of the road,' Tom remarked. 'And the house on the opposite side of the road stands well back, so it's most unlikely that they would have heard the sound of someone falling down the stairs. Is that a doctor's plaque on the gate?'

'Yes, that's where Doctor Owen lives. You will probably meet him tomorrow at St Agnes's.' Aunt Hetty lowered her voice conspiratorially, though it would have been impossible for anyone inside the house across the road to hear her. 'I suspect that he is not nearly so enamoured of Mr Pinder's new ideas as he appears to be. I think he goes along with a great deal in order to keep the peace with his sister.'

'Who is his sister?' asked Fran.

'Mrs Dulcie Smith. She has kept house for him since her husband and son died. The arrangement suits them both, I imagine, since Doctor Owen has never married.'

'Is Mrs Smith the woman you mentioned yesterday? The one who lost her husband in the war and then her son to influenza?'

'She is. You will meet her at church tomorrow, too. We turn left at the next corner and then we're almost at Mr Ripley's house. There now, you can see the chimneys from here. They're mock Tudor, the only ones like it anywhere in the village.'

Although they had walked a relatively short distance to reach the bank manager's house, the day was growing warmer and Fran was grateful to be served with a generous glass of lemon barley on arrival, served from a jug in which ice cubes chinked against the glass. Mr Ripley's household evidently enjoyed the rare luxury of a refrigerator. They had been conducted out on to the terrace, where an awning had been set up above a group of striped-canvas garden chairs. Here Mr Ripley, a slim, middle-aged man with a neat moustache and hair greying at the temples, welcomed them with what appeared to be genuine friendliness and introduced his son, Geoffrey, a precocious, skinny boy with a corncrake voice and a good deal too much to say for himself; his teenage daughter, Florence, whose pretty face was slightly spoiled by a rather sulky mouth; her governess, Mademoiselle Bertillon, whose almost flawless English was delivered with an accent that betrayed her French origins; and finally Miss Rose, a tall, broad-shouldered woman who was wearing a floral frock which did not really suit her.

'Miss Rose has kindly agreed to join us in order to even up the numbers,' announced their host, as if in doing so Miss Rose had conveyed a great favour upon them all. 'Florence and Miss Bertillon take their meals in the dining room now, but Geoffrey has only been doing so since he returned from school this summer.'

Fran noticed that in spite of the heat, Miss Rose's gloved hand seemed cool when it briefly grasped her own during the introductions. 'Mr Ripley tells me that you and Mr Dod share an interest in literature,' Miss Rose said, politely. 'And you are staying with Miss Venn while visiting a church associated with Charles Kingsley?'

'Actually, we think it is associated with the poet and children's writer, Robert Barnaby,' Fran corrected her politely. (As Tom had previously remarked, the great thing about Robert Barnaby was that he seemed to have travelled all over the British Isles during the course of his short life and could therefore provide the perfect cover story to explain a visit.to just about anywhere.)

'I don't believe I have read anything of his.' Miss Rose tilted her head slightly as she considered the point. 'Clearly an omission I ought to redress, if his merely visiting a location is enough to spark a literary pilgrimage.' She smiled as she spoke, but Fran gained the definite impression that Miss Rose did not for a moment believe in the excuse that Tom had concocted with the cooperation of his aunt.

That woman's as sharp as a tack, Fran thought. I very much doubt that anything gets by her.

Fortunately there was no further reference to the reason for their visit to Durley Dean, and once everyone had remarked on the unusually warm weather for September, Mr Ripley began to ask Tom about importing bananas and Tom in turn asked Mr Ripley about his youthful visits to St Kitts. In the meantime, Mademoiselle Bertillon and Miss Rose engaged Aunt Hetty on the plans for a forthcoming local flower and produce show. Left with Geoffrey, Fran found herself telling him about her recent visit to the lawn tennis championships at Wimbledon, with the unfortunate result that he insisted on sitting next to her at lunch so that he could regale her with a long and extremely tedious monologue about his own exploits on the tennis courts before his school broke up for the long summer vacation. Brought up in a household where children who attempted to monopolize the conversation would have been politely but firmly instructed to desist, Fran found the experience thoroughly irritating. Moreover, she felt she was missing out on a valuable opportunity to size up Mr Ripley and his prospective new partner in life, Miss Rose.

Down at Tom's end of the table, the conversation had moved away from the fruits of the Caribbean and on to the perennial issues of cricket and gardening.

'Do you play tennis yourself, Mrs Black?' Geoffrey asked, after the remains of roast chicken and vegetables had been cleared away and junket was being served.

'A little, though not exceptionally well.'

'We should get up a four after lunch. Florence – Florence, say you will play tennis with Mrs Black and myself after lunch.'

Florence turned to look at her brother with undisguised distaste, but before she could respond, Fran said quickly, 'Oh, I couldn't possibly play. I don't have the right shoes.'

'Don't be silly, Geoffrey. It's far too hot to play,' his sister said.

'Rubbish,' the boy said. 'It's good for you to get out into the sun. Vitamin C and all that. You could easily lend Mrs Black some plimsolls.' He turned back to Fran. 'What size do you take?'

'Really, Geoffrey! Don't be so rude. Take no notice of him, Mrs Black.'

'Mr Dod,' Geoffrey called down the table. 'You'll play tennis after lunch, won't you?'

'Of course,' said Tom, who had been focused on something Mr Ripley was saying about vegetable marrows and was therefore clearly unaware that the rest of the party had not committed to Geoffrey's tennis plans. 'Though I will need the loan of a racquet.'

'We've got plenty – and spare tennis shoes.'

At this point Aunt Hetty asked Mr Ripley how his dahlias had been this summer, Miss Rose complimented the junket and Geoffrey began to tuck in, so the subject of tennis was temporarily dropped – only to be revived again when Mr Ripley suggested they go back out on to the veranda for their coffee, and in the general move away from the table Geoffrey popped up alongside Tom and headed him off across the hall in search of some appropriate kit for the forthcoming game.

'I bet we'd have some shoes for you, too, Mrs Black,' Geoffrey said. 'And we've plenty of ladies' racquets.'

'Just ignore him,' Florence said. 'No one has to play if they don't want to.'

'I am afraid Mr Geoffrey is rather overbearing.' Mademoiselle Bertillon had fallen into step alongside Fran and spoke quietly enough that no one else could hear her. 'He does not mean to be rude, but he has always been indulged too much.'

'Your English is excellent, mademoiselle,' Fran said. 'Where did you learn?'

'I learned in Paris when I was a girl, but I have been living in England for nearly twenty years so there has been plenty of opportunity to practise.'

'Have you been with the Ripleys all that time?'

'No, this is my third post. I came here when Miss Florence was six years old – but soon I will need to find another young lady, because Miss Florence is to go away to finishing school in a few months.'

Good heavens, Fran thought, that's rather grand for a bank

manager's daughter. Aloud she said, 'I imagine that will be quite a wrench, after what – almost ten years?'

Florence had temporarily excused herself, and her absence left an empty chair between Fran and the governess.

'I think it is the right time to go.' Mademoiselle Bertillon glanced towards the three other adults, who were now engaged in a separate conversation, then lowered her voice to say, 'There will be changes soon, and I do not think that reminders of the original household will be welcome.'

Fran followed the other woman's glance and noticed that Miss Rose had taken charge of the newly arrived coffee pot, thereby assuming the role of hostess.

'You served the first Mrs Ripley?' Fran prompted.

'No. I was appointed after she died. The second Mrs Ripley engaged me.'

'Oh.' Fran was momentarily too surprised to say anything else. She hadn't realized that the recently deceased Mrs Ripley was not the bank manager's first wife.

Sensing her confusion, the governess said quietly, 'You are a visitor . . . and will have been told that Mr Ripley recently lost his wife, but not that she was his second wife. He has been most unlucky in his domestic affairs.'

At this point Geoffrey and Tom emerged from the house, carrying racquets which had already been removed from their presses. Tom had taken off his tie, undone his top button, rolled his shirt sleeves to his elbows and exchanged his two-tone leather shoes for a pair of slightly greying borrowed plimsolls. Looking around at the others, comfortably settled in their garden chairs, it occurred to Tom for the first time that no one else was readying themselves to play.

'I say,' he said. 'Isn't anyone else joining us?'

'I never play, old chap. Artificial leg, d'you see.' To Fran's utter astonishment, Mr Ripley lifted his trouser leg at the ankle to reveal a polished wooden calf descending into his sock and shoe. What on earth was the appropriate response to such a revelation in a social situation? Fortunately the bank manager dropped his trouser cuff again and continued, 'Car smash, back in 1914. Got me out of the Great War, of course – and gave me a lot of unexpected kudos. Young chap hobbling about on a stick in 1915, everyone assumes you are a hero and wants to stand you a drink. Every cloud has a silver lining, eh? Did you see service, Mr Dod?'

'No,' Tom said. 'I'm afraid I was too young.'

Fran noticed the way Tom's face had clouded. She too felt discomfited by their host's remarks, for – like Tom's – her own brothers had not come home from the war.

Geoffrey barely allowed Tom time to finish his coffee before chivvying him across the lawn where, after the necessary adjustments to the net, they began to knock up. By now Florence had returned to her seat, which prevented Fran from drawing out Mademoiselle Bertillon any further regarding Mr Ripley's lack of fortune in domestic affairs. Oh dear, Fran thought, our detecting is not going at all well; I can't ask the governess anything in front of the daughter, and Tom is stuck on the tennis court with Geoffrey.

It was really far too hot to play, and singles meant a good deal more chasing after the ball than a set of doubles would have done. To make matters worse there was no back or side netting, so any unreturned shots had to be retrieved by the players themselves. Tom was soon red in the face and visibly perspiring. Geoffrey's constant yelping commentary kept those sitting on the terrace appraised of the score, but after a closely fought set, Tom emerged victorious and immediately returned to the rest of the party for a well-earned glass of lemon barley.

Whereas Tom clearly felt that he had done his duty, Geoffrey had other ideas. 'It's not fair. It has to be best of three sets.'

'Oh, do shut up, Geoffrey,' his sister said. 'You can see that Mr Dod is positively done for in this heat.'

'It was a close set and could have gone either way,' the boy whined on. 'It's not sporting to refuse to give a chap the chance to redress the score.'

Fran glanced across to Mr Ripley, but his attitude to Geoffrey's behaviour never seemed to extend beyond amused benevolence.

Tom was clearly nettled by the insinuation about a lack of sportsmanship. 'Very well then,' he said, rising to his feet and picking up his racquet. 'Best of three it is.' There was a glint in his eye which Fran had never seen before.

Conversation among the spectators dwindled as the game resumed. Geoffrey was young and fit and scampered all over the court with the reckless abandon of youth, while Tom, though clearly struggling in the heat and presumably disadvantaged by a borrowed racquet, played with a do-or-die determination and looked increasingly irritated by the number of close shots his opponent was calling out. Once or twice he queried them, but Geoffrey always stuck to his guns – even when Tom hit what looked like a clear winner on game point.

'You should play a let,' Florence called from her seat on the terrace.

'It was out,' Geoffrey shouted back. 'I saw it clearly.'

After a moment's hesitation, Tom accepted the call in silence and walked back to the baseline for another serve. Possibly, Fran thought, Tom was saying nothing because he could no longer summon enough breath to protest. With the score at eight games all, Tom abruptly changed tactics, no longer looking to serve and volley but instead merely playing the ball back into the court, often directly at Geoffrey's feet.

'I think Mr Dod is becoming too tired to make his shots,' murmured Mademoiselle Bertillon.

Fran said nothing. That had been her own initial thought, but after a couple of points she realized that Tom had not capitulated but had instead developed a plan to defeat his opponent. Firstly by keeping the ball so far inside the lines that it was impossible for him to lose any further points as a result of Geoffrey's fraudulent calls, and secondly by allowing the boy to beat himself, for Geoffrey had clearly mistaken Tom's apparent lassitude for exhaustion and this encouraged him to show off, attempting overambitious shots that ended up in the net or yards out of court. Eventually a flashy forehand went flying into the shrubbery for match point, and then a mistimed smash gave Tom the match.

'Ten eight,' Tom said, politely. 'My match, I think.' He walked purposefully to the net and extended his hand. Geoffrey, as if caught unawares by the score, reluctantly walked to meet him. While at the net, Tom inclined his head and said something that was inaudible to the spectators on the terrace, at which Geoffrey abruptly withdrew from the handshake and marched, red-faced, directly into the house.

'I am afraid Mr Geoffrey is a bad loser,' remarked Mademoiselle Bertillon.

'Well played, Mr Dod,' said Miss Rose and clapped Tom back to the terrace, her applause taken up enthusiastically by the rest of the party.

It occurred to Fran that Miss Rose might not be particularly fond of her prospective stepson. She pictured her own eldest brother, another Geoffrey, who had been keen on tennis but had always played fair. Poor Geoffrey, who had not been so very much older than this brat of a boy when he went off to fight in the war to end all wars. It must never, ever, be allowed to happen again.

The three guests made their excuses soon afterwards, and once they were safely beyond the front gate and a few yards along the road, Fran asked, 'What was it that you said to that insufferable boy at the end of the match?'

'I said gentlemen do not cheat and cheats seldom prosper.'

SEVEN

By the time Tom had enjoyed a bath and a change of clothes, it was well past the usual hour for afternoon tea, but Aunt Hetty insisted on reviving him further with tea and cucumber sandwiches and after that they all sat in the drawing room, their conversation inevitably returning to the luncheon party.

'I hope you don't think I went too far in teaching that little beast a lesson, Aunt Het? I mean, I don't want you to be struck from Mr Ripley's address book on the grounds that your bounder of a nephew upset his precious son and heir.'

'Nonsense, Tom, it was just a game. Someone had to lose and anyway, I don't think Mr Ripley cared very much. When Miss Rose began to applaud, he joined in as enthusiastically as anyone. I must say, I thought it was very game of you to carry on in that dreadful heat. Of course, our family has always been noted for its sticking power.'

'You make us sound like a patent glue.'

'Foolish boy, you know exactly what I mean. Now I hope you don't mind, but I intend to be most inhospitable and leave you to your own devices this evening. These temperatures simply don't agree with me, and I intend to take a cool bath and then retire early to bed. Nora has laid out some cold meat and pickles in the dining room for supper, and you must ring for whatever you want to drink. I don't run to a cocktail cabinet but there is both whisky and gin in the pantry, and it's probably cool enough to sit out in the garden now, if you feel like it.'

They took Aunt Hetty at her word and went through the open French windows which led to the large rear garden. Although the weather made it seem like midsummer, the sun knew that it was really September and was already sinking, so by the time they strolled across the lawn the sky was losing its brightness and the birds were starting to sing their evening songs.

'I love this time of day,' Tom said. 'Have you ever noticed that roses smell best as the sun goes down?'

'Yes, lovely, isn't it?' For a dreamy moment, Fran thought he was going to slip his arm through hers. How lovely and perfectly natural it would have been – if only he had not been married to Veronica and she to Michael. 'I had a rather unpleasant encounter the other day in Ulverston,' she said. 'Someone accosted me and said I was a wicked woman.'

'Good Lord, whatever for? Who was this person? It sounds like some kind of maniac.'

'She was – is – the sister of the woman my husband is living with. Apparently they – my husband and the other woman – are going to have a child. The sister said it was wicked of me not to give Michael a divorce, so that their child would be born in wedlock.'

'A divorce would take too long for that,' Tom said, immediately focusing on the practical aspects of the matter. 'Though once the divorce came through, they would be able to get married and change the child's name. And if they did it all quietly, no one would be any the wiser as he or she grew up, I suppose.'

'I have been thinking about what she said. Michael has already asked me for a divorce, and I suppose I refused because I was so angry and did not see why I should make it easy for him. Now that a couple of years have gone by, I don't believe that I mind so much for myself, but I'm not sure my mother could stand the scandal. I know there doesn't have to be too much scandal. Divorces seldom make the papers these days unless one is particularly rich or famous, but it is still such a disgrace. If only Geoffrey and Cecil hadn't been killed in the war . . . But as it is, I am all my mother has left, and that makes it much worse, somehow.'

'And have you decided what to do?' Tom asked quietly.

'No. I don't know what to do.'

There was a pause. 'You know,' he said at last, 'that I can never leave Veronica?'

'Yes.' She tried very hard to keep her voice steady. 'Yes, I do understand.'

He reached around and squeezed her shoulder. The briefest, gentlest of movements. 'Let's sit over there, on that seat under the apple tree, and try to decide what we have discovered so far,' he said.

The wooden bench felt cool through her summer skirt. This is the sort of place where lovers sit, sharing their secrets, Fran thought, whereas she and Tom would have to make do with discussing suspicious deaths. It was better than nothing.

'I find it quite funny,' Tom said, 'that it never occurred to Aunt Hetty to mention that Mr Ripley has been married not once, but twice.'

'It's because she is working to a fixed theory,' Fran said. 'She suspects that the three deaths are all linked to things that have happened at St Agnes's, whereas we are looking at it from the opposite point of view – or at least with an open mind.'

'That's true, of course. In fact, we're disinclined to follow her theory because, having visited the place where Mr Vardy met his end, we don't think it very likely that he was murdered.'

'Quite. And if Miss Tilling's was an accidental death too . . .'

'We don't really know very much about that one, but it's hard to see what more we can find out. I wish there was some way of getting inside the house to have a look at where it actually happened.'

'I'm not sure how that would help. And it will be different now new people have moved in . . . I suppose anyone can fall downstairs.'

'I suppose so. Though the odds would surely be against clunking yourself on the head with a statue in the process. I wonder how big the statue was?'

'Your aunt would probably know – and it might have been mentioned at the inquest.'

'I don't recall that it was,' Tom said. 'Though I only saw one press clipping about it. It was a piece Aunt Hetty had saved. She sent it through the post to me when she first suggested there was a mystery to be looked into.'

'We should look up the reports of the inquests properly. There may be a lot more to Miss Tilling's death than is apparent from the one report you've seen,' Fran said. 'And there must have been an inquest for Mr Vardy as well, though not of course for Mrs Ripley as that was certified a natural death.'

'I suppose we have learned most about the Ripley case.'

'I'm not sure we've learned anything very much about that one either.' Fran sounded doubtful. 'I was monopolized by that obnoxious boy during lunch, and you were forced into playing tennis with him for the rest of the afternoon. I hardly got a chance to talk with Mr Ripley or Miss Rose during the entire visit, and in any case one could hardly raise the circumstances of his last wife's death.'

'Well, I agree our visit wasn't all that productive . . . but I think we've come away with one or two things.' Tom paused, but receiving nothing in return, went on. 'Firstly, Ripley does have a motive for wanting to be rid of his wife, because Miss Rose is obviously going to become Mrs Ripley number three. Secondly, although he could have chosen to poison his wife, he may not have had the capacity for more violent methods.'

'Good heavens, whatever do you mean?'

'I'm thinking of the wooden leg.'

'I don't think it incapacitated him all that much. I hadn't even noticed that he limped until he pointed it out. Oh dear, I won't forget the way he rolled up his trouser leg in a hurry. What on earth is one supposed to say when someone unexpectedly flashes their wooden leg under your nose?' Fran could not help giggling, though she knew she shouldn't.

Tom laughed too. 'It was a bit of a googly. Fair enough, I don't suppose a wooden leg would stop someone from batting their wife over the head. He would only be in trouble if she tried to make a run for it, or maybe threatened him with a can of woodworm.'

'Really, Tom, that is not funny.' Fran laughed just the same.

'No, I suppose it isn't. The real reason anyone would poison their spouse is that poison can be mistaken for some other illness. Whereas someone lying in a pool of blood, with their head stove in, needs a bit of explaining.'

'Unless you are an elderly lady supposedly alone in the house who has fallen down stairs, encountering a statue on the way.'

'Right. I wonder how closely the police questioned that housemaid who was supposed to have been out posting a parcel?'

'Never mind that just now. Stick with the Ripleys.'

'Yes, ma'am. So Ripley has been married twice already. Aunt Het says his first wife was killed in the same car accident that cost him his leg, so there's nothing suspicious there.'

'I was thinking,' Fran mused, 'that if it hadn't been an accident in which he was badly injured too, her death might have looked suspicious. From what Aunt Het told us over tea, his first wife had quite a bit of money and he remarried within just over a year of her death. I suppose that's how he can afford to send his daughter off to a finishing school on the Continent.'

'Surely you're not saying that he could have staged the accident somehow?'

'On the contrary, I'm saying that though it was genuine, if the circumstances had been slightly different, it could have appeared suspicious. My point is that it's very easy for something to appear suspicious when it isn't. Mr Ripley's first wife dies and he marries again after an absolute minimum amount of time has passed. Mr Ripley's second wife dies and again he remarries after an absolute minimum amount of time has passed. The same thing happens twice, but the surrounding circumstances are different – and it's only the circumstances that make it seem suspicious.'

'I see what you're getting at,' Tom said. 'But you might equally say that just because one wife dies of natural causes, it doesn't necessarily mean the other one did.'

'I didn't like Mr Ripley, did you?'

'Not particularly. Pretty bad taste, I thought, that crack about getting free drinks by pretending to be a war hero. And as for the way he indulges that boy of his . . .'

'According to the governess, Geoffrey has always been indulged. His mother doted on him and Mr Ripley seems to have carried on where she left off.'

'Let's hope his school can sort him out,' Tom said. 'Otherwise he's on course to become an insufferable bounder.'

'How about Miss Rose? What did you think of her?'

'She reminded me a bit of my father's secretary, Miss Winspear.'

'Who?'

'Miss Winspear? Terrifying woman. Frighteningly efficient and never wrong about anything. You want to know which year we bought the firm's first typewriter and how much we paid for it? Miss Winspear will tell you off the top of her head, to the month and the shilling, even though she didn't start with the firm until 1916. No one argues with her, and my father adores her because she is so capable. I swear that if he called her in and said, "Miss Winspear, I need a copy of Shakespeare's first folio on my desk in the next fifteen minutes", she wouldn't bat an eyelid. It would just be "Yes, Mr Dod", and the thing would duly appear.'

'Goodness, Tom, you do exaggerate.'

'Well, yes, for effect – but you get the picture.'

'But if anything happened to your mother . . .' Fran ventured carefully.

'Would my father marry Miss Winspear? Oh, goodness, no. Or, well . . . no, I really can't imagine it. She isn't at all pretty, and imagine being married to someone who is always right about everything.'

'Did you think Miss Rose was pretty – or let's say attractive – speaking from a male perspective?'

'Not particularly, but then both she and Ripley are rather older than you and I.'

'And of course,' Fran said, 'it doesn't matter whether we can understand the attraction or not. The fact is that Mr Ripley and Miss Rose will probably get married, but that doesn't really tell us anything about how the other Mrs Ripley died. If we assume Mr Ripley has always been attracted to Miss Rose, then he has both a motive and the opportunity. And what about Miss Rose? Doesn't she have a motive, too?'

'If we proceed on the basis that there was a long-standing attraction, then she has a motive, and since she comes across as such a capable sort, one assumes that she might have been able to manufacture an opportunity.'

'We need to know more about the circumstances. For example, who was in the house in the period immediately before Mrs Ripley died?'

'More homework for us.'

Fran stifled a yawn. 'Gosh! Sorry, I must be getting tired. It's this heat. It completely saps one's energy.'

'It's too dark for me to see the time by my wristwatch,' he said, 'but it must be getting late. Come on, let's go inside.'

It was very close in the house and, although she was tired, Fran again found herself sitting up in bed, unable to sleep. She pictured Mr Ripley and Miss Rose sitting side by side in their garden chairs, Miss Rose already taking on the role of hostess.

Florence and Geoffrey had seemed unperturbed by this, as if they found it perfectly normal. Would they have been so cheerfully indifferent if they had harboured any suspicions about their mother's death? Surely not. And although it was convenient for the bank manager and his secretary that death had removed his wife from the picture, this did not necessarily mean anything. Just as it would be fearfully convenient for herself if Veronica were to die . . .

It was such a horrid line of thought that she had previously tried to banish it. But now, in the privacy of the early hours, Fran allowed herself to explore the idea. She could not envisage ever taking the life of another human being. It was not even as if she disliked Veronica – how could she, when she had never met her and knew almost nothing about her? No, it was not dislike. Deep down, she supposed that she resented Veronica simply for *being*. Suppose the circumstances had been different and she had known Veronica, might she even have come to like her? Or would knowing her actually have made matters worse? Suppose Veronica had turned out to be one of those tiresome busybodies who was always offering other women gratuitous advice? Or a shrew who nagged her husband and spoiled her son? Or one of those hope-less women who lay on a couch all day long, pretending to be ill while eating chocolate and reading silly magazines?

Miss Rose must have known her boss's wife. Could mere resentment have grown into despising or loathing . . .? Not in a normal person perhaps, but what about a person whose outlook was a bit unbalanced? Someone who was excessively passionate in her moods and feelings? Someone with a mind capable of igniting and developing pure hatred?

EIGHT

On Sunday morning they set off for church in good time, arriving at the lychgate just as the bell summoning worshippers began to toll. St Agnes Durley Dean was a large Victorian church which occupied the site of several much earlier churches going back to the period before the Norman Conquest. The current building had a number of rather splendid stained-glass windows; and a fine marble memorial to the fallen of the Great War, mounted in the north wall. Aunt Hetty seemed to know everyone in the congregation, and exchanged nods and good mornings with all of them as she and her guests walked down the central aisle and took their seats in what Fran guessed was her habitual pew.

After hearing so much about the new vicar, Fran had been curious to see this meddlesome priest in the flesh, but she found herself oddly disappointed by the reality. Father Henry, as he liked to be known, was a nondescript man, probably approaching his fortieth year, with thinning sandy hair and a pale-pink freckled face. He looked, she thought, a singularly unlikely person to be capable of creating controversy and upheaval on any sort of scale. From the commencement of the service, however, it was evident that there were clear divisions within the congregation, with some church members ostentatiously genuflecting at every conceivable opportunity, while others very pointedly did nothing of the kind. At certain points in the service, the genuflectors dropped as one to their knees, while the non-genuflectors remained obstinately standing. When Father Pinder mounted the pulpit to deliver his sermon, while most of the former leaned forward as if in antici-pation of wondrous things to come a number of the latter set their faces into far less enthusiastic expressions, and one elderly gentleman sat back, folded his arms and glared. It made for an oddly distracting atmosphere. Certainly, Fran had never experi-enced anything quite like it. But then again, she thought, Reverend Pinder is a man who has apparently denounced members of his congregation from the pulpit, and she had never heard of anything like that before either. Not in the Church of England, at any rate.

When the sermon began, however, it turned out to be nothing remotely controversial. Reverend Pinder took Christian charity as his theme and spoke in fairly general terms of the need to be fair in all our dealings with our neighbours. Although she tried to concentrate, Fran was short of sleep, and as Father Pinder began to elaborate on rendering unto Caesar what was due to Caesar her mind began to wander, until she caught a glimpse of the silverware standing ready to be carried to the altar and the phrase 'a poisoned chalice' sprang unbidden to her mind.

Such a well-known expression – 'a poisoned chalice'. Where had it come from? Life was not always fair, she thought. It was arguable that in merely being married to the wrong man, she had herself been handed a poisoned chalice, for while the Church was prepared to forgive a whole variety of sins, its forgiveness did not apparently extend to matrimonial misjudgements. On the contrary, so far as the Church was concerned, once she had married Michael, she was bound to him for life. Even if she gave Michael his divorce, no clergyman in the land would have been willing to marry her – a divorced woman – to another man. Of course, if Veronica had not existed, there was always the registry office.

She pulled herself firmly back to the present. Hypothesizing situations in which Veronica did not exist was absolutely not the kind of thought she ought to be entertaining in church. After communion and the final hymn, Fran followed Aunt Hetty's lead and made her way down the aisle and out into the sunshine with almost unseemly haste. 'If we manage to be among the first out,' Aunt Hetty had suggested earlier, 'then we can linger in the churchyard and I can introduce you to everyone else as they are leaving.'

When Reverend Pinder had positioned himself in the porch, ready to shake hands with the departing congregation, Aunt Hetty introduced Tom as her nephew and Fran as 'Mrs Black, his fellow researcher'.

'They are on a sort of literary pilgrimage,' she explained.

The vicar frowned slightly at this and demurred that there was surely only one true kind of pilgrimage, at which point Fran suddenly saw how easy it would be to dislike this humourless man. But she smiled at him as she took his extended hand, and pretended not to be thinking anything of the kind.

'Another wonderful sermon, Father Henry,' trilled the voice of a woman who had been waiting her turn behind them. 'Fine sentiments and beautifully put.'

They stopped a couple of yards along the path and Aunt Hetty pretended to search in her handbag for something, in order to excuse them pausing. ('She's taken wholeheartedly to being a detective,' Tom had commented approvingly on hearing about this element of his aunt's plan.) The delay gave Fran an opportunity to look back towards the porch, where a small, dark-haired woman was emerging from the church with a child holding each of her hands.

'That's Mrs Welshman,' Aunt Hetty whispered, without looking up. 'Do you know, if the vicar told us to be rebaptized standing up to our necks in the river, that woman would claim it was a wonderful idea.' In a much louder, entirely different voice, she said, 'Good morning, Mrs Welshman. How is little Patricia's finger?' In a quick aside to Tom and Fran, she explained, 'The child managed to get it stuck in a knot-hole in a pew last week and it was quite badly bruised.'

One by one, Aunt Hetty managed to waylay various persons of interest as they emerged from the building. After Mrs Welshman, she introduced them to Mr Cocklington and then Miss Flowers as all the vicar's biggest supporters came by. The Ripley family greeted them as if they were old friends – all except young Geoffrey, who was evidently still smarting from his defeat on the tennis court the day before and looked rather sourly at both Tom and Fran. Then came Mrs Steadman, a garrulous lady who expressed considerable interest in their quest to visit local sites that had links with the author Robert Barnaby, thereby forcing Tom to rapidly improvise some possible connections. By the time Mrs Steadman had moved on, the members of the choir, delayed by the need to divest themselves of their robes, were leaving in ones and twos.

'Where on earth has Dulcie Smith got to?' Aunt Hetty asked irritably. 'She was definitely in her usual place in church, and I'm sure she hasn't passed us. I particularly wanted you to get a look at her.'

'You can't start searching through your bag all over again,' said Tom. 'You've had enough time to completely turn it inside out at least three times by now. Tell you what, now that the vicar's gone, why don't we slip back and see if she's still inside? You can pretend you think you've left a pair of spectacles in the pew.'

The trio headed back through the porch and into the church, which seemed dark after the bright sunlight and at first glance appeared to be deserted. It was only when they reached the pew they had occupied earlier that Tom gestured towards the east end and they saw the figure of a woman kneeling alone at the altar rail.

Aunt Hetty immediately nodded. 'Mrs Smith,' she mouthed, as she began to ostentatiously search for her missing glasses.

As they watched, the woman concluded her devotions, rose to her feet and, after making an elaborate curtsey in the direction of the crucifix, turned to walk towards them. She was a short, dumpy woman with frizzy curls which had been partially crushed beneath a summer hat.

Fran felt suddenly embarrassed. What on earth did they think they were doing, play-acting like this, in a church of all places, in order to snoop on some poor woman who had suffered more than her fair share of bereavements?

Aunt Hetty appeared to have no such reservations. 'Good morning, Mrs Smith. How are you? Is your brother well? I noticed he isn't with you this morning, but I daresay he is ministering to one of his patients as we speak. I don't think you have met my nephew, Tom Dod, and this is his friend and fellow academic, Mrs Black. They are both members of the same literary society. We have just popped back inside to see if I left my spectacles here, but I've just found them in my bag. Silly me! They must have been there all along.'

While privately wondering if Aunt Hetty had ever considered a career on the stage and simultaneously blushing at the unwarranted description of herself as an academic, Fran exchanged a limp handshake with Mrs Smith. What a contrast between Tom's aunt and her own mother, who would certainly never have told such fibs in church, Fran thought.

'Good morning, Miss Venn, Mr Dod, Mrs Black. And how

have you enjoyed worshipping at St Agnes's?' Mrs Smith enquired of the two visitors.

There was something faintly challenging in the woman's tone. Fran decided it was definitely a test. 'I found it very interesting,' she said. 'You do things somewhat differently to the church where I grew up.'

'Father Henry is the most marvellous spiritual leader,' Mrs Smith announced, with a conviction that brooked no discussion.

'I understand that he has instigated quite a few changes,' Tom said, in a carefully neutral tone.

'He has set our feet on the righteous path,' said Mrs Smith. '"He that is not with me is against me". Luke, chapter eleven, verse twenty-three. Father Henry does not approve of women wearing lipstick when they attend church.'

Fran, who had put on her Max Factor 'Geranium Charm' as usual that morning, was uncertain how to respond. The change of subject was so abrupt, and there was a quite alarming intensity in Mrs Smith's demeanour. It was like being confronted by one of those placard-waving street-corner preachers who shouted after people in the street, 'Repent and ye shall be saved!'

'I'm afraid I don't believe there is one set way to worship God,' Tom said. 'I think people find their own route to Him.' He spoke with quiet conviction. 'If you have found your glasses, Aunt Het, then we might as well be on our way. Good morning, Mrs Smith. It was most interesting to meet you.'

As they emerged into the churchyard again, blinking as their eyes adjusted to the brightness outside, Tom said, 'Bloody woman. How dare she be so rude?'

'Hush, Tom, she'll hear you,' Fran protested. 'She's probably only just behind us.'

'Now do you begin to see what I mean?' Aunt Hetty asked, keeping her voice discreetly low, though there was no obvious sign that Mrs Smith had followed them out of the church. 'Reverend Pinder has gathered this little group around him and encouraged them to act as his mouthpieces. Such rudeness is not confined to visitors. Mrs Smith has been known to approach people who have been regulars here for twenty years and castigate them about their failure to support the Reverend Pinder's ideas upon one thing or another. And some of the changes are quite troubling. As dear Miss Tilling once said, "The way things are going at St Agnes's, we will soon no longer be recognizable as part of the Church of England, for we are fast becoming the Church of Father Pinder".'

'Why don't people simply put that Smith woman in her place?' asked Tom.

'But I thought I told you that Mrs Smith has a trump card at her disposal? She has a weak heart, you see – the residual effect of suffering from influenza. It's said she must not be upset, for fear of bringing on an attack.'

'How convenient,' said Tom. 'So she can dish out her venom with complete impunity and no one can ever retaliate.'

Fran said nothing. Now that they were walking home, she found the whole business had left her feeling dispirited. It was terribly sad that a congregation should be turned against one another in this way – just the very opposite of how things ought to be. It also felt wrong that she and Tom had attended almost under false pretences. We shouldn't have come here at all, she thought. No good can come of this friendship with Tom.

'You're very quiet,' he said. 'What are you thinking?'

'I was just wondering where the expression about being handed a poisoned chalice comes from.'

'You surely don't think Reverend Pinder poisoned Mrs Ripley himself?' Aunt Hetty sounded extremely shocked.

'No. I was just thinking about the expression itself.'

'It's Shakespeare, I think,' Tom said.

'Yes, I suppose it will be. Sayings like that nearly always are.'

Aunt Hetty provided them with a hearty Sunday lunch before waving them off on their homeward journey. Over apple pie and custard, she had asked them for their view of 'the case' as she called it, but Tom merely said it was early days yet and there was still more to be done, which she accepted without further enquiry.

Only when they were speeding north in Tom's Hudson, with the open windows providing a welcome breeze, did they begin to reassess 'the case' themselves.

'I have to admit that having met this Smith woman for myself, I can see what Aunt Het is getting at,' Tom said. 'She has fanatic written all over her.'

'But religious fanatics don't murder people, surely?' Fran demurred. 'That's the exact antithesis of what Christianity is all about. "Thou shalt not kill" is one of the Ten Commandments.'

'That didn't stop the crusaders, or all that carnage in the Great War. You might justify killing someone if you thought they were doing something that was totally against what God wanted. What we encountered this morning was someone whose views have become so extreme that she's telling people off for wearing lipstick – and there's no commandment against that.'

In the brief silence that followed, Fran wondered for a moment if Tom, like herself, had been mentally ticking off the commandments and had reached the one about coveting someone else's spouse.

'At the same time,' Tom continued, 'it isn't easy to see how a woman with a weak heart could have managed to murder three different people.'

'When we tried to work out the Linda Dexter murder,' Fran said, 'we started off coming at it from the wrong way. The same could be true here. It's as we said yesterday. If you accept that three members of the same congregation have been murdered, then there's a link that leads to their church – but if you take only one death by itself, the link disappears.'

'You're putting your money on the relationship between Mr Ripley and his secretary?'

'I'm keeping an open mind.'

They continued to toss the subject back and forth for the remainder of the journey, but had got no further by the time Tom dropped Fran back at Bee Hive Cottage. He declined her invitation to come in for some tea as he had to get home. 'Three-line whip for supper at the in-laws,' he explained.

As she unlocked the front door, Fran wondered how much Veronica knew about their expedition. Would Tom talk over what he and Fran had discovered with his wife – sitting up in bed together at night perhaps, or maybe over the breakfast table? He had assured her that Veronica did not mind his periodic absences, or even his friendship with her. But was that really true? Although it had been a marriage of convenience for both of them, surely Veronica must care for Tom? Did she never experience a pang of jealousy? Could it be that Veronica put a brave face on things?

Did she resent Fran simply for *being*, in the same way that Fran sometimes found herself irrationally resenting Veronica? She reminded herself that Veronica too had been handed a kind of poisoned chalice, losing the love of her life in the war and accepting marriage to his brother for the sake of her unborn child.

She shut the door and collected the handful of letters that Ada had picked up and placed in a neat pile on the hall table. They were all communications of a routine nature except for the final envelope, which had a pretty scalloped pattern along the flap. It turned out to be an invitation to the wedding of Richard Finney, the editor of the Barnaby Society's journal, and his fiancée, Miss Julia Spencely. Fran smiled. It warmed one's heart to see that some people, at least, had found a happy ending.

NINE

Fran had not expected to hear from Tom again for a few days at least, so she was extremely surprised when her telephone rang at three the following afternoon and she heard his voice on the line. (Some people had their servants answer the telephone, but Ada was unaccustomed to the instrument and approached its use much as one might approach an encounter with a dangerous snake.)

'Hello, Tom,' she said. 'Is everything all right?'

'There's been a surprise development. Aunt Hetty telephoned just now, which she never does unless there's been a family bereavement.'

'Oh dear, has someone died?'

'No, no, nothing like that. She wanted to tell me that the police have turned up with an exhumation order for Mrs Ripley.'

'Oh my goodness!'

'It's supposed to be a secret. They're going to do it tonight, under cover of darkness, but word has leaked out somehow or other, so the entire village seems to know about it and the whole place is in a state of subdued uproar.'

'Can one have a subdued uproar?'

'Do you think this is the moment for a discussion on semantics?'

'No, of course not. So I suppose we have to wait and see what happens next?'

'I suppose so. Though Aunt Hetty said that if either of us want to go back and stay with her to do some more sleuthing we are welcome at any time. Apparently she doesn't have much faith in the regular authorities, as she thinks they have already allowed the killer to strike three times. I told Aunt Het that our next plan was to bone up on the evidence given at the inquests – and I suppose it's become more urgent now, but there's no chance of me getting away from the office until Friday at the earliest.'

'I expect I could go down there by train,' Fran said, knowing perfectly well there was nothing in her diary that could not be put off.

'I knew you'd come up trumps,' Tom said. 'Let me give you Aunt Het's telephone number so you can make arrangements direct with her.'

'I say,' Fran said, after she had written down the number on a handy sheet of paper, 'when I got home yesterday, I found an invitation to Richard Finney's wedding waiting for me.'

'Yes, we've received one too,' Tom said. 'And luckily it's a date we can make. Jolly nice of him to ask us.'

'Yes, jolly nice,' Fran echoed.

We've received one. Of course. Richard Finney and Julia Spencely would have known that Tom was married and naturally included his wife in the invitation as a courtesy, even though they had presumably never met her since Veronica did not attend Barnaby Society meetings. As she went through the motions of signing off on the phone, Fran found herself fervently wishing that her morning had been too busy for her to have already taken her little note of acceptance down to the postbox at the end of the lane. It would look odd now if she cried off, but for reasons she could not explain, even to herself, the idea of meeting the previously unseen Veronica had wrong-footed her completely.

Ada was clearly surprised when Fran explained that she was going away again at short notice, and when she passed the kitchen door she overheard the daily saying something conciliatory about 'a nice tin of sardines' to the cat. No wonder Mrs Snegglington was putting on weight.

Without Tom to drive her, it would take the best part of the day to reach Aunt Hetty's, but she knew that Tom was right about the increased urgency. If there was an exhumation in progress, things might move very fast, just as they had in various other high-profile poisoning cases during the past few years. And surely poison must be suspected, for why else would an exhumation order have been granted?

TEN

B y Wednesday evening Fran was in a position to provide Tom with her first progress report and duly telephoned him, using Aunt Hetty's wall-mounted telephone, which was even more old-fashioned than the instrument that graced her mother's home.

He greeted her enthusiastically. 'I was hoping you would call. How are you getting on?'

'Quite well, I suppose. It took me most of yesterday to get here, but this morning I took the bus into Nottingham and went to the main library there. They had all the old newspapers, just as they do in Kendal, so I made a note of all the relevant details.'

'Oh, jolly good work.'

'It didn't take long. Both inquests were pretty cursory affairs. Mr Vardy's body was found by one of his own farmworkers. He was a widower who lived alone and the woman who came in to cook and clean for him didn't generally get there until nine o'clock, whereas the farmworkers turned up at first light. When they realized that he hadn't appeared to give them any orders, some of them started on their usual tasks, but a couple of the men began to walk over the farm to look for him and they spotted him lying face down in the pond. There was an autopsy, of course, performed by the local doctor, Doctor Owen, who said that Mr Vardy had obviously drowned. There was nothing at all suspicious, and there were no signs of foul play.'

'The last person to see him alive?' Tom prompted.

'Was Mrs Morgan, keeper of the Bird in Hand beerhouse. It seems that Mr Vardy preferred the beer at Mrs Morgan's to that served at the other inns in the village, so he went to the Bird in Hand for a drink most evenings, cutting across his fields to get there. Mrs Morgan was called to appear at the inquest and she said that when he left, at about half past nine, it was not only dark but also getting foggy. He was her last customer of the night and she followed him to the front door, then watched him walk down the path.'

'Presumably the worse for drink?'

'Mrs Morgan seems to have been somewhat reluctant to confirm that, one way or the other. She said he was "no worse than on any other night", and when asked how many pints he had drunk she said – and I quote – "I don't rightly know".'

'Well, thank goodness for such a helpful witness!'

'Quite. The next-to-last customer in the Bird in Hand that night appeared as a witness too, and he took the same line. He said that he left the beerhouse about a quarter of an hour earlier than Mr Vardy, and that Mr Vardy had not drunk any more than usual that evening. On being asked the obvious next question, he affected not to have any idea how much that usually was.'

'Hmm. They do say that a publican's relationship with their regulars is bound by the same kind of confidentiality as doctors have with their patients. Perhaps a similar code is observed among fellow drinkers?'

'I think it would probably have been to spare the relatives. The newspaper mentioned that there was a married niece who had come up from Oxfordshire for the inquest, and you know how reluctant people are to speak ill of the dead.'

'Do there appear to be any relatives who might be in line to inherit the farm?'

'That's another negative. Mr Vardy was a tenant, so he had no property to speak of. He didn't have any surviving children and he hadn't made a will, so his savings will be split between quite a large number of grown-up nieces and nephews.'

'So, according to Mrs Morgan, Mr Vardy set off for home as usual?'

'That's right. It seems that he invariably walked along the lane – it would be the same lane we went along, but from the opposite direction – and then he took a shortcut across the fields, which, as we saw last Saturday, would have taken him right alongside the pond. When they found him, he was still wearing his working boots and a heavy coat. If he went too close to the water's edge, slipped in the mud and fell, it might have been quite a job for him to get out again.'

'He's sure to have had stuff in his pockets,' Tom mused. 'Pocket knife, loose change, door keys . . . and once his clothes got waterlogged—'

'And if he'd had a bit too much to drink, he could have become disorientated when he went into the water. Essentially it has accident written all over it, but there's just one little loose end. Mrs Morgan said that as Mr Vardy went out of her front gate and she stepped back and half turned to close the front door, she fancied that she heard Mr Vardy speak to someone. The coroner asked her if she'd actually seen or heard anyone else in the lane and she said "no". Apparently the local police asked around and no one came forward to say they were in the lane that night or that they saw Mr Vardy leaving the beerhouse, so in his summing up the coroner suggested that either Mrs Morgan must have been mistaken or else Mr Vardy might have made an exclamation of some kind, perhaps after stubbing his toe.'

'Stubbing his toe!'

'Stubbing his toe – or something like that.'

'So there's a faint suggestion that there was someone else around that night?'

'I've put "See Mrs Morgan" on my list of things to do.'

'Good show. Who's next?'

'Well, Mrs Ripley should be – Mrs Alice Elizabeth Ripley, to be precise. But there wasn't an inquest, because Doctor Owen had been treating her before she died and he put her death down to natural causes.'

'Which hardly squares with the police digging the poor woman up again. How's that going, by the way?'

'It's all rather horrid. Mr Ripley had to be present when the police exhumed the body on Monday night, and rumour has it that when they opened the coffin, the poor man had to confirm that the remains were those of his late wife.'

'Good God, how awful!'

'Some big cheeses from London have done an autopsy . . .'

'I bet that was fun. The body must have been in a pretty vile state of decomposition.'

'Do stop interrupting, Tom. I can't spend half the night on your Aunt Het's telephone, think of the cost.'

'Of course not. Sorry, do go on.'

'The local rumour mill has it that the London chaps have put various bits of the late Mrs Ripley into sealed jars and are taking them off for analysis, and in the meantime what's left of the body has been reinterred.'

'They must suspect poison, then? Sorry, sorry, I won't interrupt again.'

'As you know, according to Aunt Hetty, Mrs Ripley was taken ill at a lunch party, but no one else showed any symptoms. The doctor was called in – like most people in the village, the Ripleys are patients of Doctor Owen, Mrs Dulcie Smith's bachelor brother – and he didn't appear to think it was initially all that serious, but then Mrs Ripley suddenly died a few days later. I've added Mademoiselle Bertillon to my list of people to talk to, because she was living with the family at the time and it strikes me that it might not be too difficult to get her talking about what happened.'

'Good plan.'

'Finally, there's Miss Tilling. There was an inquest, of course, because it was a sudden death. Doctor Owen – he was Miss Tilling's doctor too – gave her a fairly clean bill of health. Couldn't recall any problems with dizziness, said she was steady on her feet, no previous history of falls or anything of that kind. The police couldn't find any evidence of a loose rug at the top of the stairs or anything else that might have caused an accident, so basically it's a complete mystery why she fell.'

'What about the statue?'

'Well, that's where the plot thickens. The statue hit the back of her head with sufficient force to fracture her skull, so it wasn't just a glancing blow.'

'Could someone have hit her over the head while she was standing on the landing, then staged it to look as if she had fallen down the stairs?'

'If they did, then they'd gone to an incredible amount of trouble. One of the bannister rails had been dislodged where Miss Tilling knocked into it, and a small tear in her frock corresponded with a strand of material found on a carpet tack that was slightly proud of the fifth tread up – which suggests the dress was torn as Miss Tilling came hurtling past. But the point is that if you hit someone over the head when they were standing at the top of the stairs, the chances are that they would fall from top to bottom anyway.'

'So all you would need to do to fake the accident would be to take the statue down and place it next to the body as if it had fallen on her as she came tumbling down the stairs.'

'Quite so. And if you swept everything else off the shelf too, that would add a bit of dressing to the scene.'

'Isn't it a bit strange that none of this appears to have occurred to the police?'

'My impression is that they did consider other possibilities at first, but the policeman who gave evidence told the coroner that they had ruled out foul play on the grounds that nothing within the house had been tampered with or stolen and there was no sign of a break-in. According to the maid, Miss Tilling was unusually particular about keeping her doors locked. The front door had a Yale lock and the maid had turned the key on the outside of the back door when she left the house, in accordance with the household's usual practice. She reckoned that Miss Tilling hardly ever went into the kitchen, and even if she had gone to answer the front door bell herself while the maid was out, she would never have admitted a stranger to the house when she was there on her own.'

'That only rules out people she didn't know. What about people who might benefit financially?'

'Another non-starter, I'm afraid. Miss Tilling left small legacies to her household servants, a fairly generous dollop of cash to her goddaughter who lives in Australia, a few hundred pounds to the parish church, and the remainder of her money goes to a charity which takes care of retired horses.'

'Aha. It was Dobbin what done it.'

Fran ignored the lame joke. 'It looks as if money wasn't a motive. One thought which did occur to me is that the killer must have known that Miss Tilling was alone. You couldn't risk hitting her on the head and watching her tumble down the stairs while there was someone else in the house – in case she screamed and the servants heard that or the sound of the fall, and came rushing into the hall to see what was going on.'

'You think it was an accident then?'

'Perhaps – but the statue business niggles me.'

'Well done, anyway. You've found out a terrific lot already.'

Fran smiled to herself as she ended the call. Tom would always say that, she thought, even when she had found out next to nothing at all.

Aunt Hetty was waiting for her in the drawing room. 'What does Tom make of it all?' she asked.

'It's too early to draw any real conclusions,' Fran said. 'We need to find out more about all three cases if we can.'

'Is there anything I can do to help?'

'Well,' Fran paused. After thinking for a moment, she said, 'I need to talk with Mademoiselle Bertillon, but I'm not sure how to go about it. I can't just drop in unannounced.'

'Hardly the most tactful time to make a call,' Aunt Hetty agreed. 'Your best chance of bumping into her accidentally would be in the High Street. She tends to do a little household shopping at around ten thirty, most weekdays. She uses Fulchers butchers and Mr Wainwright is their regular greengrocer.'

God bless domestic routines, Fran thought. Aloud, she said, 'Is there a tea shop in the High Street?'

'I'm afraid Durley Dean doesn't possess such an establishment, but if you want to keep her talking, you could profess to be walking the same way. I'm sure I can think of some little errand that would take you in the direction of the Ripley house. Let me think . . . That's it, you could be dropping off a chutney recipe to Miss Grimes – she lives out past the Ripleys. I don't believe she's ever asked me for one, but she's getting so forgetful that she won't question it if you turn up with one.'

'That's brilliant, Miss Venn. Thank you.'

'Goodness, all this subterfuge! It would be quite exciting if only it wasn't all so tragic. Is there anything else?'

'Only that I need to speak with Mrs Morgan, who keeps the Bird in Hand beerhouse.'

'Oh dear, I'm not sure I can help you with that. I'm not acquainted with Mrs Morgan, I'm afraid.'

'That's all right. I'm sure I'll find a way.'

ELEVEN

F ran made sure that she was lurking in the High Street well in advance of Mademoiselle Bertillon's anticipated arrival. The good weather had persisted, so all the shops had their awnings extended, providing welcome oases of shade across the pavement. She drifted from shop window to shop window, keeping a lookout for the governess while pretending to study the displays. At the stationer's, she spent such a long time peering into the window that the proprietor came out on to the pavement in anticipation of making a sale and Fran had to feign interest in a box of sketching pencils, only extricating herself by saying she would have to think about it and come back later.

From time to time she covertly glanced at her wristwatch, not wanting to be marked down as obviously waiting to meet someone. By twenty-five to eleven she had examined the wares displayed in the windows of every establishment and was just wondering whether to repeat the exercise in the opposite direction when she saw the neat, slender figure of the French governess turn the corner and advance towards the shops. Fran noted the way other passers-by turned their heads and stared – not, she was sure, in admiration of the governess's perfect deportment, but out of curiosity because of the sensation and scandal that had enveloped the Ripley household. As predicted by Aunt Het, Mademoiselle Bertillon made for Fulchers, the butchers. Once her quarry was inside, Fran strolled towards the butcher's shop at a leisurely pace, pausing when she reached the premises next door, where the rows of iced buns set out on paper-lined shelves in the window were already looking decidedly sticky in the heat.

There must have been a queue inside the shop, because by the time Mademoiselle Bertillon emerged Fran had had time to count each type of confectionary on display, the number of stripes on the red-and-white awning of the butcher's shop, and the rows of cobblestones between the drain covers in either direction. As soon as she saw the governess's reflection in the angle of the shop window, however, she immediately began to move forward again, so that it would not appear as if she had been waiting – and this resulted in a realistic-looking near-collision alongside an A-board advertising brisket at special prices.

'Oh, Mademoiselle Bertillon! I'm so sorry, I just wasn't looking where I was going.'

'It is no matter. Nothing is upset. How nice to see you again.'

'And you too. Actually, it's jolly fortunate, because I'm doing a couple of errands for Miss Venn and she has asked me to drop something at the home of Miss Grimes. She told me it was not far from Mr Ripley's and I was confident of finding it, because we walked there when we came to luncheon with you on Saturday, but on that occasion we didn't go via the High Street and I'm afraid I have rather lost my bearings.'

'Oh, it is very easy to find. I can direct you, if you like – or if you would care to wait while I call at the haberdashery shop, then we can walk back together.'

Excellent, thought Fran. Exactly according to plan. Aloud, she said, 'Oh, thank you, mademoiselle, that would be most kind.'

The errand at Miss Lumley's Haberdashery took next to no time, as the special set of buttons ordered by Florence Ripley had not come in. 'Miss Florence will not be pleased,' Mademoiselle Bertillon remarked. 'She is not a patient young lady.'

Fran could not help thinking that with the exhumation of her stepmother's body on Monday, Miss Florence might have more troubling matters on her mind than a set of buttons, but she said nothing.

'I am surprised to see you here again, Mrs Black,' Mademoiselle Bertillon continued. 'What brings you back to Durley Dean so soon?'

Although it was an obvious question, Fran had failed to anticipate it. Thrown momentarily off guard, she decided to take a gamble. 'If I can rely on your discretion, mademoiselle, the truth is that Miss Venn asked myself and Mr Dod to come here because we have had a little bit of experience in solving unpleasant mysteries. Miss Venn told us that there had been a couple of unexpected deaths among her fellow parishioners at St Agnes's, and now there's this unhappy business of Mrs Ripley's death too. Though it sounds a little strange, Miss Venn wondered if there might be some connection between the three cases.'

'Me, I am a Catholic.' The governess gave a Gallic shrug, which implied to Fran that strange goings-on were hardly to be wondered at in upstart offshoots like the Church of England. 'Tell me, are you and Mr Dod – how would you say – the not-in-uniform policemen?'

'Plainclothes police. Oh no, no. We are just, well, amateurs, but because of our success – well, sort of success – in the past, Miss Venn thought that we might be able to make some discreet enquiries . . . More to put her mind at rest than anything else.'

'Ah, yes, we would all like someone to do that for us.'

'It must be very difficult for Mr Ripley and the rest of the family at the moment,' Fran prompted, hopefully.

'Indeed yes. Difficult for everyone. Some very nasty policemen have been to the house, asking everyone questions. They have even searched Mrs Ripley's bedroom. I told them that this would be of no use at all, because the room has been tidied out and cleaned many times since Mrs Ripley died.' The governess sighed and shook her head. 'They take absolutely no notice, these . . .' she paused, perhaps searching for a word, '. . . great clodhoppers of men.'

'What were they looking for?'

'Who can tell? Poison, I think.'

The word hung in the air as they turned the corner and began to walk away from the High Street along a road lined with terraced houses.

'But surely, Mrs Ripley's death was due to natural causes?'

Mademoiselle Bertillon did not respond immediately. Fran sensed that she was struggling with the question, perhaps not for the first time.

'It was said so, of course. It was a shock to everyone at the time because it was not expected that Mrs Ripley should die, but these things happen . . .'

'But I thought – that is, when Miss Venn told us about it – that Mrs Ripley had been ill for some time?'

This time there was no hesitation. Fran got the distinct impression that the governess found it a relief to talk to someone beyond the immediate family circle about her late mistress's death.

'The circumstances are a little more complicated than that. For as long as I have worked for the family, Mrs Ripley had always enjoyed poor health. You understand what I mean by this, Mrs Black? A great many ladies in her position . . . they take to their bed and a lot of fuss is made. My own mother – a true lady – did not have time for such trivial ailments . . .

'Of course,' Mademoiselle Bertillon added hastily, 'after Mrs Ripley died, I felt much remorse that I had ever suspected her of . . . magnifying her illness in order to gain her husband's attention. Her "weak constitution", she used to call it. No doubt you think badly of me for having such thoughts?'

'On the contrary,' Fran assured her companion. 'I have an aunt who is exactly the same. She uses her health to manipulate everyone, but I have always suspected there is nothing particularly wrong with her and that in fact she will probably outlive us all.'

'Mrs Ripley, poor lady, did not outlive us all.'

'But you were surprised when she died?'

'I was.'

'It can't have been all that sudden. I mean, there was no inquest, was there? And there has to be an inquest if someone dies and it's completely unexpected.'

'Expected? Unexpected? It's difficult to say. It all began the day of the luncheon party for Mr and Mrs Craig. The Craigs were old friends of Mr Ripley from many years ago who were visiting the neighbourhood and had come for lunch with Mr and Mrs Ripley. Miss Florence and I were also there, but Master Geoffrey was away at school, so six of us sat down.'

'Everyone ate the same things?'

'Of course. We had vegetable soup, roast lamb with mashed potatoes and peas and naturally mint sauce and gravy. I did not have the mint sauce, as it is so vinegary.'

'But everyone else did?'

'Of course. The English must have their mint sauce. For dessert there was rhubarb tart and custard. Soon after lunch, Mrs Ripley complained of feeling unwell. She had only eaten the same as everyone else, but she had to go and lie down and Doctor Owen was called in. Doctor Owen diagnosed what he described as "her usual gastric trouble", prescribed her some medicine, and said he would call again the next day if she was no better.'

'Was everyone terribly worried?'

'Not at all. Myself, I had noticed that Mrs Ripley had not much enjoyed the lunch party. She did not really know the Craigs, you see. They kept talking with Mr Ripley about things that had happened when the first Mrs Ripley was alive, and even things which had taken place before that.'

'What sort of things?'

'Oh, nothing very much. Mr Craig and Mr Ripley had been boys together. It was all "You remember when old So-and-so made a lot of runs for the cricket team . . ." Nothing upsetting, you understand, but it did not concern Mrs Ripley, so she could take no part in the conversation. Miss Florence was also bored by it all.'

'And you?'

'It is not my job to be bored.'

'So you think Mrs Ripley may have pretended to be ill in order to regain the centre of attention?'

'I never said so. It is . . . possible that she exaggerated a little. Yes . . . I admit, I thought that at the time.'

'But not now?'

'Mrs Ripley is dead, is she not? Who knows what to think now?'

'And Mr Ripley was anxious enough to send for the doctor?'

'Mr Ripley always did whatever his wife asked in these situations. Mrs Ripley was inclined to call Doctor Owen out for any kind of trivial complaint. Her husband could afford it, so naturally Doctor Owen always came.'

'But this time it turned out not to be trivial?'

'I did not think it was anything serious. Mrs Ripley took to her bedroom. During the daytime she lay on her chaise longue, in her dressing gown, and carried on taking her usual medicine, and Doctor Owen popped in to see her the next day and the day after that, but on the third day after she was taken ill he had to attend a lady who was . . . confined, I believe you would say, and in his absence Mrs Ripley became very ill and went into a state of collapse. Mr Ripley was still at the bank, so I telephoned for Doctor Owen, saying that it was urgent, but he did not come immediately and only arrived just a minute or so after Mrs Ripley died. He attempted to revive her – but it was no use, she had gone.'

'So it was not really an expected death?'

'Doctor Owen said he would be able to issue the certificate of death because he had been treating Mrs Ripley for many years, so he knew that she had a weakened heart and could have died at any time.'

Fran nodded. 'It's the sort of thing any good family doctor would do. No one wants the nuisance of an inquest.'

'Going to this coroner's court, getting the family's name into the papers. That sort of thing is not respectable,' the governess agreed.

'Well, in cases of sudden death one can't always avoid it, but a good GP will help the family by issuing a certificate whenever he can. Tell me,' Fran continued, a little hurriedly, for the distinctive chimneys of the bank manager's house had come into view above the hedge, 'why have the police suddenly become suspicious?'

'According to Mr Ripley, someone has been sending anonymous letters to the chief constable alleging foul play.'

'Goodness, why on earth would anyone do that?'

'A bank manager has enemies. There are people to whom he has refused credit or loans. It is said in the village that a Mr Pascoe, whose business failed, has sworn to take revenge on Mr Ripley . . . But of course there are many stories in the village now. The cook or the maid arrives back with a new one every day.'

Mademoiselle Bertillon stopped. They had reached the front gate of Mr Ripley's house. 'Here I am,' she said. 'If you continue walking to the end of the road, then turn left, you will come to Miss Grimes's house in just a few yards. I am sure you will find your way back to Miss Venn's without a problem. I think our meeting today was no accident?'

She gave Fran a shrewd smile, before opening the garden gate and walking up the path.

TWELVE

By the time Tom arrived at his aunt's house on Friday evening, there was a great deal to tell him. He was initially perturbed to learn that Fran had disclosed the real reason for their visits to Mademoiselle Bertillon.

'Suppose she gossips? If she tells the entire district what we're doing here, it may be a lot more difficult to get anything out of anyone.'

'Really, Tom, you make us sound like secret agents or something. And anyway, I don't believe she does gossip. I think the whole reason she was happy to talk to me is because she doesn't really have anyone else to use as a sounding board. She doesn't like the police. She can hardly discuss things with Mr Ripley and Florence, and she doesn't trust the servants because she knows they *will* gossip.'

Tom nodded. 'It's always a difficult position, being a governess. Neither part of the family nor one of the servants.'

'Exactly, and I don't think she has any particular friends in the locality to confide in. There's no one else in an equivalent social situation in Durley Dean – at least not that your Aunt Het knows of. And of course, she's a foreigner as well.'

'So after your encounter with the governess, what happened next?'

'I took the chutney recipe round to Miss Grimes.'

'Hardly worth the bother, I'd have thought. Particularly as Mademoiselle what's-her-name had seen straight through you.'

'As it happens, it *was* worth the bother, because Miss Grimes told me something interesting about Miss Tilling.'

'Really? What?'

'It seems that Miss Grimes was a friend of Miss Tilling and when I casually dropped her death into the conversation—'

'As one does . . .'

'She said she had imagined poor Miss Tilling looking at a book as she came downstairs and missing her footing because she wasn't concentrating on where she was going.'

'Why looking at a book?'

'Exactly what I said. Miss Grimes said it was just the way she imagined it, although it was probably quite different in real life, but whenever she thought of Miss Tilling going upstairs in the middle of the day she always associated it with books.'

'I suppose this does all have a point to it?'

'Yes, it does. Or at least maybe it does. I eventually got out of Miss Grimes that Miss Tilling had inherited quite a library of books from her father, the late Reverend Tilling. There were a lot of devotional books among them, as you would expect. The sort of thing not generally found in the public library, Miss Grimes said. Miss Tilling kept all these books on shelves in one of her spare bedrooms, and people were in the habit of borrowing them from time to time. I asked Aunt Het if she knew anything about this and she confirmed it, but said she hadn't mentioned it to us previously because she didn't see what it had got to do with Miss Tilling's demise.'

'I have to admit that I'm with Aunt Het on this one.'

'Bear with me. Miss Grimes said that if people were interested in borrowing something from the collection, Miss Tilling would take them upstairs to find the book they wanted. In most households there would be absolutely no reason for a visitor to be standing on the upstairs landing in the middle of the afternoon in a position to bonk an old lady over the head or give her a helping hand down the stairs, because in most households visitors are received in the drawing room – but in this case the Reverend Tilling's library would provide a perfect excuse to get our villain and our victim on to the upstairs landing.'

'Ah, now I'm with you.'

'Right ho. So after seeing Miss Grimes, I came back to have a bite of lunch with Aunt Het. Then I went out for another walk, beyond the place where we cut across the field to see Mr Vardy's pond, and carried on along the lane until I found the Bird in Hand beerhouse. It's a rather out of the way place and a real throwback to the old days, but it seems there are still a few farm labourers who like to have a drink there rather than going to the pubs in the village.'

'You didn't go in there, did you?'

Fran suppressed a smile at Tom's evident surprise.

'Of course I did. How else was I going to get Mrs Morgan to talk to me? It's quite titchy inside. Mrs Morgan serves the drinks in the passage and the customers sit in the parlour where there are a couple of tables and some chairs and benches. I imagine it's pretty cosy in there on a winter night when she has the fire burning. I walked up the path, stepped into the passage, and rang the little brass bell. Mrs Morgan popped out of a door at the back and looked pretty surprised to see me standing there.'

'I don't wonder,' said Tom. 'You're probably the first woman, aside from Mrs Morgan, who's ever set foot in the place.'

'Luckily it was such a hot day that I had my excuse ready prepared. I said I'd been walking and had come over a little faint, and could I possibly buy a mineral water or something? Mrs Morgan seemed to be a bit flustered by the idea, but then she reeled off this list of things I'd never heard of and I chose something called a raspberry champagne, which turned out to be a nasty sugary concoction. Before she fetched it for me, she insisted on carrying a chair out into the little front garden so that I could sit down. There were two regular customers having their beer in the parlour, and Mrs Morgan said, "You won't want to be sitting in there alongside of them, Mum". Which, of course, suited me very well, because I wanted to get Mrs Morgan on my own.'

'That's jolly plucky, you know,' Tom said. 'Not many women I know would go waltzing into a beerhouse all on their own.'

'Goodness, Tom, what on earth do people imagine is so dangerous about beerhouses?' Fran said briskly, pretending not to understand what he meant while imagining her mother reaching for the smelling salts at the very thought of her daughter going into a male-only establishment. 'Anyway, I thanked her and said I was sure I would feel much better once I'd had a nice cool drink. I'd already worked out how I was going to draw her into a conversation about how much business she did and whether she had regular customers and so on and so forth, and in no time at all we'd managed to get round to Mr Vardy.'

'You are such a cunning woman. Remind me to never get on the wrong side of you.'

'Apparently, Mrs Morgan was rather fond of Mr Vardy. She referred to him as "a nice old gentleman who had no airs about him". I suspect he was probably the only customer she had who could have been called a gentleman, and what she really meant was that unlike the other farmers in the neighbourhood he wasn't too proud to drink with the ordinary farmworkers.

'I asked her if it was true that she had been the last person to see him and she said, "That's right". And then she hesitated and said, "It's a funny thing you should ask that, because at the time I thought there was someone else in the lane".'

'Which is what she said at the inquest.'

'Yes. The thing is that Mrs Morgan seemingly doesn't keep regular opening hours the way a public house would. Once the last of her regulars leaves, whatever time in the evening that happens to be, she shuts the place up for the night and retires to bed. On dark nights, she usually keeps the door open for a moment or two, so that the hall lamp lights up the path for her departing customer, and then she closes it when they reach the gate. That's what she was doing, as usual, when Mr Vardy set off for home.'

'And she thinks that when he got to the gate he met someone in the lane?'

'She thought he spoke to someone – greeted them as if he knew them.'

'By name?' Tom couldn't keep the excitement out of his voice. 'Did she tell the police about this?'

'She did. But the trouble is she isn't at all sure now that she heard exactly what he said. Apparently it sounded to Mrs Morgan as if he said "Hello, Saul", followed by something else she didn't catch because by then she was already stepping backwards and shutting the door.'

'How did he sound? Surprised? Alarmed?'

'Just ordinary, according to Mrs Morgan. Like someone greeting a friend.'

'Saul's a most uncommon name.'

'Yes. And that's the problem. You see, according to Mrs Morgan, there used to be a man called Saul working on Mr Vardy's farm, but he passed away a couple of years ago. Needless to say, Mrs Morgan is now torn between thinking that perhaps she imagined the whole thing, or alternatively, that Mr Vardy had encountered the ghost of his old farmworker by way of a presentiment of his own impending doom.'

'And what did the police think? Or don't we know?'

'I don't think they are much enamoured with the idea of a ghostly encounter in the lane. According to Mrs Morgan, the police assumed that Mr Vardy was drunk and didn't know what he was saying, but she doesn't go along with that. "Mr Vardy might have been a bit unsteady, but he wasn't ever one to go ranting to hisself," she said.'

'A dead farm labourer,' Tom mused. 'That doesn't seem to take us very far.'

At that moment Norah rang the bell summoning them in to dinner, and Aunt Het turned the conversation to family matters that kept them going until after they were well on with their dessert. Fran was just finishing a spoonful of lemon soufflé when they heard the telephone bell ring, quickly followed by Norah's brisk footsteps along the hall and then her special telephone voice as she recited the number. There was a pause, then she said, 'Yes, Mr Dod is here.' A moment later she appeared in the doorway of the dining room and announced, 'It's for you, Mr Tom.'

Fran and Tom exchanged anxious looks. 'Something must have happened at home,' he said, as he got to his feet and hurried into the hall.

Although she knew it was rude to eavesdrop, Fran strained her ears and caught the words, 'Of course. We will come right away.'

We?

She did not have long to wait for elucidation.

'That was Florence Ripley. Her father has been arrested on suspicion of murdering her stepmother.'

'But . . . why on earth is she telephoning here?'

'It seems that Mademoiselle Bertillon told Florence of our interest in the case and she wants to know if we can help.'

'And can we?' Fran hesitated. Until now, although these supposed murders were a serious matter, detecting had been a kind of game. She and Tom were not professionals. 'Tom, are you sure we can get involved? We mustn't mislead the Ripley family about how much we might be able to help them.'

'Mademoiselle Bertillon knows we're not professionals,' he said. 'If they are desperate enough to call on us, it probably means they don't know where to turn for help. Excuse us, Aunt Het. Come along, Fran. We'll get there quicker if we drive. Young Florence Ripley sounded absolutely beside herself.'

THIRTEEN

F ran and Tom's arrival at the Ripley household on Friday night could scarcely have been more different to their previous visit just six days before. The maid who opened the front door was white-faced and looked like a frightened rabbit. She had evidently been told to expect them for she showed them straight into the drawing room, where Mademoiselle Bertillon and Florence Ripley were already on their feet, waiting to greet them. A palpable sense of shock hung over the room.

It was the governess who spoke first. 'Thank you so much for coming, Mr Dod, Mrs Black. Since the police came for Mr Ripley, we have scarcely known what to do.'

Tom took in the situation immediately. 'Has a solicitor been appointed to attend the police station on behalf of the family?' he asked.

'Daddy's solicitor is Mr Gaffney, of Frampton and Gaffney in Southwell,' Florence said, 'but the police didn't come until after office hours.'

'Then we must roust out Mr Gaffney at home. Do you think your father will have his private telephone number?'

'I'll check in Daddy's desk.' The girl hurried from the room. She seemed to be encouraged by the opportunity to contribute some help, however small. Fran noticed that she suddenly looked much younger and less self-assured than she had done at the luncheon party. Poor girl, she was obviously worried out of her mind.

Tom turned next to Mademoiselle Bertillon. 'Are there any close relatives who could come and stay with yourself and Miss Ripley?'

'Mr Ripley's only sister is in South Africa.'

'I see. How about Miss Rose? Has she been told? And young Geoffrey? Where is he?'

'Mr Geoffrey went back to school at the beginning of the week.'

'Then we must call the headmaster. It's vital that he gets word to the boy before some fellow pupil spots something in the newspapers. How about Miss Rose?'

'I did not know what to do about Miss Rose.' The governess hesitated. 'She is not really a member of the family. The police have been asking questions about her.'

'What sort of questions?'

'Whether there was anything improper going on between herself and Mr Ripley before his wife died.'

'And was there?'

Fran was impressed by the way Tom managed to make it sound like the most ordinary enquiry in the world.

'Most definitely there was not.' Mademoiselle Bertillon was so emphatic that it might have been her own reputation which was in question.

At that moment Florence appeared in the doorway, holding an open leather-bound address book in her hand. 'The number's in here.'

'Good show,' Tom said. 'Just leave this to me.'

He took the book from Florence and headed into the hall, closing the door behind him. Fran could see that his purposeful way of taking charge had already begun to calm the situation somewhat. Taking up his lead, she said, 'Why don't we have some tea? Mr Dod will make the telephone calls and, in the meantime, we had better compose a cable to Mr Ripley's sister, or she too will only learn of his arrest via the newspapers.' As Mademoiselle Bertillon rose to ring the bell for Martha, Fran went on. 'Now there is also the question of Miss Rose . . .'

'I hesitated to call Miss Rose,' the governess said carefully, 'because I did not want to suggest to the police a connection which was not there.'

'That was very sensible,' Fran said, 'but she will have to be told what has happened.'

'Poor Miss Rose,' Florence said. 'She thought she was going to be engaged to Daddy and now . . . and now . . .'

The governess reached out a comforting hand. 'Florence, my dear, I know this is hard, but it will not help us to give way to the emotions. Please can you ring the bell for Martha, and then go into the study for some paper so that we can compose a cable as Mrs Black suggests? And remember that Mr Dod and Mrs Black are going to help us.'

Again Fran felt the mantle of responsibility descending on to their shoulders. She half-wished now that she had not been so open with Mademoiselle Bertillon. It might have been better to have stuck to their story about doing some literary research. The awful reality of Mr Ripley's situation had infused the very house itself with tension. The Ripleys' electric lights were harsher than the oil and gas lamps which she was more accustomed to. Their artificial brightness seemed to make everyone's faces paler and the unusually warm evening even closer.

By the time the maid, Martha, had brought in a tray of tea and biscuits, Tom had made his telephone calls, a cable had been composed and sent to Florence's aunt in South Africa, and both Florence and Mademoiselle Bertillon had been calmed to some degree by Tom's positive, businesslike air.

'When I gave Miss Rose the news, she wanted to come over immediately,' Tom told them, 'but I assured her there was nothing she could do to help this evening. As she is Mr Ripley's secretary and a family friend, it will be perfectly natural for her to call here tomorrow, whereas coming round tonight may suggest a very close relationship to the police, which would not be helpful at the present time. Now, Mademoiselle, Miss Ripley, I know you must be tired of questions, but if Mrs Black and I are to be of any help I'm afraid we are going to need to ask you some more.'

'Of course,' Florence leaned forward, eager to help. 'Ask away.'

'First of all, do you know what made the police suspicious in the first place, and what grounds they have for arresting your father?'

'That's an easy one.' Florence sounded almost disappointed. 'Some nasty gossip wrote an anonymous letter to the police claiming that my father did away with my stepmother so he could be free to marry Miss Rose.'

It occurred to Fran that if anything ever happened to Tom's wife, a similar allegation could be made. It was the poisoned chalice again – wrong place, wrong time, wrong circumstances.

'Miss Ripley, please understand that I am not trying to be offensive in any way, but if Mrs Black and myself are to be of any help whatsoever, we need to understand the situation as fully as possible. Do you feel that there was anything at all in your father's dealings with Miss Rose before your stepmother died which could have given rise to such a suspicion?'

It was Mademoiselle Bertillon who answered. 'We understand perfectly, do we not, Miss Florence? You must ask these questions, and we must put our trust in you and answer them as truthfully as we possibly can.' She turned to Florence. 'Mr Dod and Mrs Black are not like the policemen, trying to twist the meaning of our words.'

Florence nodded. 'I don't believe there had ever been anything improper between Miss Rose and my father. We all liked Miss Rose and she was sometimes invited here to make up the numbers for dinner and things like that, particularly if Daddy was entertaining customers from the bank, as he occasionally did. Miss Rose and Daddy have the same sense of humour, and occasionally something would make them laugh. They've worked together for years, you see – and although you wouldn't think it, funny things do sometimes happen at the bank. If someone who didn't know them had seen them together, I suppose they might have thought there was more to it.'

'And your stepmother didn't seem to mind them sharing these jokes together?' Fran prompted.

'Not in the least.'

'So no one ever suggested that your father and Miss Rose might have been in love with one another at that time?'

'Goodness, no.' Florence all but laughed at the suggestion. 'It isn't as if Daddy and Miss Rose are *in love* at all. They're rather old for all that sort of thing. It's more a matter of convenience and common sense, I would say. Miss Rose lost her sweetheart in the war and has been all alone since her father died. And now that my stepmother has died, Daddy is alone too and needs someone to run the house. I don't suppose Miss Rose really likes having to work at the bank every day – who would?' The girl turned to her governess, as if in search of confirmation, but Mademoiselle Bertillon's expression was unreadable.

'So,' Tom moved on. 'A local gossip wrote to the police, the police exhumed your stepmother's body, and found what? Do you know?'

'The police inspector who came to arrest Daddy told him that the analyst found a large quantity of arsenic in my stepmother's body.'

'Arsenic?'

'Yes. They are saying my stepmother was poisoned with arsenic.'

'So she could have taken it herself, either accidentally or deliberately?' asked Fran.

'Madame Ripley would never have taken her own life,' Mademoiselle Bertillon cut in swiftly. 'It was completely against her beliefs.'

'And anyway, why ever would she?' Florence agreed. 'She was a perfectly happy person.'

'Although her health was poor?'

'My stepmother was never happier than when her health was poor.' Florence gave a little laugh. 'She would lie up in her room and be waited on hand and foot. Annie – that's our cook – would make all her favourite dishes, my father would go up and read to her, and mademoiselle or I would play the piano for her. She adored being the centre of attention.'

Fran observed that none of this was said unkindly. If anything, Florence appeared to have been completely tolerant of these foibles. 'You mentioned Mrs Ripley's beliefs,' she said. 'We've heard that she did not see eye to eye with the local vicar.'

'The Reverend Pinder?' Florence responded. 'No, she didn't like him very much. She said he was causing a lot of division among the congregation. Some people were upset by the changes he made and they left. We have a motor car, so we could have gone to St Bartholomew's – that's the next parish – but Daddy said that one can't make too much of a stand on religious issues when one is the bank manager. "Better to keep our heads down", he said.' Florence paused. 'Only my stepmother didn't. She signed a letter to the bishop, which Daddy was rather cross about.'

'Was there a row about it?' asked Tom.

'Oh, no. Daddy never rowed with her, because that might have made her feel ill. He just said, "Oh dear, I wish you hadn't, my love", or something of the kind.'

'Now if your stepmother was poisoned,' Tom said quietly, making it sound as if this was the most normal thing in the world, 'and she didn't deliberately take the poison herself, who else had access to your stepmother's food and drink?'

'Only the family and the servants,' Florence said. 'That's what makes me think the whole thing must be some sort of ghastly mistake.'

Mademoiselle Bertillon interposed helpfully. 'There were only Mr and Mrs Ripley, Miss Florence, myself, the cook and the maid here at the time. Master Geoffrey was away at school and Binks – the handyman gardener – doesn't live in and has nothing to do with what goes on inside the house.'

'Annie and Martha have both been with us for years and are completely above suspicion,' Florence put in firmly.

'What about visitors?' asked Tom. 'Weren't there some guests present when Mrs Ripley was first taken ill?'

'Yes. Mr and Mrs Craig, but that was what . . . two . . . three days before she died. Up until the last day, she didn't seem particularly poorly. Doctor Owen came to see her, but I don't believe there were any other visitors.'

'Not Miss Rose?'

'Definitely not. She never came unless invited. My stepmother died on a weekday, so both Daddy and Miss Rose were at the bank.'

FOURTEEN

I t was after midnight when Tom and Fran eventually drove back to Aunt Hetty's house. The hall light had been left burning for them and, after Tom had opened the front door with the key which his aunt had previously provided, he and Fran crept into the hall and up the stairs in silence, closing their respective bedroom doors with elaborate care, having already agreed that they ought to suspend any further discussion until the morning.

It was an absolutely stifling night, Fran thought, as she undressed. She had never known such warm weather to last right up until the end of September. There was probably going to be a thunderstorm. Even after throwing off the blankets and eider-down, she was still far too hot. She tried to lie still and relax but sleep would not come, and after a few minutes she extended her hand and felt around on the nightstand until she found the matches and managed to relight her candle. After that she slipped out of bed and tiptoed across the room to pull the sash window up as far as it would go in search of some breathable air. She took firm hold of the lower frame with both hands and heaved it upwards, hoping it wouldn't rattle, but she need not have worried, for any noise from the window was drowned by a sudden drum roll of thunder, so loud that she only just managed to stop herself from squawking in surprise.

The storm must be quite close, she thought, though presumably the lightning was only visible from the other side of the house. At that moment, however, there was a flash beyond the curtains, almost instantly followed by another explosion of sound. Fran returned to bed, smiling as she slid back under the top sheet and remembered how she had stopped being afraid of storms after her brother Geoffrey – who had been so very different to young Geoffrey Ripley – had told her that the thunder was only the giants at the top of their beanstalks having a game of rugger.

She sat waiting for another flash or rumble, but the next sound she heard was something much closer – a gentle tapping on her bedroom door. Two raps, followed by another two, Tom's signature knock.

'Come in,' she said in a voice barely above a whisper, and then watched as he eased the door open by inches, came into the room, and shut the door with equal care behind himself before he spoke.

'Are you all right?' he stage-whispered. Tom was hopeless at whispering.

'Perfectly.'

'Ah . . . the thunder doesn't worry you then? Veronica is rather bothered by it. I thought perhaps it was a female thing.'

'Not this female.' Seeing him hesitate, she added, 'You might as well come in and talk now you're here. Neither of us will be able to sleep while all this racket is going on.'

As if to underline her words, a prolonged series of rumbles and crashes intruded through the open window, so Tom came over and sat down on the bed beside her. She hoped he couldn't see how fast her heart was beating, with just the bedsheet and her cotton nightdress between herself and Tom's paisley-patterned dressing gown and silk pyjamas.

Just for a moment, as she watched his face in the glow of the candlelight, she imagined he was going to lean in and kiss her, and she had already made up her mind not to resist, but instead, he said, 'I'd say that things are looking pretty bad for Mr Ripley. The police won't view his relationship with Miss Rose in the same light as his daughter does. I'm afraid the poor child completely fails to see that falling in love is not confined to the very young.'

'She's rather typical of her age group,' Fran said, while privately thinking that in the various moments when she had imagined Tom entering her bedroom it had certainly not been in the script for him to be talking about other people falling in love. 'I expect I was the same at her age. I thought twenty-one was terribly old, and thirty positively decrepit.'

'Even so, Miss Rose appears to be out of it, as she was nowhere near the house at any point during the victim's final illness. I can't imagine a motive for Mademoiselle Bertillon or the servants, but I suppose we can't rule out Florence herself.'

'Why? I mean why would she do it?'

'It's a real long shot, but maybe she never liked her stepmother. Perhaps the stepmother had always favoured her own son, the odious Geoffrey?'

'Girls are often used to that sort of thing.'

'Whatever do you mean?'

'You don't have any sisters, do you? In most families it's the boys who get the best of it – much more fun and licence to do all kinds of things, while the girls have to stay at home, minding their manners and keeping their frocks clean. We are destined to become good girls, from the cradle to the grave. Pleasing our parents, keeping our husbands happy, never expecting to put ourselves first. Not that some of us don't occasionally decide to kick off the shackles and behave a little naughtily.'

'The trouble is that I can't imagine Florence Ripley being naughty enough to poison her stepmother,' Tom said. 'I know I said it's a possibility, but it's a real long shot.'

Tom was evidently not open to any hints about behaving naughtily, Fran thought. He really had come in only because he thought she might be afraid of the storm. Perhaps if she had pretended to be afraid, he might have put his arms around her . . .

'Listen,' he said. 'It's starting to rain. That will cool things down a bit.'

The sound of rapid heavy drops hitting the stone terrace below the window was clearly audible. Fran sighed. She knew they had to keep their relationship on the same footing that it had always been, but knowledge did not still the longing.

'Sorry,' Tom said. 'You must be awfully tired. I'd better go back to my room.'

'Oh, please don't. I'm not tired at all. I was just sighing with relief that it's begun to rain. I can't bear it when the weather is so close. Do go on talking – I won't be able to go to sleep for ages yet.' Just having him there, so close, was better than nothing.

As the thunder continued to grumble around the rooftops, they batted ideas and information to and fro until Fran was suddenly aware that a weight had shifted from the bedclothes and she heard Tom saying, 'I said you were too tired for this. Goodnight, Fran.'

She opened her eyes, which she had not realized were closing, and saw that he was already at the door. He hesitated and then said, 'I'd better blow that candle out.'

'Aren't you going to kiss me goodnight?' she mumbled, before she could stop herself.

If he answered she didn't hear him, and next morning she couldn't decide whether or not she had imagined the touch of his lips on her forehead as the bedroom candle was snuffed out.

By the time Fran got downstairs for breakfast next morning, Tom had already eaten his eggs and bacon and gone out for a walk.

'He said he wants to think,' Aunt Hetty explained. 'Just like a man. Personally I have always been able to think perfectly well while deadheading the roses or dusting the breakables, but men seem to find the process easier if they are stamping about. I assume that you two detectives have not found an answer yet?'

Fran again felt that worrying weight of expectation. 'I don't believe we are any further forward at all,' she said. 'And I do hope people aren't expecting too much. This is a really serious situation. A man is likely to be standing trial for his life. Our other murder wasn't like that.'

'Even the day after the exhumation, some people in the village were already starting to speak as if they thought Mr Ripley might be guilty.' Aunt Hetty's tone was carefully neutral. 'It will be even worse now he has been arrested.'

'He is the obvious suspect.' Fran was equally non-committal.

'The trouble is,' Fran said to Tom later that morning, as they sat under the apple tree in Aunt Hetty's garden, 'that he might be guilty. I feel as if Florence Ripley and the governess are relying on us to produce some evidence which will acquit him, but suppose he did it?'

Tom thought about the question for a moment. 'We're doing our best to discover the truth. If what we find out points to Mr Ripley's guilt, we can't help that.'

'Poor Florence Ripley.'

'Even Florence herself is a suspect.'

'So you said last night, but I thought we'd agreed that she doesn't seem to have particularly disliked her stepmother.'

'People's motives aren't always entirely obvious,' Tom said. 'Suppose Florence didn't much care for either of her parents and thought it would be rather nice to come into her inheritance as soon as she came of age?'

'Well, yes . . . If her father was blamed for the murder of her stepmother, she could kill two birds with one stone,' Fran mused. 'But it's almost five years before she reaches twenty-one – and that's assuming Mr Ripley hasn't tied his money up so that she doesn't inherit until she reaches thirty, or gets married, or some scheme like that. Besides which, if that was her plan it went all wrong, because Mrs Ripley's death was originally assumed to be from natural causes.'

'And so things would have continued if someone hadn't written anonymous letters to the police . . .'

'You mean Florence herself could have written them? Gosh, yes, Tom, that is a clever idea.'

'Though probably not the right one.'

Fran nodded. 'If Florence herself is responsible, then she must be a jolly good actress.'

'It's just an idea to keep in mind.'

'We don't have very much to go on, do we?'

'Well, there's your ghostly farm labourer, Silas . . .'

'Saul,' Fran corrected.

'And the possibility that Miss Tilling was running some kind of religious lending library, which may have been patronized by our friend Reverend Pinder.'

'I wonder what happened to Miss Tilling's cook and maid?' Fran said. 'I wish we could talk to them.'

'Why not ask Aunt Het? She might know,' suggested Tom.

Aunt Hetty did not know where either of the two women were currently working, but Fran's interest in the late Miss Tilling's domestic staff led Tom to suggest that Florence Ripley might be willing to let them interview the servants in the bank manager's household, and with this in mind they set out on foot to call at the Ripley house for the second time in less than twenty-four hours.

Florence Ripley and her governess seemed pathetically pleased to see them.

'Mr Gaffney has already called to see us this morning. He is going to do his best for Daddy and told us not to worry,' Florence said, 'but unfortunately he spoke in that prepare-yourself-for-the-worst sort of way which is of no comfort at all. We've also had a telegram back from Aunt Caroline, to say she is going to come as soon as she can. Of course, it's a jolly long way from South Africa and I expect Daddy will be freed and everything sorted out long before she gets here. Mr Gaffney thinks it's important that she comes, however, because he says that mademoiselle cannot be counted as my official legal guardian, though in the meantime she is going to take over most of the running of the household and I will do the rest. Mr Gaffney is going to organize things with Daddy so all the bills get paid . . . Oh, yes, and everyone has agreed that it will be far better for all concerned if Geoffrey simply stays at school. He will only make a nuisance of himself here.'

Fran was surprised to find herself feeling almost sorry for young Geoffrey, even if his sister's assessment of his potential usefulness was absolutely spot on.

When Tom explained their desire to interview the servants, Florence agreed with alacrity, fetching the cook and the house-maid and instructing them to give every possible assistance to Mr Dod and Mrs Black, who were, she said, 'helping the family'.

Florence had suggested that they use her father's study to conduct their interviews, but Tom declined this offer, saying that he would much prefer to use the kitchen, where, although Annie, the cook, initially protested, he insisted she take the rocking chair next to the range while he and Fran occupied the upright chairs that normally stood to either side of the scrubbed wooden table. Although clearly agog and hoping to stay, Martha, the maid, was told she could continue with her household chores elsewhere until she was required.

Tom began gently enough, eliciting the information that Annie had been with the family for almost twenty years.

'This is a terrible business, sir,' she said. 'As if the poor master hasn't had enough trouble already, losing Miss Florence's mother in a motor accident – and his leg, too – and then Master Geoffrey's mother last spring, and now all this nasty affair with the police. I always thought you could trust the police. Why, the times I've given Police Constable Godfrey a cup of tea when he was passing of an evening. There'll be no more tea after this, I can tell you! And as for all the rock buns and biscuits . . .'

Tom decided that the time had come to politely interrupt the flow. 'Now, Annie – I may call you Annie, I hope – I want you to cast your mind back very carefully to the few days before Mrs Ripley died. You remember, don't you, that the Craigs came to lunch?'

'They did, sir. I gave them roast lamb and no one but Mrs Ripley was taken poorly, so it was nothing against my cooking, you see.'

'No, of course not. I am sure there is no question of that. Now, how about things to drink? Did they have sherry beforehand, wine with lunch perhaps?'

'Martha would be the best person to tell you about that, sir. You see, she carries the food to the table and clears up afterwards, so she would know who'd had what in their glasses.'

'Of course. We must ask Martha. Now Mr and Mrs Craig left after lunch, and Doctor Owen was called in some time the same afternoon. That's right, isn't it?'

'The same day, yes. Martha heard Mr Ripley using the telephone, and she came into the kitchen and told me Mrs Ripley had a touch of the usual trouble.'

'And what was the usual trouble?'

For the first time, Annie looked uncomfortable. She fidgeted her hands and failed to meet her interrogator's eye. 'I don't rightly know, sir.'

Tom momentarily caught Fran's eye, before saying gently, 'Remember, Annie, that Miss Florence has asked you to tell us the full truth about everything. It's perfectly all right to say things to us about Mrs Ripley which you wouldn't normally tell anyone else. Things that you might be too polite or too discreet to say.'

Annie hesitated. 'Well,' she said at last. 'I know it was very wrong of us, sir, madam, but me and Martha never thought there was very much wrong with Mrs Ripley. We took her for one of those ladies what likes to rest up and have the doctor in attendance every so often. I know it was none of our business to think like that . . .'

'It's perfectly all right, Annie.' Tom had adopted his most reassuring tone. 'Believe me, this is exactly the sort of thing we need to know. So when Mrs Ripley was taken ill, none of the household were particularly worried?'

'No, sir.'

'And when Mrs Ripley was having these little episodes of illness, was it usual for her to receive callers?'

'Well, that would all depend on the caller.'

'So if it was someone Mrs Ripley liked and enjoyed seeing,' Fran suggested, 'then she might feel well enough to see them in her room?'

'That's exactly it, madam. Yes.'

'So who might be admitted to the sickroom?'

Annie promptly reeled off a list of half-a-dozen names, none of which meant anything to Fran, though she dutifully jotted them down in her pocket book.

'And did any of these people visit during her final illness?'

'No, sir, none of them.'

'How about Miss Rose?'

'Oh, no, sir. Miss Rose was just Mr Ripley's secretary. She got invited to lunch sometimes, but she didn't ever make social calls, not back then.'

'So there were no visitors to the sickroom apart from the immediate family?'

'And Doctor Owen.'

'Doctor Owen,' Tom concurred. 'Of course.'

'And the vicar, sir. It was my half-day, the day she died, but Martha told me afterwards that the vicar came to give her the last rites.' The cook punctuated this sentence by dabbing her eyes with her apron. 'I'm sorry, sir,' she said, 'but she was a nice lady and she didn't deserve to go that way. It wasn't her time. She couldn't have been more than forty-five.'

Tom nodded sympathetically. 'He is quite new here, isn't he, your vicar?'

'He's not my vicar, sir, begging your pardon. I was brought up chapel, you see, and I go to the early service there of a Sunday, and Martha comes as well. Mr and Mrs Ripley have never made any trouble about it, for all that they're staunch Church of England. In fact, I think it suits them, as us going off to the early service doesn't cause any lateness with Sunday lunch.'

'But, of course, you knew that Mrs Ripley didn't like the new vicar.'

Annie looked uncomfortable again. 'I don't know what

she thought of him, I'm sure. This isn't the sort of household where the staff go listening at doors, nor discussing matters that aren't their concern.'

'Oh, I'm sure that isn't what Mr Dod is suggesting, is it, Tom?' Fran put in quickly. 'But sometimes it is impossible not to over-hear things when you live under the same roof. And sometimes things are said outside, too. Miss Florence gave us to understand that some of the congregation at the parish church were so unhappy with things that they'd begun to go to the chapel, instead of the parish church.'

'Not to the early service.' Annie had adopted a rather stub-born tone, but then, as if having second thoughts, she abruptly relented. 'Alice Phillips, who used to work for Miss Tilling – she always came to the early service – talked quite a bit about how the new vicar was upsetting folks.' Annie lowered her voice and glanced around, as if excluding any possible eavesdroppers from a confidence. 'Alice found it rather amusing, I'm afraid. She's a terrible gossip, and she was rather irreverent about it all.'

'What sort of things did she say?'

'Oh, nothing very specific. Though she did say once that it served Miss Tilling right – her being so smug about the Church of England and them ending up with all this bother and some folks leaving and all.'

'You said she found it funny,' Fran prompted. 'Why was that?'

'Well, you see, madam, when Alice went for the job, Miss Tilling asked about her religious habits, and when Alice said she didn't attend the parish church Miss Tilling seemed to hesitate about giving her the position. "I'm the daughter of a vicar", Miss Tilling said to her. "I've never employed a Wesleyan before". In the end she gave Alice the job because the only other applicant was that girl Ruby Stainforth, and she's the sort who would turn up to an interview with a stain on her coat and dirty nails. But that's why Alice found it funny, you see – Miss Tilling setting such store by getting an Anglican and then the Anglicans all falling out with one another and deserting the ship, so to speak.'

'Alice must have needed to find another situation after

Miss Tilling died,' Tom said. 'Do you happen to know where she works now?'

'I don't, sir, but I'm sure Martha would know where she went, because their afternoon off used to coincide and they would sometimes take the bus into Southwell or Nottingham together, there being not very much to do in Durley Dean.'

FIFTEEN

When Annie went off to fetch Martha, Fran could not help but laugh about Miss Tilling's comment regarding the employment of a Wesleyan. Tom agreed. 'From what little I hear about such domestic matters, good help is so hard to come by these days that even a girl with dubious fingernails might be regarded as a find. Imagine asking someone which church they go to!'

'Miss Tilling evidently belonged to the generation which hasn't quite caught up with modern employment realities,' said Fran.

Martha was a somewhat different proposition to Annie. Skinny where the cook was plump, and garrulous where Annie had attempted to be discreet. While she was eager to help, it soon became clear that Martha was not gifted with a precise memory.

'What did people drink that particular lunchtime, sir? Well, I expect some would have had sherry before they sat down. Which ones? Well, mademoiselle always took a sherry when one was offered, her being French, I expect. Miss Florence wouldn't have been allowed it at that time, so it would probably have been a glass of lemon barley for her. Mr Ripley and the guests had sherry, I reckon, for Mr Ripley usually has sherry when there are guests. If it's just the family, he might have a glass of beer – though sometimes in the winter he has a whisky . . . a little tot, he calls it – and he is very partial to a special hot toddy mixture, which Annie—'

'And Mrs Ripley?' Tom cut in quickly.

'Sometimes she used to have a sherry. Well, most times, really. She was very particular about the brand too. Mr Binns – we always shop with Mr Binns – delivered the wrong brand once and Annie had to pull him up sharp. Mrs Ripley would have known at once, she said, if she'd tried to serve that up – decanted or not! Now when it came to cooking sherry—'

'So you can't be sure whether Mrs Ripley had sherry or not on the day she was taken ill?' Tom interposed, somewhat firmly.

'No, sir.' Martha caught the tone and was temporarily silenced, but brevity was not her strong point and when she was asked what everyone ate at the lunch party, she was off again, wanting to explain just how the master liked his vegetables served – and before they knew it, she had managed to digress on to the subject of young master Geoffrey's favourite puddings.

When it came to the period after Mrs Ripley had been taken ill, Martha couldn't remember which days Dr Owen had been to see her mistress, or whether there had been any other visitors or not. As Fran said afterwards, the only really useful information Martha was able to provide was the whereabouts of Alice, Miss Tilling's ex-maid.

'Annie told us that you and Alice sometimes used to spend your half-days together,' Fran said. 'Do you still meet up with her?'

'Oh, no, madam. We could do, because Alice has only gone to Epperstone – which is no more than ten miles away from here and she could easily catch the bus into Southwell – but since I've started walking out with Mr Hall I always spend my half-day with him.'

'Mr Hall?' Fran enquired politely.

'Harry Hall, madam. He's the gamekeeper at Welstone Lodge. He lodges with Mr and Mrs Brewster at present, but there is a nice little cottage coming up on the estate, he says, and after that . . . well, we'll see. Not that I haven't been very happy in my situation here, but a woman needs to consider her future. It isn't a secret, for I've mentioned it to Mademoiselle Bertillon and it's common knowledge in the village. It isn't like the old days, when a young woman in service dared not let on that she was walking out with a chap, lest she be dismissed and the spot. Why, I remember at my first place . . .'

'Poor Mr Hall,' Tom said later, as they were walking back towards his aunt's house. 'There's no hope for the poor fellow, unless he has some kind of hearing impediment and a deaf aid that can be switched off.'

'Don't be unkind,' laughed Fran. 'Martha did her best to help, and she's going to write to Alice so we can arrange to see her.'

'Annie described Alice as a gossip,' Tom said. 'Which could be extremely useful from our point of view. I say, isn't that Reverend Pinder approaching?'

In the same moment they had both seen the vicar of St Agnes's come into view, accompanied by a large black Labrador on a lead.

'A dog,' murmured Tom. 'A dog is always a useful diversion.'

As each of the men tipped his hat and said 'Good morning', Fran – who fortunately liked dogs – reached out her hand and offered it to the Labrador for him to sniff, prior to stroking his head.

'What a lovely dog,' she said. 'How old is he?'

Reverend Pinder, who might otherwise have passed on with just a greeting, had no alternative but to pause. 'He's seven now – or is it eight? Time moves on so fast, doesn't it?'

'I bet he takes a bit of walking,' said Tom.

'Morning and evening,' the vicar responded briskly. 'It does me as much good as it does him, of course. Fresh air and exercise hurt no man.'

'Yes, indeed. Nothing to beat a bit of exercise,' Tom agreed. 'I'm afraid the motor is my downfall. I really ought to walk more. You know, I was quite embarrassed at how out of puff I got playing tennis at the Ripleys' on our first visit here. Dreadful business, isn't it, Mr Ripley being arrested like this?'

Reverend Pinder's expression hardened slightly. 'One must not make judgements too quickly,' he said. 'But Mrs Ripley stood out against the Lord's ways, and one cannot expect to escape the consequences of one's actions.'

'But surely, Reverend Pinder,' Tom attempted to keep the shock out of his voice, 'you don't believe that Mrs Ripley's death and her husband's arrest can have anything to do with a petty quarrel at the parish church?'

'There is nothing petty about God's church, Mr Dod. Come, Saul, we must be getting on our way.' He gave the dog's lead a slight jerk. 'I am invited to dine with the Welshmans and I must not be late for luncheon.'

Fran and Tom stood watching the departing figure in his black floor-length cassock, his light-coloured hair mostly hidden by a black homburg hat. For a second or two they were both too shocked to speak. But then, as if pulled by a single thread, they pivoted to face one another and whispered in unison, 'Saul!'

SIXTEEN

Aunt Hetty left Tom and Fran to their own devices after lunch, as it was her afternoon to help out at the Cottage Hospital, where church ladies took it in turns to visit and read aloud, wind wool, or otherwise assist any patients who had no other visitors and were therefore in need of such acts of kindness. Over lunch Tom had casually mentioned their meeting with Reverend Pinder and his dog, and thereby ascertained that the dog's name was common knowledge among his parishioners.

'It is extremely difficult to believe that a man who has devoted his life to serving God could be going around bumping people off,' Fran said after they had drunk their coffee and said goodbye to Aunt Hetty.

'He seems a rather peculiar man,' Tom said.

'Well, he's not like any vicar I've ever met before,' Fran agreed. 'Even naming his dog Saul seems a little bit odd, somehow.'

'Probably some kind of ecclesiastical joke.'

'Does Reverend Pinder strike you as a man who makes jokes – ecclesiastical or otherwise?'

'Not really. Singularly lacking in any sense of humour, I'd say. But I do agree, one can't imagine a clergyman being a murderer.'

'I doubt there has ever been one,' Fran said. 'Not even in fiction.'

'Oh, well, you're wrong there,' Tom said. 'There was at least one. When I was about twelve years old I read a book in my grandfather's library that was all about a wicked priest. Actually, I'm not sure whether he was a priest or a monk, but anyway he was a terrible fellow who went about murdering people and having his way with women and goodness only knows what.'

'Good heavens! What a very peculiar book for a twelve-year-old to be reading.'

'Ah.' Tom looked a little shamefaced. 'I wasn't supposed to be reading it. Or at least . . . no one ever specifically told me not to read it. My brother Will came across it on a rainy day at grandfather's house, and once we discovered that it was jolly near the knuckle, of course we used to go and read bits of it whenever we were unsupervised and at a loose end. You know what boys are like.'

'What on earth was your grandfather doing with a book like that?'

'It was a very old book and I suppose rather valuable, so I expect it counted as art. You know how it is with art. Copulation and nakedness are fine providing that they were happening to someone else a long time ago. That makes it perfectly all right to sculpt it, paint it or write about it, whereas a photograph of Mata Hari without her clothes would be filthy pornography.'

'I think that we are getting somewhat off the subject.'

'Well, you brought it up.' Tom laughed. 'Anyway, even if there has never been a case of a murderous minister before, there's always a first time for everything. As soon as I mentioned the dog, Aunt Het came out with his name; and if Aunt Het knows the dog's name, then you can bet that old Mr Vardy did too. The dog needs to be walked morning and evening, as the vicar said himself, so it's perfectly feasible that the old man could have walked out into the lane and met Reverend Pinder and Saul on their evening stroll.'

'And we know that Reverend Pinder was the only outsider apart from the doctor to be admitted to Mrs Ripley's sick room.'

'And he might easily have borrowed books from Miss Tilling's father's library, which probably contained some pretty obscure material that might easily have been of interest to a fellow clergyman.'

'I agree that it's all awfully suggestive,' Fran said. 'I wonder if the maid Alice will know who used to borrow books from Miss Tilling? I do hope Martha manages to arrange something with Alice quickly, as I absolutely have to get home for my mother's birthday the day after tomorrow.'

'It's no use expecting anything to be arranged on a Sunday morning,' Tom said. 'There's no help for it – I will have to drive you back home tomorrow afternoon, and we'll both have to get back here again later next week. Now that the crisis over the stock market has died down a little bit, I'm sure I can be spared from the office for a few days.'

'I know it's been all over the newspapers, but I'm afraid I don't understand this business about Mr Hatry and the London Stock Exchange,' Fran said. 'What does it all mean?'

'Now that the fraud has been exposed and Hatry arrested, it looks as if there will be a continuing loss of confidence in the market, and that means a general downturn. Fortunately for W.H. Dod and Sons, we aren't in Queer Street, like some firms, and of course there will always be people who want fruit and veg, but I'm afraid it's going to mean more hardship for a great many people.'

Fran shook her head. 'I hate to see those poor ex-servicemen selling matches on street corners and queuing at the Labour Exchange. This isn't what our men fought for.'

When she came downstairs for breakfast next morning, however, it was to find that something much closer to hand had pushed Mr Hatry and his cronies on to the inside pages.

Aunt Hetty was in a virtual state of shock, and a glance at the front page of the Sunday newspapers was enough to tell Fran why.

'Poor, poor Florence Ripley,' Aunt Hetty all but whispered, as she pushed the paper in Fran's direction. '"Bank Manager's Wife Poisoned – Another Arsenic Sensation" – banner headlines, my dear, and people all over the country reading about one's family. How ever will they bear it?'

'It's horrible,' Fran agreed.

In fact, the situation was far worse than she had imagined, for when they arrived at St Agnes's that morning they found the churchyard bristling with reporters, jostling for places on the path and all but tumbling over the gravestones in their enthusiasm to catch a glimpse of Florence Ripley and her governess, who arrived in Mr Ripley's motor car. In the absence of Mr Ripley, it was being driven by Binks, the handyman, who had exchanged his usual flat cap for a faded bowler in honour of his new temporary status as chauffeur.

As the two women in the car took in the crowd of waiting pressmen, who were shouting questions and letting off flash-bulbs, Tom and several other male parishioners came to the rescue, virtually shouldering reporters out of the way in order to take the women's arms and shepherd them into the building.

While most of the worshippers attempted to ignore this invasion of their usually tranquil church grounds, Aunt Hetty made a spirited swipe at one photographer with her umbrella, saying, 'Have some respect, young man!' as she marched towards the porch with a stern look in her eye.

The interior of the church had been dressed for the Harvest Festival, and the font was surrounded by oversized vegetables artfully arranged among miniature sheaves of corn. There was a magnificent sheaf-shaped loaf before the altar, and great bunches of orange and gold chrysanthemums beamed down from every window ledge. As the beleaguered remnants of the bank manager's household made their way to their accustomed pew, they found themselves the objects of numerous kindly gestures and encouraging words. At least this unexpected adversity has brought people together, Fran thought, for the atmosphere within the building seemed much friendlier than when she had previously attended.

Fran recognized most of the congregation from their previous visit, but immediately noticed a man she had not encountered before sitting alongside Mrs Smith. She decided that this must be the woman's brother, Dr Owen, who had been absent from church the week before. Like his sister, the doctor was not overly endowed with inches and appeared to be not much taller than Fran herself. It was impossible to determine whether he had escaped the frizzy curls sported by his sister, as premature baldness had taken most of his hair and he had chosen to keep that which remained cut unusually short and close to his head.

Fran and Tom had already discussed the somewhat difficult position in which Dr Owen now found himself – for clearly, if Mrs Ripley had been poisoned, his original diagnosis and subsequent decision to issue a death certificate without first performing an autopsy would be regarded as a serious error.

When the service concluded, Fran's supposition about the man's identity was confirmed by Aunt Het, who managed to time her exit so that they came face-to-face with Dr Owen in such a way that introductions naturally occurred. Now that she could see his face, Fran decided there was a distinct resemblance between brother and sister, though she gained a fleeting impression of two very different personalities. Whereas Dulcie Smith seemed to radiate an ill-suppressed excitement or agitation of some kind ('nerves' Fran's mother would have said), Frank Owen had a calm, kindly voice and the air of a man who knows what he is doing. The hand he extended was steady, and his grip warm enough for friendliness without any danger of overfamiliarity. The perfect family doctor, Fran thought. I wonder if that manner came naturally or whether he had to learn it? If Dr Owen was worried about his certification of Elizabeth Ripley's death, or indeed anything else, she thought, he did not show it.

Tom – suitably primed in advance by Aunt Hetty – contrived to involve the doctor in a conversation about cricket, but this was cut short by the realization that Florence Ripley and her governess were about to leave.

'We need to keep those hounds from the press at bay,' Tom said. 'Shall we walk one on either side, Owen?'

The doctor caught on immediately. 'Hold on a moment, Miss Ripley,' he called. 'Let's just make sure that Binks has the car drawn up and ready, then Mr Dod and I will see you down the path.'

Left with Mrs Smith, Aunt Hetty began by complimenting the Harvest Festival decorations, telling Fran, 'Mrs Smith is now the leading light in our flower-arranging team.'

'It all looks lovely,' Fran agreed. 'It was absolutely delightful, walking in to so much colour this morning.'

If she had been hoping to win Mrs Smith's favour she was disappointed, for the woman responded by staring pointedly at Fran's mouth and saying, 'I see that you have not heeded Father Henry's views regarding lipstick, Mrs Black.'

'I think God cares more about what is in our hearts than about what we are wearing on our bodies, Mrs Smith,' Fran snapped back, before she could stop herself.

'Oh dear,' Fran said, as they rejoined Tom beside the lychgate, where the scrum of reporters was already dispersing back to the various vehicles that had transported them into the village. 'I really oughtn't to have spoken like that. Mrs Smith seems very close to Reverend Pinder, and I suppose she might have been a source of useful information if I could only have befriended her. But instead I've gone and alienated the woman.'

'Nonsense,' Tom said. 'She didn't like you anyway, you lipstick-wearing hussy.'

'And you were quite right to stop her in her tracks,' Aunt Hetty agreed. 'Such rudeness to a visitor. Besides which, my dear, the look on her face was priceless. It's such a long time since anyone has stood up to that woman – she is far too accustomed to having it all her own way.'

'Oh dear, that's another thing,' said Fran. 'She isn't supposed to be upset, because of her weak heart.'

'Rubbish!' said Tom. 'I'll bet that in the entire history of medical science, putting forward a contradictory point of view has never been known to bring on a heart attack. It's just a ruse to get her own way all the time.'

'There have been occasions,' Aunt Hetty hesitated, perhaps not wishing to upset Fran, 'when Mrs Smith has taken to her bed following some kind of upset or disagreement.'

'Probably just sulking.' Tom was brisk in his dismissal. 'Or bonkers. I have to say that there's something pretty odd about that woman. If you ask me, I'd say she was a bit unhinged.'

'She was always thought a rather peculiar child,' Aunt Hetty said. 'Her mother was extremely strict and not, I imagine, the easiest person to live with. I think Dulcie has inherited something of that dogged . . . dare one say . . . fanaticism.'

It took them a little under ten minutes to reach Aunt Hetty's house. Tom held the gate open for his aunt to precede him. 'Just time to wash our hands and have a small sherry before luncheon,' she said. 'And then, of course, you will have to be on the road again.'

SEVENTEEN

Fran had not expected to receive any gratitude for booking a table at the Golden Ball and organizing a taxi to convey them there from her mother's house for a birthday lunch, but it was still galling when her mother chuntered about the expense.

'I cannot see how you can afford this sort of thing on your income, Frances. You must learn to avoid needless extravagance, or you will very soon find yourself in difficulties.'

'Don't be silly, Mummy. It's meant to be a treat for your birthday. Please do relax and try to enjoy yourself. Look at this lovely menu.'

'It's all so expensive.' The disapproval in her mother's tone was unabated. 'It came to me over the weekend that you might have been planning something of the sort, and I tried to telephone you, but I could get no reply.'

'I was away . . . staying with some friends in Nottinghamshire.'

'Really? I wasn't aware that you had any friends in Nottinghamshire. I do wish you would keep me appraised of things like this. I was really quite perturbed when I could not get hold of you on the telephone. I wondered if you had been taken ill or something. Who are these people in Nottingham?'

'I was staying with Miss Henrietta Venn. I got to know her through a friend in the Robert Barnaby Society.'

'Is she a respectable person? Why have you never mentioned her to me before?'

'Of course she's respectable. I didn't mention her because it didn't occur to me that you would be interested.'

'Naturally I am interested. You seem to forget that you are all I have left in the world. Why didn't you tell me you were going away to Nottinghamshire?'

Because I am an independent, grown-up woman and I have no intention of keeping you posted on my every movement, Fran thought. Aloud, she said, 'Goodness, Mummy, you make it sound as if Nottinghamshire is at the ends of the earth. Oh, look, they have Dover sole on the menu – one of your favourites.'

Her mother was not to be so easily deflected. 'A woman in your position has to be careful of her reputation. Have you called on Mr and Mrs Chancellor yet?'

'I'm afraid I haven't got round to it,' said Fran, who privately had no intention of ever calling on these old acquaintances of her mother. Since separating from Michael and moving to Bee Hive Cottage, she had not even bothered to have any calling cards printed, as she considered the whole palaver of formally making and receiving calls a huge bore and completely outdated.

'Do try to decide what you want to eat, darling. The waiter will be across any minute and you've hardly glanced at the menu.'

'Oh dear,' laughed Mo, when Fran told her about the episode of the birthday lunch while they were having tea at Fran's cottage the following day. 'Was she like that the whole time?'

'Well, no, not the whole time. She did soften up a bit after eating her dessert, dabbing her eyes, as is customary on these occasions, and saying she could never really enjoy a birthday again now that Geoff and Cec weren't there to share it.'

'Oh dear,' Mo repeated in a completely different tone of voice.

'I know it seems mean of me, but it just made me crosser. She thinks that I don't understand how hard it is to lose your sons in the war, but it never seems to cross her mind that I miss them too. Or that she might be kind enough to remember once in a while that I don't need to be forever reminded that a surviving daughter is only a poor third prize.'

'I take it you didn't mention Michael and Winnie's expected child? Or that you are thinking about getting a divorce?'

'How could I? It would have been a terribly unkind thing to do on her birthday.'

'Agreed. When will there be a good time to tell her?'

'Never! But I can't leave her to find out via some third party. That would be even crueller. I've decided to wait until I know for sure what I'm going to do. Once I've made up my mind, then I'll either break the news about the baby, or else tell her about the baby *and* the divorce at the same time – to get it over with in one fell swoop, as it were.'

'You still haven't decided about the divorce?'

'No. But I have been looking into it. After I'd finished with the birthday celebrations, I had an appointment with Mr Long, the solicitor in Ulverston, and he explained what is entailed. He said it can all be done fairly quietly, but there are a couple of complications. As you know, the couple can't be seen to want a divorce or to be colluding in any way in order to get one. So Mr Long said that since Michael has obviously gone off to live with Winnie and there's a babe on the way, we can't go down the road of a put-up job, with Michael being caught staying at a hotel with some floozy. Instead I have to write to Michael, telling him that I want him to come back to me and then when he doesn't return to the marital fold, I can divorce him on grounds of his desertion and adultery with Winnie.'

'I bet her family won't like that.'

'Too bad. That's the deal, take it or leave it. If she didn't want to be cited in a divorce, perhaps she shouldn't have run off with someone else's husband.'

'Quite. You said there are a couple of complications.'

'The other is that before we can get the decree absolute, we have to keep the court convinced that there's no collusion, so my behaviour will be under scrutiny as well.'

'It's so ridiculous,' Mo declared. 'The law lets people marry each other perfectly freely. If people can decide to be together without the interference of a blasted judge, then why on earth shouldn't they be equally free to part when they both want to? The divorce laws in this country are incredibly stupid!'

'I know. It's utterly illogical and completely horrid,' Fran agreed. 'For most people, it means that in order to get a divorce they have to involve themselves in a level of deceit that's an absolute anathema to anyone who is halfway decent. But if one wants a divorce, that's the way it is. Apparently someone called the King's Proctor will be keeping an ear to the ground and if there is any rumour that I am romantically involved with someone else, that's it – no divorce.'

'Which means you and Tom would have to stop seeing each other.'

'Not because there is anything going on between us,' Fran said bitterly, 'but because some nasty-minded person called the King's Proctor might *think* there was something going on.'

'The King's Proctor,' Mo mused. 'The name puts one in mind
of some kind of unpleasant medical procedure.'

'As if the King would be remotely interested in what anyone
was doing in their private life,' Fran said. 'I expect His Majesty
is far more interested in his stamp collection.'

'Stamp collection?'

'Yes, didn't you know that the King collects stamps?'

'No, I didn't. What extraordinary bits of information you sometimes come up with. Talking of which, how is the investigation
going down in Nottinghamshire?'

Fran spent a few minutes bringing her friend up to date,
concluding with the information that according to the newspapers
an inquest into the death of Alice Elizabeth Ripley had been
opened and adjourned, and her husband had been formally
charged with her murder and remanded by the magistrates' court.

'Not much point in having an inquest,' Mo remarked. 'Given
that the police have already leaked the findings of the analysis
and arrested Mr Ripley for murder.'

'It's just a formality,' Fran said. 'It will probably be postponed
until after Mr Ripley has been tried and then the coroner's jury
just has to replicate the trial jury's verdict. In the meantime, Tom
and I are supposed to be finding out what really happened.'

'Well, the vicar is odds-on favourite,' Mo said cheerfully. 'With
the Ripley daughter a good outside bet and Saul, the ghostly
farm labourer, currently at 1000 to 1.'

'It's all very well making a joke of it, but I feel awfully
responsible. It's as if we've made a sort of promise to help when
actually we aren't in a position to do anything of the kind. Neither
of us is even on the spot any more, and Tom rang last night to
say that he can't get away until the end of this week after all.'

'Can't you go back to stay with his aunt?'

'She's told me I'm welcome at any time, but I don't see what
good going back there will do. I can't just go around questioning
people, the way the police would.'

'Why not? People often employ private detectives to investigate
things on their behalf.'

'Don't be silly, Mo. Tom runs a wholesale fruit-and-vegetable
business and I am . . . well . . . a sort of housewife without a
husband, I suppose.'

'I don't imagine there are any special qualifications for setting up as private investigators. If you were able to tell people that Florence Ripley has commissioned you to investigate on her behalf, that would give you the perfect excuse to contact whoever you want and ask them questions. I bet a lot of local people would cooperate if they thought it might help the Ripley family – and even if some said "no", you wouldn't have lost anything by it, as those sorts of people wouldn't have talked to you anyway. Why don't you get Florence Ripley to agree to it?'

'Goodness, I don't know. It seems very forward and it can't be right, pretending to be detectives.'

'Investigators,' Mo corrected. 'You wouldn't be pretending because you *are* investigating. That's why you went down there in the first place, isn't it?'

'I suppose so. I'll talk to Tom about it when I telephone him again tonight.'

EIGHTEEN

Somewhat to Fran's surprise, rather than ridiculing Mo's idea, Tom took it up with alacrity, and by the end of the evening he had discussed it by telephone not only with Florence Ripley herself, but also with Mademoiselle Bertillon and the Ripleys' solicitor, Mr Gaffney.

'I thought Gaffney might be a bit stuffy about it,' Tom told her, 'but he seems to feel that there's nothing against it. According to him, the police have made up their minds and don't appear to be making any further enquiries, so in the absence of appropriate professional intervention the Ripleys have nothing to lose by engaging amateurs.'

'How is Mr Ripley doing?'

'Gaffney reckons he is still in shock and simply can't believe what is happening.'

'I can understand that. I mean, even to us, it doesn't feel quite real, does it? Someone you were eating lunch with not a fortnight ago is now on the point of standing trial for murdering his wife?'

'Let's hope it doesn't come to that,' Tom said. 'There are quite a few hurdles to get over before being sent for trial. First there's the inquest and then the formal committal proceedings at the magistrates, and then the case won't actually be heard until it's been approved by a grand jury at the next assizes.'

'But they have adjourned the inquest and hardly any murder cases ever get thrown out at any of those other stages,' Fran said.

'No.' Tom's tone grew sober. 'Hardly any.'

'So it's agreed then,' Fran said as brightly as she could. 'I'm to go back down to Nottinghamshire on the next possible train.'

When her taxi drew up outside Aunt Hetty's on Thursday afternoon, Fran experienced a strong sense of *déjà vu*. Everything in the spare bedroom – the paper-lined drawers of the dresser, the floral-patterned bowl and jug on the washstand, even the little tin of biscuits on the night table – looked just the same. And yet, Fran thought, things are different. As the page of the calendar had turned to October, so the weather had abruptly changed: the long Indian summer had given way to rain and gales. The flowers in Aunt Hetty's borders looked forlorn and battered, the trees across the road were starting to show their autumnal tints, and a cardigan was a definite requirement. Other things had altered, too. There had been a certain larkiness to their original arrival. Aunt Hetty's suspicious deaths had been no more than a puzzle to solve, whereas now a man's life was at stake. Suppose everything she and Tom uncovered merely pointed to Mr Ripley's guilt? Although there was no money involved, she and Tom had sought their commission on the basis of helping rather than hindering the bank manager's cause, and yet they could not be sure that he stood on the side of right.

Added to this was the faint worry that her name might somehow become publicly linked with the case. The press had given up besieging Durley Dean for the time being, but no doubt the furore would erupt all over again the moment there were any fresh developments. Fran could well imagine her mother's reaction to an appearance in the papers by her only daughter in connection with something as sordid as an alleged murder.

It had been arranged via Tom that Florence Ripley would contact various people to whom he and Fran wished to speak, so after eating supper with Aunt Hetty, Fran walked the now familiar route to the Ripleys' house to learn the results of this operation. She was admitted by Martha, as usual, and shown straight into the drawing room, where she found not only Florence and her governess but also Miss Rose.

'Miss Rose wants to help in any way she can,' Florence explained. 'Knowing that you would need to see her, she offered to come over this evening, because of course she is still working at the bank during the day.'

'And there is no convenient place for a private interview at my boarding house,' Miss Rose intervened. 'When the police came to see me, my landlady was rather difficult about it. Nor does she like her lodgers receiving telephone calls. Obviously she takes the respectability of her establishment very seriously – we are all unmarried ladies, of course – and she feels that the arrival of the local constabulary casts quite a slur upon her premises. Fortunately I have been able to persuade Inspector Donaldson, who seems to be leading the police investigation, that if he needs to speak with me again, it would be far better achieved by attending my place of employment.'

'Thank you, Miss Rose. I would appreciate talking to you, of course.'

'Here is the list of people Mr Dod asked me to contact.' Florence handed across a sheet of paper, adding, 'No one has refused.'

Fran cast her eyes down the list. 'Goodness,' she said. 'You have done well. Reverend Pinder has agreed, I see.'

'Well, of course. He's our vicar, after all. And it's a good idea, going to talk with him, because vicars tend to know all sorts of things, don't they? Especially vicars who encourage people to go to confession.'

'The confessional is sacred, Miss Florence,' Mademoiselle Bertillon reproved. 'Anything said to a priest in such circumstances would never be revealed.'

'Well, not revealed as such, no,' Florence said. 'But surely Reverend Pinder could drop a hint if he knew something important, rather than just letting Daddy go ahead and be hanged?'

'Miss Florence!'

The girl tossed her head and said almost angrily, 'It's no use pretending to be shocked. We all know what will happen to Daddy unless we can find out what really happened to my stepmother.'

Fran could see that beneath the bravado Florence was close to tears. 'I'm sure it isn't going to come to that,' she said quickly, with far more confidence than she felt.

'Why don't we go into the study, Mrs Black?' Miss Rose suggested. 'Florence has kindly put the room at our disposal and I'm sure some tea can be sent in, or coffee, if you would prefer it.'

Fran noticed the way in which Miss Rose – who had once virtually assumed the role of hostess – was now deferring to Florence as the head of the household. She immediately agreed to both suggestions, with the result that in a matter of a few minutes the two women were settled in the bank manager's study, with Miss Rose taking an armchair to one side of the fireplace and Fran taking the other.

Fran had decided to adopt a similar line to that which she had seen Tom employ and, making it sound like the most natural enquiry in the world, she began by asking, 'Do you think Mr Ripley could have killed his wife, Miss Rose?'

It was a calculated risk, but to her relief the other woman replied in a completely level voice. 'That rather depends on what you mean. If you are asking *could* Mr Ripley have killed his wife, meaning did he have the opportunity to do so, then the answer is "yes". But if you mean was Mr Ripley *capable* of killing his wife, then I would answer emphatically "no".'

'What makes you say that?' Fran asked politely.

'Horace Ripley and I have worked together for just over seven years and during that time we have got to know one another very well. As you must be well aware, I am very fond of him, and I am sure that he is very fond of me – but I believe he was equally fond of his late wife and extremely loyal to her. She could at times be an extremely exasperating woman, rather selfish and self-centred, but he tolerated all of that and, although we became good friends during our time working together, there was never a hint of impropriety between us. The other thing . . .'

Miss Rose hesitated, received an encouraging nod from Fran, and continued. 'The other thing is that Horace Ripley is not a brave man. I don't mean that unkindly, Mrs Black, but . . . well . . . I think it takes a certain amount of nerve to commit a murder and Horace is not that kind of man. I don't mean to say that he is a coward. I daresay,' she hastened on, perhaps fearing she had made a bad impression, 'that had it not been for his being unfit for service, he would have answered his country's call. However, he is conventional. He worries over the slightest lapse at the bank. Even blots in the ledger, or a farthing out of the final balance is a source of agitation. Such men do not go looking for perilous situations. They are not – in my opinion, at least – the stuff of which murderers are made. Finally, as someone who knows him well, I would say that his shock and grief on learning of his wife's death were absolutely genuine.'

Fran found herself nodding, as if in comprehension. 'Were you present when he heard that his wife had died?'

'It was me who broke the news to him. The governess, Mademoiselle Bertillon, telephoned from the house, and when I told her Mr Ripley was rather tied up, she said that in any case it might be better if she spoke with me. I was extremely surprised, because I could not imagine why she would prefer to speak with me, and such a thing had never occurred before. Then she told me that Mrs Ripley had taken a sudden turn for the worse and died. She said Mr Ripley was needed at home, and asked my advice as to how we might break the news, so I offered to inform Mr Ripley, and she accepted. I went into his office and told him that he must prepare for some bad news. He was shocked, of course, and asked me at once what had happened. I told him that Mademoiselle Bertillon had just telephoned to say that his wife had died a few minutes before.'

'Can you remember what he said in reply?'

'Not the exact words, no.' Miss Rose paused, thinking. 'He made some kind of exclamation. He was obviously shocked and surprised. He said something like "Impossible!" or "Surely not?", and I said I was terribly sorry but it was true and that he would be needed at home. Then he just sat at the desk for a moment and tears came into his eyes. I said I would tell Mr Johnston – he's our chief clerk – that he would have to take over for the rest of the afternoon, and Mr Ripley just nodded, and then I went out and explained the situation to Mr Johnston. Mr Johnston and I agreed between us that we would not say anything about Mrs Ripley's death to the junior staff, as it was only a couple of minutes to closing time and there was no point in people becoming distracted from their work just then. I was on the point of returning to Mr Ripley's office, to ask if there was anything he would like me to do, when he came out wearing his hat and coat and gave me a brief nod before he left the building. I honestly believe he was too much overcome with emotion to have said anything more to me just then.'

'Mrs Ripley's death seemed to you to have been completely unexpected?' Fran prompted.

'Goodness, yes. I don't imagine Horace would have come into the bank that morning if he had thought for a moment that his wife was dying. He may be very conscientious about his duties, but he is not such a cold fish as that!'

'And yet Doctor Owen issued a certificate,' Fran said thoughtfully.

'Oh, but that would have been perfectly proper,' Miss Rose said. 'Before I was with the bank, I worked for a time as a hospital secretary, so I know a little bit about the regulations. Providing the doctor who issues the certificate has been treating the patient in the run up to their death and there are no suspicious circumstances of course, then a certificate can be issued without an inquest.'

Fran could not help thinking that if someone wasn't expected to die and then suddenly did, that was in itself a slightly suspicious circumstance, but she kept the thought to herself. Instead, she asked, 'When was the last time that you saw Mrs Ripley, before she died?'

For the first time, Miss Rose had to stop and think for quite a long time. Eventually she said, 'Do you know, I'm not really sure. It would have been in some quite ordinary way I expect, such as meeting one another in the High Street, for example.'

'You didn't go to see her when she was ill?'

'Goodness, no. We were sociable with one another, but we were not friends.'

'You didn't like her?' Fran suggested.

'I didn't dislike her, if that's what you mean. She was Mr Ripley's wife, so of course I was respectful and showed her the degree of friendship appropriate to our relative positions.'

Since Miss Rose did not seem in the least upset or offended by these questions, Fran decided to probe a little further. She was conscious that it was not polite to do so, but then she remembered that private investigators were not necessarily expected to be polite. 'Do you think Mrs Ripley realized you were fond of her husband, and he of you?'

'I think you have perhaps overestimated the level of fondness which existed before Mrs Ripley's death,' Miss Rose said. 'I have no doubt Mrs Ripley was aware that her husband and I got along well and that he appreciated my efficiency as his secretary, but there was nothing in our relationship which would have given Mrs Ripley any cause for concern. It was all very proper, I assure you.'

'And that was as far as I got with Miss Rose,' Fran told Tom, when he arrived on Friday evening. 'She continues to insist that there was nothing but normal friendliness between herself and

her employer until after his wife had died. She also claimed that
Mrs Ripley was still an extremely beautiful woman, to whom
her husband appeared devoted. "If anyone had suggested to her
that her husband was in love with his secretary, she would have
laughed in their face", were her final words on the subject.'

'I hadn't realized that Mrs Ripley was a looker,' said Tom.
'And poor old Miss Rose isn't exactly a beauty queen.'

'That might make it worse,' Fran said thoughtfully. 'I mean,
suppose you were a slightly dull-looking secretary, wildly in love
with your boss, but his relationship with you was no more than
friendship because he adored his utterly gorgeous wife . . .
Wouldn't that make you all the more eager to get rid of her?'

'Because you weren't satisfied with just being good friends
and wanted something more?' Tom's question hung in the air
for a moment before he added, 'But surely Miss Rose is
completely out of it, because she was never anywhere near the
house during Mrs Ripley's last illness? Though she could have
been somehow in cahoots with Mr Ripley, I suppose. We only
have her word for it that he adored his wife and took no romantic
interest in his secretary until after his wife's death. It could all
be a double bluff. Perhaps Miss Rose is just putting on a front
in order to protect her lover?'

'Except that after Miss Rose had gone, I spoke to Mademoiselle
Bertillon again and she essentially confirmed what Miss Rose
had said about Mr Ripley being pretty devoted to his wife. Don't
forget that Florence took exactly the same line. It had obviously
never occurred to her that her father might have wanted her
stepmother out of the way in order to marry Miss Rose.'

'So we're no further forward so far as the Ripley ménage is
concerned.' Tom sighed. 'Never mind,' he said. 'We have lots
more people to talk with tomorrow.'

NINETEEN

Their first port of call on Saturday morning was in Epperstone, a village about ten miles away, where permission had been given for them to interview Alice, one-time housemaid to the late Miss Tilling, who was now working for a retired major and his wife.

Alice was, as her friend Martha had warned them, a great gossip; and if anything, she was even more garrulous than Martha herself had been. Alice had evidently heard all about the troubles at St Agnes's, but it had never occurred to her to associate the death of her previous mistress with them. All the same, when encouraged to speak freely, she had a good deal to say about various parishioners, most of it garnered from her acquaintances who worked below stairs in Durley Dean. 'Mr and Mrs Cocklington, now, they are as nice folk as you would ever care to meet and would do anyone a good turn. Real Christians they are and no mistake. Their cook, Flora, told me that they have refused to take sides over all this business at the church and just carry on as they always did, being kind and generous to everyone what crosses their path.'

'How about Mr Vardy? Did you know him?'

'I can't say as I know much about Mr Vardy,' Alice conceded reluctantly. 'My cousin Wilf worked for him a couple of years back and reckoned he was a fair old tyrant, but then it's always been said in the family that our Wilf's a right lazy lad, so it would be small wonder if Mr Vardy hadn't got on to him.'

Miss Flowers was 'a funny old stick' according to Alice, and so prim and proper that she still had the newspapers ironed each day, while Mrs Welshman was 'a fairly peaceable sort', though she had engaged in a long-standing dispute with Mr Sopwith, the butcher, over a Christmas goose which had been past its best, with the result that she had taken her business elsewhere. Miss Grimes had fallen out with Miss Flowers back before the war, though no one could remember what it had been about, and they hadn't spoken to one another in the best part of twenty years. 'Mind you, it's no wonder Miss Grimes can't remember the cause of their rowing, because she is so forgetful now that she can't remember anything much, poor old soul.'

Given half a chance, Alice would have worked her way through all the inhabitants of Durley Dean, providing details of their minor squabbles and domestic mishaps going back over the last couple of decades, and Tom had to keep dragging her back to more relevant areas.

Asked whether the various members of the congregation of St Agnes's had been in the habit of visiting Miss Tilling and perhaps borrowing some of the books which had belonged to her late father, Alice agreed at once that there had been plenty of callers connected to the church. 'Though I wouldn't know about the books, sir, as Miss Tilling would have taken folk up and down the stairs to look at them herself.'

'You dusted the books, I suppose? Would you have noticed which books were borrowed and returned?'

'I did dust them, of course, sir. But there was an awful lot of them, and I wouldn't have known from one time to the next what was there and what wasn't.'

'Did Reverend Pinder ever call?'

'Oh, yes, plenty of times. Miss Tilling used to invite him round for afternoon tea quite regular. Myself and Cook couldn't decide if it was two-faced of her – seeing as how she couldn't stand the man – or properly Christian to welcome him in spite of her feelings.'

Repressing a smile at the thought of this pseudo-theological debate going on in the kitchen, Fran said, 'Supposing Reverend Pinder had rung the doorbell that afternoon when you were out taking the parcel to the post office, would Miss Tilling have let him in?'

'Oh, yes, I'm sure she would. I doubt she would have made him any tea, though. Not with me being expected back presently. She would have waited and rung the bell for me when I got back in.'

'How about other people she knew?'

'It would have been the same,' Alice said. 'Miss Tilling wouldn't have made them any tea. She would have waited until

I got back to do it. She never went into the kitchen herself, except occasionally to issue orders, and even then she'd usually ring for one of us to go into the drawing room or the morning room. You see—'

'But she would definitely have opened the front door to someone she knew if you weren't there to do it for her?'

Alice adopted the patient look of a put-upon servant humouring an extremely stupid question. 'Well, yes, sir, of course she would have let them in. You wouldn't leave friends and acquaintances standing on the doorstep, but she wouldn't have made any tea and I doubt she even knew where to lay a hand on the biscuits . . .'

'So in spite of her disagreements with Reverend Pinder, she still invited him and his supporters for tea?' Fran reiterated.

'I don't know about his supporters.' Alice hesitated. 'There had been a few harsh words exchanged, and feelings were running high. Of course, some people just invited themselves. That Mrs Smith from across the road. Not once but twice she turned up at the door when Reverend Pinder was there. Sweet on him, I reckon. Cook said she thought it more than a coincidence, and that she wouldn't be surprised if Mrs Smith hadn't seen the Reverend arrive through her front window and made some excuse to come across.'

'Could Mrs Smith see Miss Tilling's front door from her window?' asked Tom, catching Fran's eye and trying to keep a note of heightened interest out of his voice.

'Oh, yes – she lives right opposite with her brother, the doctor. She was always a bit of a nosy parker, begging your pardon. I reckon she knew a good deal too much of people's business already, being the doctor's sister and him probably telling her all sorts about his patients. There's not much goes on that passes Mrs Smith by – why, she was forever sitting in that front window. She cracked on to Maisie – that's their cook – that she sits there to get the best light for her needlework, but I've got my own opinions on the subject.'

'Could Mrs Smith have seen someone come to Miss Tilling's house that afternoon, do you think?' Fran asked Tom as they were driving away. 'If she did, surely she would have said something about it?'

'Mrs Smith can't spend her whole life looking out of the front window, whatever Alice may think. But if she was looking out and did see someone approaching Miss Tilling's door, then I suppose there are two possibilities. One is that she didn't appreciate the significance of what she'd seen, or two, that she stayed silent in order to protect someone.'

'And that someone could have been Reverend Pinder. The man with the dog called Saul.'

'He's on our list. What say we go to see him next?'

TWENTY

F ran felt absurdly nervous as she and Tom drove in through the gates of the large Georgian rectory, but the visit quickly turned into an anti-climax, for the maid who eventually answered the clanging doorbell informed them that the Reverend Pinder was out on parish business.

'Blow it,' said Tom when they were back in the car. 'Who should we try next, do you think?'

Fran glanced at her wristwatch. 'It's getting on for twelve,' she said. 'It's not very good form to drop in on people just before lunch.'

'You're right. I wonder what time Doctor Owen and his sister Mrs Smith sit down? But perhaps we'd better leave them until this afternoon. Hello . . . Who's this?'

Tom's eye had been caught by a man wearing rather shabby tweed plus fours and a matching jacket who had paused in the act of walking his spaniel past the rectory gates. He now appeared to be hesitating, as if unsure whether to enter or not. As Tom pulled the car forward a few yards and nosed it out into the road, the stranger waited, with the obvious intention of initiating a conversation, so Tom wound down his window and said good morning.

'Good morning. Pardon my asking, but would you be the young persons commissioned by Miss Florence Ripley to look into her stepmother's death?'

'Tom Dod.' Tom removed a hand from the wheel and extended it in the stranger's direction. 'And this is my companion, Mrs Black.'

'I see, I see.' After fumbling the dog leash from one hand to another, the man clasped Tom's proffered hand for a brief reluctant shake, rather as if he suspected a trick of some kind, then said, 'You've just been to visit the Reverend Pinder, I see.'

'He wasn't at home,' Tom said. 'I don't think we have been introduced?'

'Pascoe. Frederick Pascoe. I daresay my name has already come to your attention.'

'I can't say that it has, Mr Pascoe.'

'Oh . . .' The man seemed momentarily taken aback. 'Then I suppose you haven't spoken to that bossy harridan at the bank yet. You should not take any notice of a word she has to say about me, Mr Dod. Not a word. I am a wronged man – a thoroughly innocent party, that's what I am. And if people are talking about the sending of the letters, well it turns out that I was right all along!'

'I'm sorry, Mr Pascoe, but I'm afraid I have no idea what you are talking about,' Tom said. 'Perhaps you would care to explain.'

'There is no explaining to do!' the man burst out. 'That's the whole point, sir. I know that wretched woman at the bank will try to foist the whole blame on to me, somehow or other, but the point is that I did not know for sure when I sent the letters. Only now, of course, with everything being looked into and that woman at the bank wanting to lay the blame elsewhere, I know it is only a matter of time before she will have her say. She knows what was said, you see.'

'What was said about what? Which woman do you mean?'

'There is only one woman at the bank, you dunderhead,' thundered Mr Pascoe, who had gone so red in the face that he looked about to explode.

Sensing his master's mood, the spaniel gave a couple of indignant barks, as if by way of corroboration.

'Do you mean Miss Rose?' asked Tom, but the man was already walking off down the road, carried mostly on the tide of his own indignation.

'What a peculiar fellow,' said Fran. 'You know, now I come to think of it, I'm sure that someone has mentioned the name Pascoe before, but I can't remember how it came up. Was he one of the disgruntled parishioners?' She was fumbling for her notebook as she spoke. 'He certainly isn't on the list of people Florence Ripley has made arrangements for us to talk with.'

'Mmm. He doesn't strike me as someone who'd be particularly enthusiastic about having a tête-à-tête with us. Let's go back to Aunt Het's for a bite of lunch. Then we can ask her to elucidate on the peculiar Mr Pascoe. He must be a local if he's walking his dog along here, and I bet there's no one in Durley Dean that Aunt Het doesn't know.'

Aunt Hetty had laid on cold meat and pickles, 'so that you can tuck in whenever it is convenient'. As for Mr Pascoe, 'I've never thought him particularly odd,' she mused, 'though he does have a very short fuse and is the sort who easily falls out with people.'

'Indeed he does,' Tom said. 'I doubt that we'd managed to exchange more than a dozen words before getting into his bad books. And he certainly has it in for Miss Rose. He called her a bossy harridan. Has there been some kind of problem between himself and Miss Rose?'

Aunt Hetty laughed. 'Lots of men don't particularly like Miss Rose. She is very firm and capable, you see, and men like Mr Pascoe expect all women to behave just as their wives do, saying, "Yes sir, no sir, three bags full, sir". It would not go down at all well if, for example, Miss Rose refused them admission to Mr Ripley's office at the bank.'

'I think I've got it now,' Fran said. 'On the morning when I met Mademoiselle Bertillon in the village, she told me that when a Mr Pascoe's business failed he blamed Mr Ripley and swore to take revenge on him.'

'Oh, yes,' said Aunt Hetty. 'There was talk of something like that. One doesn't know all the details, but Mr Pascoe's business did go under a year or two ago and I believe their circumstances have been somewhat straitened ever since. They had to let their cook go and they have stopped entertaining altogether since Mrs Pascoe has been doing the cooking.'

'And is it true that he swore to take revenge on the Ripleys?'

'Well, Tom dear, I really don't know anything about that, though it would be easy to imagine Mr Pascoe saying something of the kind in the heat of the moment. He's such a blustering type of man.'

'We need to ask Miss Rose what he's talking about,' Fran said. 'It might be significant.'

'There now!' Aunt Hetty pretended to smack the back of her own hand. 'I almost forgot to tell you. Mr Hargreaves came here this morning hoping to catch you. Like Mr Pascoe, it seems that word of your mission on behalf of Mr Ripley has reached him, and he said he would like to talk with you. When I explained that you were already out, he said he would appreciate your calling on him this afternoon, if you can spare the time.'

'Hargreaves . . . Remind me where he fits in,' requested Tom.

'I am not sure where Mr Hargreaves "fits in", as you put it. He is a regular worshipper at St Agnes's and not at all enthusiastic about all the changes.'

'Wasn't he one of the signatories to the letter of complaint which was sent to the bishop?' asked Fran.

'He is the only surviving complainant,' said Aunt Hetty. 'Or at least the only one who still attends St Agnes's. Mr and Mrs Brayshaw were the others, but they have left.'

'Gosh,' said Tom, as he piled piccalilli on to his plate. 'We'd better get to him before someone bumps him off, too.'

'Really, Tom!' his aunt objected. 'One oughtn't joke about such things.'

'Now my dear,' she turned to address Fran. 'You really must have more than that for your lunch, or you will simply waste away.'

'Leave her alone.' Tom laughed. 'You are always trying to feed people up. Tell me, did Mr Hargreaves give you any idea what he wants to talk to us about?'

'I think it may have been something to do with Dulcie Smith. He said, "I suppose you've told them about Mrs Smith?" and then he gave me a sort of knowing look. I didn't know quite what to say to that. Then he said, "It was just something she said the other day. It troubled me, but I don't want to go to the police, you see". So I said, "The best thing will be to tell my nephew and his colleague, Mrs Black. They will know what to do".'

'It sounds as if Mr Hargreaves thinks that Dulcie Smith knows something about the murders,' Fran said. 'Miss Venn, you once said you had your suspicions about a particular person. That was Dulcie Smith, wasn't it?'

'I do hope this isn't going to go beyond these four walls.' Aunt Hetty spoke reluctantly. 'It does seem so dreadful to suspect anyone. And, of course, there is no evidence whatsoever. It's just instinct really. One feels there is something . . . not quite right . . . about that poor woman.'

'Poor woman, my eye,' Tom remarked, when they were

climbing back into the car in readiness for their afternoon house calls. 'It seems to me everyone falls over themselves to make allowances for that woman and be nice to her, despite the fact that she's quite venomous to other people.'

They decided to call on Mrs Smith and her brother first, but met with disappointment when the maid, a timid-looking girl with a lisp, informed them that the doctor had driven into the city in order to watch Nottingham Forest play, and his sister was not at home either, having gone to help hand out the hymn books at a wedding in St Agnes's.

'Bother! That means Father Pinder will be tied up too,' said Fran. 'I can't say the happy couple have chosen the best weather for their big day. It looks as if it's going to pour down again in a minute. Let's try Mr Hargreaves next, as he was so keen to see us.'

'It's quite surprising, isn't it?' said Tom. 'We thought it might be difficult to get people to talk to us, but instead even people who aren't on Florence Ripley's list, like Mr Pascoe and Mr Hargreaves, are positively seeking us out.'

In order to reach Mr Hargreaves' cottage they had to backtrack towards the church. They initially had some trouble locating the address, which turned out to be a modest dwelling tucked down a little alleyway at the rear of the churchyard. As the path was too narrow for a motor car, the Hudson was left on the main road and they undertook the fifty or so yards on foot. It turned out to be another wasted journey, for although they allowed plenty of time for Mr Hargreaves to respond to their summons on the door knocker, it soon became apparent that there was not going to be an answer.

'Dear me,' said Fran. 'We really should have made firm appointments with people. We're wasting an awful lot of time, just traipsing around not finding people at home.'

They had more success when it came to gaining an audience with Clara, Miss Tilling's one-time cook, though she could add nothing to what Alice the ex-housemaid had already told them. Clara was now working for Mr and Mrs Cocklington, who insisted on providing them with tea and cake and were very keen to help, though they had no real information to give.

After that they called on Mr and Mrs Brayshaw, who also

plied them with tea and cake, but although the Brayshaws had
been the other signatories to the letter of complaint to the bishop
regarding Father Pinder, they too had little to add to what was
already known.

'I'm sure you will think this a strange question,' Tom said,
'but did you ever think it a little odd that several of the people
who signed that letter have died unexpectedly?'

'It is a strange coincidence,' Mrs Brayshaw said. 'Of course,
people in country districts like this are inclined to get all sorts
of silly superstitious ideas into their heads. Personally I have
never given any credence to that kind of nonsense, but I daresay
that if you asked Harriet, our parlour maid, she would say that
someone had put some kind of curse on the signatories. I'm
afraid poor Harriet is much addicted to attending these wretched
séances which are all the rage nowadays. One tries to discourage
it, but discipline among domestic staff is so much more difficult
to achieve than it was in the old days.'

'I don't believe we'd made any connection between the three
deaths and the fact that they all happened to be party to the letter
until Mrs Smith pointed it out,' said Mr Brayshaw. 'Mrs Smith
came up to my wife in the village one morning and made some
foolish remark about Mrs Ripley's death being another sign, but
that's exactly the sort of silly thing Mrs Smith would say, I'm
afraid, and we didn't take any notice. I feel sorry for Doctor
Owen. He's a good sort of chap, and I think he has a lot to put
up with. Imagine listening to that sort of drivel over the breakfast
table.'

'There was a lot of stupid talk when Mr Vardy died, too,'
Mrs Brayshaw said. 'It was the fault of that woman who keeps
the beerhouse, saying he'd seen a ghost in the lane, or something
of the sort.'

'I'm not sure she actually said that, my dear,' Mr Brayshaw
demurred.

'Well, that was the interpretation some people put on it. I
distinctly recall Reverend Caswell saying something about the
danger of falling prey to old superstitions when he conducted
Mr Vardy's funeral. I'm sure he meant all the talk that went
round among the labouring classes about there being ghosts in
that lane. Although Mr Brayshaw and I were no longer regular

worshippers at St Agnes's, we naturally attended the funeral as we'd known Mr Vardy for years, and it was particularly nice that Reverend Caswell came back to take it. Quite like the old days.'

In response to gentle probing from Fran about Mr Vardy's drinking habits, however, Mr and Mrs Brayshaw emphatically denied any knowledge of his private life. Nor did they know anything about Miss Tilling's private lending library.

'Not really up my street,' Mr Brayshaw admitted. 'I must say, I prefer good old Raffles and Bulldog Drummond, myself.'

'I'm sure you're right about there being no connection between these sudden deaths and the letter to the bishop,' Tom said. 'But I wonder if you can clarify something for me? How was it that these particular people came to sign the letter? I mean, did you have some sort of meeting to discuss it?'

It was Mr Brayshaw who replied. 'No, no, nothing as formal as that. I believe the letter was originally Miss Tilling's initiative. There had been a lot of upset, people were leaving the parish church, and there had been one or two private conversations between what might be termed the dissenters about what could possibly be done about it. Being a daughter of the manse herself, so to speak, Miss Tilling thought of appealing to the bishop. It was fairly well known within the congregation which of us supported Reverend Pinder wholeheartedly and which of us did not. Several people, my wife included, had crossed swords with the vicar over one thing and another. My wife had taken issue with him after he refused to baptize an infant over some technicality or other—'

'No babe should be denied a Christian baptism,' Mrs Brayshaw put in.

'So when Miss Tilling composed her letter, my good lady here was an obvious person to approach as a co-signatory and, naturally, I said I would be happy to sign it too. I believe Mr Hargreaves, Mr Vardy and Mrs Ripley were all approached by Miss Tilling on a similar basis.'

TWENTY-ONE

After calling on the Brayshaws, Tom and Fran returned to the home of Dr Owen, where they found that Mrs Smith had completed her duties at the parish church and was settled in front of a brightly blazing fire in the drawing room. No sooner had they been ushered in than Mrs Smith insisted on ringing for tea and cakes, which Fran would have preferred to decline, but the atmosphere in which they were received was already frosty, the blazing fire notwithstanding, and she decided it would be unwise to give offence by refusing them.

'Florence Ripley said you were going to assist their family in some way by talking to people about Mrs Ripley's death,' their hostess said. 'Though I can't see why she would think your intervention likely to be of any assistance. Naturally I have agreed to see you, because one can only feel sorry for that poor child in her time of need. However, as I said to Father Pinder this morning, when he called into church while I was titivating the flowers, I am extremely hesitant to cooperate with people who may have been involved in some kind of deception.'

'What deception do you mean, Mrs Smith?' Tom asked politely.

'I'm sure someone originally told me that you had come to stay with Miss Venn for reasons entirely unconnected with Mrs Ripley's death.'

'Miss Venn is my aunt,' Tom said. 'So I hardly need to invent a reason for coming to stay with her. As for Mrs Ripley's death, the official doubts about what happened to her have only surfaced since we first came to visit. Mrs Ripley was originally believed to have died of natural causes.'

'Mrs Ripley died because she stood against the Lord's true way,' Mrs Smith declared emphatically. 'Her death is a sign, just as the others were.'

'The others?' Fran prompted. Privately she and Tom had already speculated about how, when they were supposed to be talking about Mrs Ripley, they might manage to persuade Mrs Smith to speak about the deaths of Miss Tilling and Mr Vardy, but now Mrs Smith herself had just made it easy for them.

'James Vardy and Ellen Tilling. The Lord moves in mysterious ways and we are all His instruments,' Mrs Smith said firmly.

'But surely, those deaths were accidents?'

'There is no such thing as an accident, Mrs Black. The Lord's hand is everywhere. He watches our going out and our coming in.'

'Well, of course,' Fran said carefully, deciding this was no time for a theological debate as to whether or not God ought to get the blame for everything. 'I didn't mean that God isn't with us at all times, but I find it a little hard to believe that He would strike someone down just for having a disagreement with the vicar.'

'Father Pinder is no ordinary priest. "The Lord revengeth and is furious. The Lord will take vengeance on his adversaries". Nahum, chapter one.'

Out of the corner of her eye, Fran could see that Tom was itching to disagree with this uncompromising view, but it was vital to try and keep Dulcie Smith onside, so she said quickly, 'I must say, I found Father Pinder's sermon on charity quite an inspiration. The point about Mr Vardy's and Miss Tilling's deaths, though – setting aside our acceptance that God's hand is everywhere – is that to the lay person, as it were, they could both be described as accidents, couldn't they, inasmuch as it appears that there was no human agency involved?'

'James Vardy drank too much, everyone knew it,' Mrs Smith said. 'He walked too close to the edge of the pond, slipped in the mud and fell in. He couldn't get out, of course. Not with that great heavy coat and his working boots. Unless you were standing in the lane, you couldn't hear him shout. There's nothing closer than the Bird in Hand beerhouse, and they heard nothing there.' There was a grim satisfaction in her voice. 'That was the first of the signs. As it says in Deuteronomy, "Take heed and hearken". But, of course, no one did.'

'Didn't Miss Tilling fall down the stairs?' Fran prompted.

'Miss Tilling lived at the house opposite, didn't she?' Tom put in, gesturing toward the bay window as he spoke. 'You have an excellent view of it from here. I suppose you would have been able to confirm that there were no visitors to the house that afternoon.'

'I could do nothing of the sort.' Mrs Smith seemed affronted by the question. 'I was asked the self-same thing by the policeman who called here the day after they found her. Anyone hearing him might have thought I spent half my life gazing out of the window, when nothing could be further from the truth. I told him that I am a very busy woman. I run this house for my brother, often taking his telephone calls and assisting with his appointment diary, and at very busy times I have even helped in the dispensary on a few occasions. As if that were not enough, I have many responsibilities at the parish church and I am frequently out of the house on a variety of errands, usually doing the Lord's work. That is why I was out of the house when Miss Tilling died.'

'Of course,' Fran said. 'How silly of me. I suppose it was just that sitting here, with the front door of Miss Tilling's house plainly in sight, I sort of pictured you sitting where you are now and able to see people come and go.'

'Imagination,' sniffed Mrs Smith, 'is a very dangerous thing.'

'And anyway, no one really believes that someone came along that afternoon and *pushed* Miss Tilling downstairs, do they?' Tom said.

'Don't they? I have no idea what anyone else thinks.'

'May I ask what you think?'

Mrs Smith looked Tom straight in the eye. 'I know that the Lord's hand was at work.'

Oh dear, Fran thought. We seem to have come full circle. Aloud, she said, 'The situation with Mrs Ripley is very different, of course. We know that Mrs Ripley's death was not an accident. The analyst has found arsenic in her remains.'

'The death of Mrs Ripley is a sign, nonetheless.'

Tom managed to stifle a sigh. 'Did you happen to call on Mrs Ripley yourself during her last illness?'

'I understood that Mrs Ripley was not well enough to see me when I called at the house.'

'Your brother had been attending her, I believe.'

'Frank attends all the people of quality in the village – and a great many of lesser status too.'

'I suppose you knew Mrs Ripley fairly well?'

Mrs Smith considered this for a moment before she said, 'No, I did not know either of the Ripleys particularly well. Mr Ripley grew up in a village not far from here, I believe, but we didn't know his family. He and his wife moved into the village in 1921, I think it was, when Mr Ripley replaced old Mr Dukes as manager at the bank. My brother deals with all financial matters, so I seldom came into contact with Mr Ripley, and although they attended the parish church, I had very little to do with Mrs Ripley either, since she seldom helped with good works or any fund-raising on account of her supposed poor health.'

Dulcie Smith sniffed expressively. 'Mrs Ripley found standing behind the handicrafts stall for a couple of hours too much of a strain for her, though of course nothing ever stopped her from jaunting off down to Eastbourne for her summer holiday. To think that a person who did almost nothing for the church thought she could put her name to a letter attacking its spiritual leader!' Mrs Smith's frizzy curls positively bounced with indignation.

'You never took her illnesses particularly seriously then?'

'Our Lord instructed us to care for the sick and the weak, Mr Dod. Naturally whenever I heard that Mrs Ripley was unwell, I called to enquire after her health, and sometimes left her a pot of quince jelly or some elderflower cordial, both of which are very soothing to invalids.'

'Which was most generous of you,' Tom said. 'Particularly if you suspected that she was shamming.'

'I never said such a thing.'

'Pardon me, but I got the impression that you thought Mrs Ripley had sometimes exaggerated her condition. Did your brother share that opinion?'

'That is hardly for me to say. In any case, Frank is thoroughly professional and never discusses his patients with me. Have some angel cake, Mrs Black. You will find it's very good. Maisie has a very light touch.'

'I suppose Maisie wouldn't have seen whether anyone called on Miss Tilling on the afternoon she died?' Tom ventured. But Mrs Smith dismissed the idea at once, firmly stating that the staff would always be at the rear of the house at that time of day and, as for her brother, he had been out on his afternoon house calls.

TWENTY-TWO

'**W**ell,' said Tom, after they were safely back in the Hudson and the front door of the doctor's house had been closed behind them. 'I'm not sure that got us anywhere. Where next? Should we try the rectory again?'

'I think it would be better to try Mr Hargreaves. We're less likely to be offered tea and cake there. If I have to eat another thing this afternoon, I may be sick. It was so hot and stuffy in there, too. Who on earth lights a fire in the middle of the afternoon at this time of the year?'

'Very well then, Mr Hargreaves it shall be.'

'Sorry,' Fran said, a few minutes later, as they made their way back towards the car after another fruitless wait on Mr Hargreaves' doorstep. 'We should have gone to the rectory after all.'

'Not your fault. How were you to know there'd still be no answer?' Tom replied. 'I think it's pretty bad form, asking us to call and then not being at home all afternoon. We might as well leave the car here and walk over to the rectory. It's only a matter of yards on the other side of the churchyard.'

They were more fortunate at the rectory, where Reverend Pinder himself came to the door to admit them. 'I hope you won't mind conducting your interview in my study,' he said as he ushered them through the first door on the right of the hall, which led into a book-lined room dominated by a huge wooden desk covered in papers. 'Basket, Saul,' he said firmly, as the dog came forward to greet them.

The rector took his usual seat on one side of the desk while Tom and Fran occupied the pair of upright wooden chairs facing him – just like a couple coming to ask about being married, Fran thought. When they had declined his offer of tea, Father Pinder said, 'When Miss Ripley telephoned to let me know you might be calling, I naturally expressed willingness to assist in any way. The family are of course part of my flock and I want to stand by them in their hour of need. However, though I expressed no reservations to Miss Ripley, I will say frankly to you that I have no idea in what way I can possibly help. When all is said and done, the murder of Mrs Ripley is a police matter and I consider that they are the only appropriate authority to investigate it.'

'I understand what you are saying, sir,' Tom said. 'But the fact is that the police have occasionally been mistaken in these matters. Mrs Black and I became involved in a case earlier this year – the Linda Dexter murder, which you may have read about in the papers – where if the police had been left to conduct the investigation alone, her murderer would have got off scot-free.'

'I'm afraid I know nothing about the case you are alluding to.' The vicar folded his hands on the desk as he spoke. 'I have very little time to read the scandal sheets. However, even assuming that your opinion on the matter is correct, I cannot imagine every police force is as incompetent as you suggest. Mrs Ripley was poisoned, and I'm sure the police would not have arrested her husband without very good reason. I daresay they have some evidence against him of which you are unaware.'

'So far as we understand it, Reverend Pinder, the police are basing their case on the fact that very few people were in a position to administer arsenic to Mrs Ripley, and the assumption that Mr Ripley wanted her out of the way in order to marry his secretary.'

'The ninth commandment condemns the married man who even contemplates adultery,' the rector said.

There was a moment of awkward silence, before Fran said, 'But there is no evidence at all of Mr Ripley's contemplating any such thing. Everything we have uncovered so far suggests that Mr Ripley was devoted to his late wife.'

'You may be right, of course,' the clergyman said mildly. 'Though none of us can say what is in another man's heart, for the secrets of the heart are known to the Good Lord alone.'

'We have just been to see Mrs Smith,' Tom said. 'She told us that she thinks Mrs Ripley's death was one of a series of signs. Her idea seems to be that Mrs Ripley was struck down because, like Mr Vardy and Miss Tilling, she took a stand against some of the things you have introduced since your arrival at the parish church.'

To their surprise, Reverend Pinder continued to sit looking at them, his hands calmly folded, and made no response at all. There was quite a lengthy silence, and when he eventually spoke again, it was in the same level tone as before. 'I understood that you had come to ask questions pertaining to the death of the late Mrs Ripley, rather than seeking my opinions as to what my parishioners may or may not think about various things.'

Tom changed tack. 'I believe you went to the Ripleys' house on the day Mrs Ripley died?'

'That is correct. I received a message that Mrs Ripley was extremely ill, and of course I responded immediately.'

'Was it a telephone call?' asked Fran.

'No. There is no telephone installed at the rectory. Mr Binks came for me on his bicycle. You have met Mr Binks? He is a sort of gardener and odd-job man who lives in the village and works for Mr Ripley.'

'When you got to Mr Ripley's house, can you remember who was there?'

'Certainly. The door was opened by the housemaid and Florence Ripley was waiting behind her in the hall. She – the maid, that is – took me straight up to Mrs Ripley's bedroom, where Mademoiselle Bertillon was sitting with Mrs Ripley, who was in a state of complete collapse.'

'There was no one else there at all?'

'Not then. Florence Ripley was in and out of the room, and I understood that both Mr Ripley and Doctor Owen had been sent for but neither of them had arrived. Doctor Owen was attending a confinement some distance away, and Mr Ripley was presumably on his way back from the bank. The Ripleys' cook was also somewhere on the premises, I assume, as I suppose was Binks, but they were not actually in the bedroom. As I attempted to administer the last rites to Mrs Ripley, I heard a motor car drawing up outside and a few moments later Doctor Owen entered the room, just as Mrs Ripley died. I remained at the house for some time afterwards, attempting to offer what comfort I could.'

'Did you form any opinion about the cause of Mrs Ripley's death?' asked Tom.

'My calling relates to the spiritual needs of my flock, Mr Dod, not their corporeal needs.'

'Did you see much of the family in the following days?'

'A certain amount. There were the funeral arrangements to be made and it is my role to offer comfort in times of trouble.'

'Did you conduct Mrs Ripley's funeral yourself?'

'Naturally.'

'Her illness and death were quite sudden, weren't they? Had anyone made you aware that she was very unwell prior to receiving that summons to her bedside on the day of her death?'

'Let me think . . . I am fairly certain that Mrs Smith mentioned that Mrs Ripley was unwell, probably a day or so before she died. I am afraid that I did not take too much notice at the time, perhaps because Mrs Ripley was something of a martyr to her health and quite regularly required the services of Mrs Smith's brother. It would have been just a casual remark, made in passing, while Mrs Smith and I were engaged in some parish duties, no doubt.'

'So you had not visited Mrs Ripley at all during her illness?'

'Not prior to the afternoon of her death, no.'

'You remember the deaths of Miss Tilling and Mr Vardy, of course,' Tom continued in a somewhat more tentative tone.

'Not in any particular sense, no. Forgive me, Mr Dod, but over the course of any year my ministry brings me into contact with rather a lot of deaths. The churchyard is the principal resting place for anyone who dies in Durley Dean and does not specifically identify with our friends in other denominations. Parishioners who never attend here at all as a general rule still look to us for the rites of baptism, marriage and burial.'

'Miss Tilling and Mr Vardy were regular worshippers at St Agnes's,' Fran said.

'I understood from Miss Ripley that it was her stepmother's death which interested you.' Reverend Pinder carefully unfolded his hands and rested them, palms down, on the desk as he rose from his seat. 'I trust you will forgive me if I say that I think we have covered that subject as fully as we can, and I am afraid I still have a good deal to do before supper time. The lamps will need to be lit shortly and, as I live alone, once my daily help has gone home for the day all the domestic duties devolve on to me, so if you will excuse me . . .'

Fran and Tom had no alternative but to accept that the interview was over. They said their thank-yous as they were escorted to the front door, which had closed behind them before they got more than a yard or two down the drive.

The overcast sky was bringing the dusk more swiftly.

'That's a big gloomy house for one man to rattle around in on his own,' Fran remarked. 'Shall we try Mr Hargreaves one last time, as we're so near?'

But there was still no answer at Mr Hargreaves' cottage, so they drove back to Aunt Hetty's house, where Fran positively groaned at the suggestion that Nora should bring in some tea and cake.

TWENTY-THREE

'We've done really well,' Tom said, in answer to Aunt Hetty's request for a progress report. 'The only people on our list left to speak with are Doctor Owen and the elusive Mr Hargreaves.'

'I do find it quite extraordinary that Mr Hargreaves was not at home,' Aunt Hetty said, after Tom had told her about their three attempts to call on him. 'I cannot imagine where he would have been on a Saturday afternoon.'

'He's not a soccer fan, is he?' asked Fran, thinking of the absent Dr Owen.

'Not so far as I know. And surely, if he had known he was going to be away from the house, he would have mentioned it when he called this morning?'

'Perhaps he had forgotten he was going out,' suggested Tom. 'Isn't he quite elderly?'

'Elderly and senile are not the same thing,' harrumphed his aunt. 'As for Doctor Owen, why not telephone him and ask if you can call there this evening? He will have been back from Nottingham long ago by now. They can't play football in the dark. And I suggest you stress that it's to be a private word,' she added, by way of an afterthought. 'Otherwise you will have Dulcie hanging on every word. I regret to say that she has always been rather inclined to eavesdrop.'

'Yes, ma'am, right away.' Tom pretended to salute as he marched off in the direction of the telephone.

He returned a few minutes later to say that Doctor Owen would expect them after supper, at around nine o'clock.

'And now,' said Aunt Hetty, 'I will leave the two of you alone to discuss your findings. I'm burning with curiosity, but it's far better I don't know anything, because that way I can't accidentally give something away in the village. In detective stories, that's always a danger, isn't it? An innocent remark into the wrong ears and hey presto, there's another corpse. Also . . .' She hesitated.

'Go on,' Tom prompted.

'Well, I was thinking things over while you were out and realized it was very wrong of me to suggest that Dulcie Smith could in any way be a suspect. She's a rather foolish, misguided woman, but she has always been perfectly harmless. One should not point a finger just because one doesn't much like a person, or thinks them a little extreme in their views. I'm afraid you must both think rather badly of me for suggesting she might be involved.'

'It's perfectly all right to have suspects,' Tom said. 'Someone has to be the guilty party. And if you don't think it's the Reverend Pinder . . .'

'He is our vicar, Tom, a man of the cloth.'

'And you don't think that Mr Ripley poisoned his wife . . .'

'Mr Ripley has always seemed such a nice man and he has been a very generous benefactor to St Agnes's in one way and another. He has always been noted for his sociable tendencies too. Look at the way he invited you both to lunch.'

'Well, someone must have done it!' Tom exclaimed.

Aunt Hetty stood in the doorway of the drawing room, a troubled look on her face. 'You know,' she said, 'I almost feel as if I have been in some way responsible for bringing this trouble down on the village. Perhaps I ought never to have asked you to look into all this. Perhaps it is all in my own imagination.'

'Don't be silly, Aunt Het. Mrs Ripley was poisoned. That is definitely not in your imagination.'

'I suppose not.' His aunt appeared slightly mollified. 'Yes,' she nodded, 'Mrs Ripley was definitely poisoned. There is that, of course.'

'And that is still just about the only fact at our disposal,' Fran said, as Aunt Hetty closed the door behind her. 'I've consumed heaven knows how many calories to hardly any benefit whatsoever. If our investigations continue along these lines, I won't be able to fasten my skirts.'

'Nonsense,' said Tom. 'A few slices of cake and the odd scone never did anyone any harm. For goodness' sake, don't turn into one of those women who's banting the whole time. It's such a bore. Not that you could ever be a bore,' he added hastily.

Fran tried not to blush, because it was silly to react like a schoolgirl, but she felt the unwelcome warmth rising in her cheeks all the same, so she kept her head down and focused on the notebook in which she had attempted to scribble down the substance of their various conversations. 'So,' she said, after flicking back a page or two. 'From the maid, Alice, we learned that Miss Tilling would definitely have admitted Reverend Pinder if he had called while Alice was out posting the parcel.'

'And Mrs Smith says she was out that afternoon, so she wouldn't have seen any callers.'

'Right. In fact, there's anecdotal evidence that if Mrs Smith *had* spotted the vicar arriving at Miss Tilling's, she might have found some excuse to invite herself over. My next note is headed "Pascoe". We need to ask Miss Rose about him.'

'Bearing in mind,' Tom said with a wry grin, 'Mr Pascoe's contention that we ought not to believe a word Miss Rose tells us about him.'

'Immediately under Mr Pascoe's name, I've got Mr Hargreaves. It's most vexing that he has something which he wants to say to us and yet after three visits to his cottage, we still haven't managed to hear what it is.'

'It may well turn out to be nothing,' Tom said. 'According to Aunt Hetty, it's about something odd that Mrs Smith said to him. But as Mrs Smith is given to saying odd things to people at just about every opportunity, it's probably of no significance at all.'

'It may be no more than that Mrs Smith is claiming the three deaths are all connected to the problems at the parish church. Mr Hargreaves probably doesn't realize she's told lots of other people exactly the same thing already.'

'That's true. We know that Mrs Smith has been suggesting this to all and sundry, because she made it her business to share her ideas with the Brayshaws too.'

'Do you think she hoped to frighten them?' Fran asked. 'After all, both the Brayshaws and Mr Hargreaves signed the letter to the bishop, which puts them next in line for this supposedly divine retribution.'

'I think it's more likely that she singled them out in the hope that it would persuade them to change their ways and put their wholehearted support behind Reverend Pinder.'

'As for Mrs Smith herself,' Fran scanned her notes as she spoke, 'we really got nothing useful out of her at all.'

'She's such an infuriating woman,' Tom said.

'She's not very likeable, I agree, and she hardly ever appears to have a good word to say about anyone . . . with the exception of Reverend Pinder, of course.'

'We didn't exactly learn much from him,' Tom said.

'Oh, I don't know. Firstly, I've noted that he was quite reluctant to speak with us at all. It was also interesting to hear what he had to say about the sequence of events on the last day of Mrs Ripley's life. According to Reverend Pinder, he only arrived a very short time before Mrs Ripley died. If that's so, then he can't have slipped her a fatal dose of arsenic – or at least, if he did, it was academic, as she was dying anyway.'

'Which rather messes up the theory that Reverend Pinder is our murderer,' Tom said.

'Something else I noticed,' Fran said. 'According to Reverend Pinder, as well as sending for Doctor Owen, the family had also sent word asking Mr Ripley to come home from the bank, which would be the natural thing to do. But according to Miss Rose, the message she took from Mademoiselle Bertillon didn't tell him to come home because Mrs Ripley was very ill, but to come home because Mrs Ripley was dead.'

'That's an important discrepancy. Something else to ask Miss Rose about.'

'Then there's the fact that if Reverend Pinder is right, Doctor Owen didn't see Mrs Ripley on the final day of her illness until he arrived that afternoon, by which time she was already dying – and that puts Doctor Owen out of it, as well.'

'I hadn't realized that Doctor Owen was *in* it,' Tom said. 'Or at least no more so than anyone else.'

'But don't you see, Tom, that if you take our conversation with Reverend Pinder at face value, it pretty much excludes all outsiders. If he is right, then only someone within the Ripley household could have got the poison to Mrs Ripley.'

'We've never taken Mademoiselle Bertillon through precisely what happened that day,' Tom said. 'I suggest we need to talk to her again.'

'I agree.'

'So our list of interviewees is down to Doctor Owen and Mr Hargreaves, after which we need to revisit Mademoiselle Bertillon and Miss Rose.'

'And Florence too,' Fran said. 'To see if she and Mademoiselle Bertillon's accounts of Mrs Ripley's last day agree.'

TWENTY-FOUR

T om and Fran arrived at the doctor's house on the dot of nine o'clock. In spite of the darkness and the pouring rain, the drawing room curtains were still open, so Dr Owen and his sister were aware of their arrival and the doctor had the front door open for them as they ran up the path from the car.

'Do come in. That's right, Mrs Black – pop your brolly into the bottom of the hat stand. Here we are, let me take your coats . . .'

After a moment or two of cheery bustle, Dr Owen led them through a door on the opposite side of the hall to the drawing room. 'Then we won't trouble my sister, who is listening to a play on the wireless – we got a new Bakelite one last Christmas, a marvellous instrument. Now, Mr Dod, will you have a whisky and soda? And what can I offer you, Mrs Black? Or perhaps, like my sister, you don't partake?'

'A gin and lime would be very nice, if you have it.'

'Of course. Of course.'

While Dr Owen clinked about with bottles, tumblers and the heavy glass soda syphon, Tom asked whether he had enjoyed the football match.

'I didn't catch the score. How did they get on?' Tom asked.

'It was a draw.' The doctor's hand hovered over the bottles in his drinks cabinet. 'Do you follow football, Mr Dod?'

'Not really. I'm more of a cricket man myself, and Mrs Black is tremendously keen on tennis. Though of course one notices the results. Forest got a terrible drubbing last week, as I recall.'

'Yes, we conceded five goals to Southampton. I'm afraid we haven't won a match yet this season. If we carry on like this, we will very likely be relegated.'

As the doctor kept up a cheerful banter with Tom about football and cricket, Fran took in the room into which they had been shown. She had half expected it to be the doctor's consulting room, or else a book-lined working study, like the one where they had been received by the vicar earlier in the day, but she quickly realized that it must be the doctor's private retreat: a small sitting room, with a comfortable three-piece suite uphol-stered in a masculine plain brown, some pot plants in brass containers and a half-read detective novel lying on a side table. A modest fire burned in the grate, just enough to cheer the spirits and take the chill off the room without raising the temperature to subtropical, which was evidently the way his sister liked things. This is where he comes to escape, Fran thought, while his sister listens to the wireless.

Once they were settled, Dr Owen taking one chair, Tom the other and Fran seated on the central sofa, the doctor raised his glass, said 'Chin-chin', and took a sip of his whisky before asking in a friendly tone, 'Now then, what can I do for you? I should perhaps mention before we begin that I may not be able to answer everything you ask, because I am naturally bound by medical ethics and patient confidentiality. That being said, you are here on behalf of Mrs Ripley's next of kin – which allows me a little leeway, I suppose – and since we all want to get to the truth, I will endeavour to help in any way I can.'

'I think we'll be on safe ground with my first question,' Tom said with a smile. 'Your sister said this afternoon that she thought the deaths of Mr Vardy and Miss Tilling might be linked in some way to the death of Mrs Ripley. What would your opinion be about that?'

'My sister is of course entitled to her views.' The doctor smiled. 'As you know, I issued all three death certificates – and so far as I am concerned, these are three unrelated deaths which came about in three completely different sets of circumstances. Mr Vardy and Miss Tilling died as a result of unrelated tragic accidents, and until the recent exhumation I believed Mrs Ripley's death to be due to heart failure following a bad dose of gastro-intestinal trouble.'

'Just so that we have the details straight,' Tom said, 'is it possible for you to tell us what you recall seeing when you attended the deaths of these three people, perhaps starting with Mr Vardy?'

'Certainly.' Dr Owen paused, as if recalling the scene to mind. 'It was around mid-morning, I think, when I was called out to

Mr Vardy. I was informed that he had been found dead by some of his workers. By the time I arrived, they had fished his body out of the water – they had quite a job, I believe, as his clothes were waterlogged and very heavy – and he was lying on his back on the ground. He was obviously dead and everything suggested that he had been that way for some hours, because he was completely cold when I first saw him. I had the men take him back to the farmhouse and conducted a fuller examination there. The coroner had to be informed, of course, and an inquest held. I could find no signs of any violence or a struggle and the jury delivered a verdict of death by misadventure, which I believe was entirely correct.'

'Thank you,' Tom said.

'Miss Tilling's death was a rather odd business,' Dr Owen continued. 'It was quite well on in the afternoon and I had not long returned from a call and was still in my consulting room, at the side of the house, sorting out some paperwork, when Dulcie came rushing in, saying that she thought she had heard screams coming from the direction of Miss Tilling's house. I was about to follow her through to the drawing room when Clara – Miss Tilling's cook – came hammering on the front door to say the maid had just found Miss Tilling lying at the bottom of the stairs.

'I grabbed my bag and rushed across the street, but the old lady was already dead and had been for probably an hour or so. It's very difficult to be absolutely precise about a time of death, as I expect you know. The maid was in absolute hysterics – it was her cries that had initially alerted Dulcie – and at first she was no help at all. In fact, from the situation as I first saw it, I was extremely suspicious of the maid, because Miss Tilling had a large wound on the back of her head which I quickly realized had been inflicted by a hefty-looking ornament. So my obvious instinct was that someone had bonked her on the head and since there must have been quite a noise when all that paraphernalia came crashing down on to the tiles in the hall, I had to ask myself why the servants had not come through straight away to investigate? I ought to explain that Miss Tilling was lying face down surrounded by various bits of broken glass and china, with this statue of some half-naked chap lying right beside her head.'

'So you thought at first that Miss Tilling had been attacked?'

'That was my first impression, yes. But once the police turned up and the housemaid calmed down and was able to tell us what had actually happened, everything began to appear in a somewhat different light, as both the servants claimed to have been out during the course of the afternoon. Naturally, the police didn't just take their stories at face value. I know they made some enquiries and established that Clara, the cook, had definitely been out that afternoon, and they also confirmed that the housemaid had dropped a parcel off at the post office – just as she said she did – which meant that Miss Tilling had indeed been left alone in the house for a period of at least half an hour. There was no suggestion of a break-in, and under the circumstances I was prepared to agree that, in spite of initial appearances, Miss Tilling's death had been the result of a freak accident, having fallen downstairs while alone in the house.'

'In spite of the head wound?'

'All the items found lying on the hall floor had come from a shelf built into a small alcove towards the top of the stairs. The police concluded that as Miss Tilling fell she had cannoned into the shelf and that had set off a sort of chain reaction, bringing everything falling down on top of her, with the statue unfortunately crashing on to her head as she reached the ground.'

'And you were satisfied with that explanation?' Tom asked, his voice carefully neutral.

'All the circumstances appeared to bear it out.'

Fran took a turn to ask a question. 'Was she killed by the fall, or by the blow to the head?'

For the first time, Dr Owen looked a touch impatient. 'My dear Mrs Black, I am not Sir Bernard Spilsbury. I cannot say precisely which injury resulted in Miss Tilling's demise, because no one knows in which order these things happened. It is entirely likely that the injuries sustained in the fall, which included a fractured pelvis and a serious contusion to the front of the skull, would have been sufficient to cause death without the damage sustained from the blow inflicted by the statue to the back of the head, and vice versa. For me, it was sufficient that death had been due to multiple injuries sustained during a fall.'

'Let's move on to Mrs Ripley, shall we?' Tom said. 'I believe you were called in to attend Mrs Ripley on the afternoon following a luncheon party for some old friends of Mr Ripley?'

'I'm afraid I have no idea who the other participants of the luncheon party were. My sister took the call, as I recollect, and she passed on the request for a visit as soon as I returned home from seeing another patient. I'm sure of that, because I particularly remember that I went straight out again to see Mrs Ripley.'

'I think we've been told that Mrs Ripley was not seriously ill at that stage . . .' Tom prompted.

'Mrs Ripley had a somewhat delicate constitution and these little digestive upsets were not unusual. I asked her a few questions, undertook a brief examination and recommended rest and a light diet for a couple of days. I also said I would drop some medicine round to her later. In fact, my sister was kind enough to deliver it to the house on my behalf as I was tied up with another case in the afternoon. I have a fair-sized practice here and things can sometimes get pretty busy.'

'Do you mind my asking what the medicine was?'

'Not at all. It was a mixture of powdered rhubarb, soda and bismuth. I had regularly prescribed it for Mrs Ripley and it always had a beneficial effect. I made up a couple of days' supply.'

'And when did you next see Mrs Ripley?' asked Fran, who had now recovered from Dr Owen's rather crushing earlier reply.

'I called on her at around eleven, next morning. Mrs Ripley was a somewhat overanxious patient and she liked the reassurance of regular visits if she was feeling under the weather.'

'And how did she seem?' Tom resumed the role of questioner.

'Oh, considerably better. I went to see her again the next day. It was probably after lunch. She told me she felt so much better and wondered whether she could abandon the invalid diet, as we called it, and start taking the same meals as the rest of the household. I confirmed that she could, and didn't do much more than check her pulse and prescribe some more medicine, just to reassure her that all was well.'

'Did you tell her to stay in bed?'

Dr Owen smiled. 'Mrs Ripley was not in bed at that point. She had a chaise longue in her bedroom, which she used when resting up during any period of illness. I had never told her to stay upstairs, I just recommended rest. It was up to Mrs Ripley how she interpreted that and whether or not she decided to come downstairs.'

'So she did not appear to be seriously ill at that stage?'

'No, she did not.'

'But she must have taken a turn for the worse?'

Dr Owen looked from Tom to Fran and back again. 'Mr Dod, I see no point in beating about the bush. You know as well as I do that the Home Office analyst has found arsenic in Mrs Ripley's remains. We therefore know that in all likelihood Mrs Ripley was not fatally ill when I saw her, but that at some point following my visit she took or had administered to her a substantial dose of arsenic. I was called back to see her the next day and arrived to find her in a state of complete collapse. She died within minutes of my arrival and her death had all the appearances of heart failure following a return of the original gastric illness, so I had no hesitation in issuing a certificate – a decision which is going to cause me some considerable professional embarrassment.' He punctuated the sentence by draining the last of the whisky from his glass.

'From what little I know of these matters, I'm sure it is the sort of mistake which any medical man might make under the circumstances,' Tom said, while shaking his head to decline the doctor's gestured offer of a top-up. 'What else can you tell us about the final day of Mrs Ripley's life?'

'Not a great deal, I'm afraid. I had planned to pop in and see her during my rounds, but immediately after morning surgery word reached me that another of my patients, Mrs Canning, had gone into labour. There were complications and I was asked to attend, so I drove out to Elton Heath, where the Cannings live, and I was detained there for some considerable time. Sometime after midday one of their servants came up to tell me that my sister had telephoned to say there was a request for me to visit Mrs Ripley, but by then things were at a critical stage and I could not leave my patient, so I sent word back that I would be there as soon as I could.'

'Can you recall what was said about Mrs Ripley's illness at that point?'

'I'm afraid I can't be exact. Possibly no more than that she had taken a turn for the worse, something like that. Things were touch and go with Mrs Canning, so I didn't go down to take the call myself. It must have been a good thirty minutes later when her child was delivered, a little girl, Violet – she's doing very well now, I'm pleased to say – and it was a while after that before I was confident enough of the mother's condition to be able to leave her in the hands of Mrs Nicholson, our local midwife. I do recall that in the meantime a second call had come in, this time directly from the Ripley household – my sister had obviously told them where I was – stressing the urgency of Mrs Ripley's condition. Again I did not actually go to the telephone myself, but sent word that I would get to them as soon as I possibly could.'

'I don't see how you could have done any more,' Tom said. 'When two seriously ill patients are simultaneously in need of your services it places you in an impossible position.'

'It doesn't happen very often,' Dr Owen said. 'But you know the saying, "It never rains but it pours".'

'And eventually you felt you could leave Mrs Canning and her baby?'

'Yes. After I was sure they were both out of the woods, so to speak, I gave my hands another scrub, packed my bag, grabbed my jacket and all but ran to the car. You can't get up much of a speed between Elton Heath and Durley Dean, I'm afraid. The furthest stretch of the lane is still unmade and it's a real switchback of a road, as you may know, so it must have taken me at least a quarter of an hour, maybe twenty minutes, to reach the Ripleys' place.'

'Can you remember who let you into the house?'

'I haven't the slightest idea, old boy. One of the servants, I imagine. I went straight up to Mrs Ripley's room and she was lying on that couch of hers, with Father Pinder on one side and the French governess on the other. I remember that as I approached the bed Father Pinder said, "I think she's gone, Doctor". He'd jumped the gun slightly, because I managed to find a faint pulse, but she was failing and I'm afraid none of my attempts to revive her bore fruit. She died a couple of minutes after I got there.'

'Were you surprised?'

'You do see some unexpected things in general practice, so in a way nothing much surprises you after a while.'

'And – believe me, I imply no criticism here – you had no hesitation in issuing a death certificate?'

'It's the duty of a good doctor to prevent unnecessary suffering,' Dr Owen said. 'That extends to avoiding the unpleasantness of a post-mortem examination and an inquest, if at all possible, so one does not go looking for problems. I had not anticipated Mrs Ripley's death, but I knew she had a weak heart and concluded that I had underestimated the seriousness of her illness. After enquiring with the governess, I established that after her lunch Mrs Ripley began to display quite alarming symptoms of gastric illness, violent vomiting and so forth, and that she quickly became exhausted and suffered a major collapse. Let me put it this way: I would not have issued the certificate if I had suspected for a moment that Mrs Ripley had been murdered.'

'You say murdered,' Fran put in. 'Does that mean you would completely rule out the possibility of suicide?'

Dr Owen paused a moment to consider his response. 'Under the circumstances, I suppose one cannot rule anything out. But I thought I knew the Ripleys fairly well and I had never considered Mrs Ripley the suicidal type, whereas we have now all realized that her husband had a motive for putting her out of the way.'

'You mean his relationship with Miss Rose?'

'I do.'

'You say "we have now all realized", so can I take it that you never noticed anything untoward between Mr Ripley and his secretary before Mrs Ripley's death?'

'I don't think anyone did. But, of course, none of us knew what might be going on behind his office door at the bank.'

'So you suspect that Mr Ripley killed his wife?' asked Fran.

'It's not a pleasant thought, I know. But let us face facts, my dear Mrs Black. The poison got into Mrs Ripley's system somehow, and who else could possibly have put it there? Who else would have wanted the poor lady out of the way?'

'Well,' Tom said, after a lengthy pause. 'Thank you so much for finding the time to see us and being so helpful. Jolly bad luck about Forest only drawing this afternoon. Better luck next week, eh?'

The doctor saw them out himself. The rain had subsided to drizzle, but Tom still needed to use the windscreen wipers.

'Look here,' he said. 'It's still only half past nine. Why don't we go and give Mr Hargreaves another try?'

'It's a bit late to be making calls,' Fran protested.

'But the old boy wanted us to call on him. Come on, let's give it a go.'

TWENTY-FIVE

After Tom had parked the Hudson, they made their way up the alley alongside the churchyard that led to Mr Hargreaves' cottage. A gas lamp stood close to where Tom had parked the car, but within a matter of yards the footway was in darkness and, when Fran's foot found a puddle, it splashed water up her stockings as far as the knees. To their left a series of grey, indeterminate shapes melted into the general blackness of the churchyard, while to their right rose the solid wall of the first cottage in the High Street. When they reached Mr Hargreaves' gate, they could see that the cottage was in darkness.

'No lights showing at all,' Tom said, his normally cheerful voice subdued. 'I don't like the look of this.'

They entered at the gate and approached the front door.

'The curtains aren't drawn, I don't think,' Fran said. 'But it's really difficult to tell in the dark.'

Tom banged on the door, and after the shortest of intervals followed that up by calling 'Mr Hargreaves?' through the letterbox, which also elicited no reply.

At that moment, Fran gave a squeak of fright, cut off almost immediately, as she looked down and made out the shape of a cat weaving round her ankles. 'Sorry,' she said. 'I felt something brush against my legs and it startled me.'

She put down her hand and stroked the cat, who mewed rather desperately and butted her calf with its soft furry head.

'Sounds hungry,' she said.

Tom tried the front door. 'It's unlocked,' he said, stepping inside as he spoke. 'Mr Hargreaves . . . Mr Hargreaves, are you at home?'

Before Fran had time to question the propriety of entering uninvited, Tom had already crossed the threshold and she could sense, rather than actually see, him feeling around the walls.

'Can't find a light switch. He's probably not connected. Blast, I wish we'd thought to bring the torch out of the car. Hold on . . . Now look out, puss cat, you're going to trip someone up if you go on like that . . . Ouch! Now my foot's gone slap into a chest of drawers or something.'

'Mr Hargreaves,' Fran called from the doorstep. 'Are you there, Mr Hargreaves?'

'There's sure to be a candle and some matches, if he's got no electricity. No, wait, here it is.'

As Tom spoke, the little room was swathed in the yellowish light of a forty-watt bulb, which was suspended from twisty brown flex in the centre of the room. He and Fran stood blinking at each other for a moment, while the cat increased the volume and frequency of its complaints.

'Stay here,' Tom said. 'I'm going to have a look round.'

It took him only a moment to mount the rickety wooden staircase, which climbed out of the principal downstairs room.

'No one up there,' he said. 'And no sign of anything amiss. What's through here, I wonder? Aha, the kitchen. And the back door is standing open – and has been for quite some time, judging by how wet the kitchen flags are. Can you see a torch anywhere? I think we'd better take a look outside.'

'There's one here, by the door,' Fran said.

'Good show. Don't want to waste time fetching mine from the car.'

Tom switched on the torch and swung the beam to and fro across the width of Mr Hargreaves' back garden. Although the cottage itself was extremely modest in size, the garden ran a long way back and was evidently employed as a productive plot. Cane wigwams, waist-high fruit bushes and the shape of an ancient apple tree momentarily glistened damp and dark as the beam passed over them. Tom began to advance down the central cinder path and, although the rain had begun to beat down a little harder, Fran followed him, not least because she had no desire to be left in the cottage on her own.

'Oh, no!'

Even as she heard Tom's exclamation, Fran saw him drop to crouch beside what looked for a moment like a pile of old clothes. There was no room to get alongside him without clambering into a cold frame, so Fran could only ask, 'Is it Mr Hargreaves?'

'It must be. He's still breathing. Quick, run to the nearest house and send for Doctor Owen.'

She did not need to be told twice. Fran raced back through the cottage and down the alleyway, heedless of the puddles, barely checking when she almost fell as her foot encountered a loose stone and slid sideways. Beneath the street lamp, the Hudson stood oddly serene, as if it belonged to another, calmer world. In the dark it was very difficult to see which, if any, of the houses had telephone wires running into them, and in this part of the village she thought the chances of finding someone who was a subscriber were very low. The nearest large property was the vicarage, but she remembered just in time that Reverend Pinder had told them only that afternoon that he was not connected. Therefore, following Tom's urgent instructions, she ran up the path of the first house in the small terrace, whose wall enclosed one side of Mr Hargreaves' alleyway. As she stood panting on the step, she grabbed the knocker and gave the door the battering of its life.

It seemed to take an age for anyone to come and as she waited it flashed through her mind that, although she hadn't driven for a long time, Cec had taught her, in their father's car, back when she had still been in her teens, and she supposed she could probably manage the Hudson in an emergency such as this. Tom did not know that she could drive. If he had, perhaps he would have told her to fetch Dr Owen herself. She took the idea no further, for at that moment an elderly woman, whom she half recognized as one of the congregation at the parish church, appeared on the doorstep, looking bemused.

'Please can you help?' Fran said. 'My friend and I have just found Mr Hargreaves lying in his garden. He's in a very bad way and I need someone to fetch the doctor.'

To her relief, the woman on the doorstep immediately took in the urgency of the situation and, without hesitation, roared in a voice louder than Fran would have thought possible, 'Jackee . . . JACKEEEE!' Turning back to Fran, she said, at normal volume, 'Lucky my grandson's here, miss. He'll go. He's right fleet of foot, our Jack is. He'll have the doctor here in two ticks.'

'Jackee,' she instructed a slender boy of about ten or eleven years old who had appeared beyond her shoulder, 'get yourself to Doctor Owen and tell him he's needed at Mr Hargreaves' at once.'

Clearly the entire family were quick on the uptake, for the boy was out of the door in a matter of seconds, still jamming a cap on his head.

'Would you like to come in here out of the rain, miss, while you wait for the doctor?'

'No, thank you. I ought to go back. There may be something I can do to help.'

'You're right, of course. I'll follow you round,' the woman said. 'I'll just get my coat and shoes on.'

When she got back inside Mr Hargreaves' cottage, Fran paused to look for an improvement on the torch. Hanging on a nail in a cupboard under the stairs, she found an old hurricane lantern that still had some oil in it. There were matches on the mantelshelf, and she was therefore able to return to the back garden bearing a far superior source of light.

'A boy from the house next door has run for Doctor Owen. How is Mr Hargreaves?'

'Gosh, you were quick, well done,' Tom said. 'I'm afraid he's in a bad way. He's breathing, but he's unconscious and very cold. He must have been lying out here for ages in the cold and rain.'

'How awful!' Fran said. 'Do you suppose he's been here all afternoon and evening, maybe each time we came to the house?'

'I'm afraid so. I daren't try to move him on my own, because if he's broken something I might jolt him about and make it worse, but maybe we could try to get him a bit warmer.'

'Of course. Have my coat – no, wait – our coats will both be wet. I'll go inside and grab whatever I can.'

Having handed the lantern over to Tom, Fran ran back into the cottage. There was nothing obviously suitable in the downstairs room or the kitchen, so she ran up the stairs and into the main bedroom. She had been about to denude the bed of its coverings when she realized that a made-up bed might be needed, and turned instead to a big linen chest that stood at one side of the bedroom. Here she was rewarded with a whole pile of blankets, which she carted downstairs and out into the garden at top speed. As she hastened through the kitchen, she found that the woman from next door had let herself in and was filling a large kettle at the sink.

'Tea is always what's wanted in situations like this.' The woman nodded, giving Fran a grim half smile.

Good heavens, Fran thought, from what Tom says I should imagine the last thing Mr Hargreaves needs just now is a cup of tea.

However, some forty-five minutes later, sitting with a hot strong brew warming her hands, Fran privately admitted to herself that Mrs Snook, as the next-door neighbour turned out to be called, was absolutely right. In the course of any emergency, the moment for a cup of tea would inevitably arrive.

Mrs Snook had also provided a towel from somewhere so that Fran could rub down the bits of her – hands, face, legs – that had got so wet while she held an umbrella over the doctor in the garden during his preliminary examination, prior to Tom and Dr Owen carrying the old man as gently as they could upstairs. Here Tom had left the doctor and the district nurse – summoned, on Dr Owen's instructions, by the indefatigable young Jack Snook – still attending their patient.

'The trouble is,' Mrs Snook was saying, 'that the garden's not overlooked by anyone. It's the churchyard on the one side and Major Fullerton's orchard wall on the other, so once poor old Mr Hargreaves had fallen no one would see him.'

'I wonder what he was doing out in the garden on such a nasty day?' Fran ventured.

'Ah, but it didn't turn really bad until late on, did it?' said Mrs Snook. 'Mr Hargreaves was always out in that garden of his, in pretty much all weathers. Trimming and pruning, he'd likely be at this time of year, I expect, for his fruit crop is probably in already. Or digging potatoes maybe, or some other veg. He used to sell some stuff to Mr Winterton, the greengrocer, and a lot of it he just gave away. A nice man, Mr Hargreaves. I hope he's going to pull through.'

'We came to see him earlier on,' Tom said, 'but he didn't answer the door. I'm afraid he may have already been lying unconscious outside.'

Mrs Snook was not convinced. 'It might be as you say, of course. But Mr Hargreaves didn't always hear the knocker if he was right down by his sheds. Folks who knew him mostly used to give him a shout and then walk through into the garden. They knew they'd find him there ninety-nine times out of a hundred.'

At that moment Dr Owen appeared at the top of the stairs. Before he was halfway down, Tom and Fran had chorused their enquiries and Mrs Snook had risen to provide the doctor with a cup of tea.

'He's still unconscious,' Dr Owen said. 'We've done what we can to make him comfortable, and Nurse Goodall is going to sit with him. The worst problem is the shock, brought on by lying outside in the cold and wet for so long. The head wound isn't actually as bad as it looks.'

'So what happened to him, in your opinion?' Tom asked, as Dr Owen sat himself in a rocking chair that stood close to the recently kindled fire.

'My guess would be that he missed his footing and fell, hitting his head as he went down. There's a sort of decorative stone edging all the way along the path, and if you came a cropper against that you'd know about it. The initial knock on the head must have concussed him, or he may have been conscious initially but passed out later. It doesn't seem all that cold to us, but an elderly person's temperature can soon drop to a dangerously low level when they're exposed to cooling temperatures combined with the shock of a fall.'

'If he was working out in the garden,' said Fran, 'then I can't understand why he was only in his shirtsleeves.'

'Who said he was working in the garden?' the doctor asked. 'As he hadn't got his coat on, I think it much more likely that he'd slipped outside to fetch something from one of his sheds, or had maybe gone to use the outside privy. You'd be much more likely to sustain a fall if you were hurrying to avoid getting cold.'

'There's no question of this not being an accident?' Tom asked.

Dr Owen raised his eyebrows. 'Are you implying that someone may have banged Mr Hargreaves over the head and left him for dead, Mr Dod? I think we must be careful not to let our imaginations run away with us, don't you?'

TWENTY-SIX

Reverend Pinder included Mr Hargreaves in the intercessions for the sick during the Parish Communion service next morning. Dr Owen was sitting alongside his sister in a front pew, and Tom was able to speak with him afterwards and ascertain that he had high hopes of Mr Hargreaves pulling through.

'He regained consciousness, but he was in a lot of pain and rather inclined to ramble. The fall has knocked him for six, of course – bruises everywhere, as well as that very nasty bump on the head – so I've given him a good, large dose of dope. That way he will get plenty of rest and give his body a proper chance to recover.'

'I don't suppose there's any chance of us having a chat with the poor old chap?'

The doctor was emphatic. 'Not a hope, I'm afraid. He needs complete rest in order to have the best possible chance of recuperating. In any case, he'll be pretty much out of it, thanks to the morphine. Even if he did say anything to you, you wouldn't be able to rely on it. None of my business, of course, but why the interest in talking to Mr Hargreaves, anyway?'

'We thought he might have a theory,' Fran interposed. 'He was another signatory of the letter to the bishop, you see.' She glanced around hastily to check there was no one else within earshot. 'The letter signed by Mr Vardy, Miss Tilling and Mrs Ripley that so annoyed Reverend Pinder.'

'Dear me.' Dr Owen shook his head. 'You really are clutching at straws, aren't you?' He lifted his hat to them, then turned to walk away.

In the meantime, Tom had spotted Mademoiselle Bertillon and Florence Ripley.

'Come on,' he said. 'Let's see what can be fixed up for this afternoon.'

The two women were waiting for Binks to arrive with the

family car and appeared to be in the process of some kind of disagreement. 'Well, I hate the way people are watching us all the time. I don't know why you're so keen on coming here, anyway. Why can't we go to your church, then you can take communion and I'll watch?'

'Now, Miss Florence, that is not the way things are going to be. People here have shown you the utmost kindness.'

'Excuse me, Miss Ripley, Mademoiselle Bertillon.' Tom lifted his hat.

'Mr Dod. Good morning.'

'Mrs Black and I were wondering if we might come and ask you some more questions this afternoon. And also whether it would be possible to contact Miss Rose for a further interview?'

'Miss Rose's landlady is being rather difficult about telephone calls, but I'm sure we can get a note to Miss Rose asking her to come round this afternoon for tea,' Florence said, glancing at her governess as she spoke and receiving a nod of confirmation. 'As for ourselves, we are completely at your disposal, of course.'

'Thank you,' said Tom. 'Shall we say three o'clock? That will allow us all plenty of time to get Sunday lunch out of the way.'

Fran wondered who would be employed as the messenger to Miss Rose, thinking that the fleet-of-foot Jack Snook would make an ideal candidate if the distance was short.

Whoever had been chosen for the mission, the summons had evidently worked, for Miss Rose arrived ahead of them and was already seated in the drawing room, along with Florence and Mademoiselle Bertillon, when Tom and Fran were shown in.

Mutual pleasantries were exchanged. Fran asked after the progress of Florence's aunt and was told that she had managed to book a passage and was now on a ship, two days out of Cape Town. In response to a further enquiry from Tom, Mademoiselle Bertillon told them that young Geoffrey was still at school, as there seemed nothing to be gained from bringing him home at this stage. 'He is far better at school, where he will be fully occupied,' mademoiselle said firmly. 'And now Mrs Black, Mr Dod, how is it that we can be of help?'

'Since we have been asking different people about what happened to Mrs Ripley, a few new questions have arisen. These things might turn out to be useful clues or might turn out to be nothing at all, but if we could ask each of you in turn to think back and tell us what you remember on various points, it may help to resolve things.'

'I assume it's going to be separate interviews and no conferring,' Florence said. 'I'll go first, shall I?'

Privately Tom and Fran had previously agreed a different order of priorities, but Florence was already on her feet, so Tom said, 'Yes, of course. Are we using your father's study again?'

However, once they were seated in the now-familiar room, Florence's apparent enthusiasm to be of assistance evaporated at once. She stared at the rain cascading down the window panes and said without looking at them, 'It's hopeless, isn't it? Going over the same things again and again.'

'Not necessarily.' Fran tried to sound a note of optimism. 'Sometimes going through things again, you come across something that you missed first time.'

'A sort of key to the whole mystery?'

'You could put it that way, yes.'

'But you haven't found the key so far?' As Florence turned back to face them, Fran noted the clear hint of reproach in the girl's tone.

She remembered Mademoiselle Bertillon telling her that Florence Ripley was not a particularly patient young lady.

'Shall we start with one or two matters that need to be cleared up following on from what various other people have said to us?' Tom suggested. 'First, were you ever aware of anyone threatening your family? Your father in particular, or maybe even your mother?'

Florence shook her head. 'Don't you think I'd have told you right at the start if there had been anything of that kind?'

'Have you ever heard of anyone called Pascoe?' Tom refused to be ruffled.

'Of course I have. There are people in the village called Pascoe. He sometimes used to walk his dog past our gate and let it do its unmentionables there, until Mr Binks threatened to tip a bucket of water over him.'

'Did you know that your father had refused Mr Pascoe an overdraft or a loan?'

'Daddy never talked about business at home.'

'So you didn't know that Mr Pascoe had made some threats against your father.'

'No. Haven't I already said so?'

For someone who had initially expressed willingness to be questioned, Florence had abruptly transformed into a most reluctant subject.

'I know it's difficult and painful,' Tom went on patiently, 'but I'm going to ask you to cast your mind back again to the period of your stepmother's final illness. She became ill after the luncheon party and Doctor Owen was called. That's right, isn't it?'

'Doctor Owen wasn't called right away. At the end of the meal we went into the drawing room for coffee and my stepmother commented that she was feeling unwell and would have to go and lie down. She said her farewells to the guests and went upstairs. Everyone just thought it was one of her usual turns and no one actually suggested calling a doctor. It got rid of the Craigs anyway – they were fearful old bores – and once they'd finished their coffee and been seen off, Daddy went up to see that Mummy was all right. (I used to call her Mummy, even though she wasn't my real mother.) When he came back down, he said that Mummy thought she would like to have Doctor Owen and he went into the hall and telephoned. I heard him say it was a touch of the usual trouble and nothing urgent, and Doctor Owen turned up a bit later and went up to see her in her room. I think he was having a busy day, because it was his sister, Mrs Smith, who dropped off some medicine later on in the afternoon. I happened to be crossing the hall when she turned up and asked after my mother, and I told her she was already much improved.'

'And was she?'

'Was she what?'

'Already much improved?'

'Of course.' Florence tossed her head. 'I wouldn't have said so, otherwise. Daddy had sent out specially for some of that ginger cordial she liked and everyone had been making the usual fuss of her generally, and of course the tiresome visitors had gone too, which was enough to cheer anyone up.'

'So what happened next?'

'Well, nothing very much. We all had supper as usual, though

I think Mummy only had a little bread and butter. Daddy went up to her room and read to her for a while. Then we all went to bed. Next day was just as usual, too. I remember that Doctor Owen came again. In the afternoon I played the piano for Mummy and mademoiselle read to her. In the evening, Daddy played cards with her and let her win, which always pleased her immensely. Oh, yes, and I remember her telling mademoiselle to be sure to tell Cook that from the following day she was to have small portions of the same things everyone else was having, rather than the white fish and milk puddings she'd had that day. The police particularly wanted to know what she'd been eating and drinking,' Florence added, by way of an afterthought.

'So on that final day, when she suddenly became so ill and died, Mrs Ripley had eaten absolutely nothing except the same food and drink that everyone else in the house had?'

'That's right.'

'What about the ginger cordial?' asked Fran.

'Funnily enough, although Daddy got it in specially for her, she said she didn't fancy any just then and it got put away in the pantry. Annie found it weeks later, standing unopened on a top shelf and it sent her into floods. I expect it's still there. No one except Mummy ever drank the stuff, you see.'

'What about her medicine?' asked Tom.

'Well, that's what the police think it was,' said Florence. 'You see, it would have been very difficult to slip a large dose of arsenic into the food while it was being prepared in the kitchen without us all getting poisoned as well – and we weren't even a little bit ill, any of us. And it would have been pretty difficult to get anything into the food once it was on the plate and being carried up to Mummy's bedroom.'

'Whereas if you added poison to the medicine, you could do it at any time between doses, knowing that only one person would take it,' Fran finished for her. 'How often did the medicine have to be taken?'

'One dose each mealtime and a final spoonful with a milky drink at night.'

'So on the last day Mrs Ripley had her breakfast then took her medicine, and she seemed to be all right during the morning?'

'So far as I know. I popped my head in first thing after breakfast, and Daddy slipped in to say goodbye before he went off to the bank. I had to do lessons with mademoiselle until the middle of the morning, then I saw Mummy again for a few minutes just before lunch and she was doing some crochet and seemed perfectly cheerful. After that, I ate my lunch with mademoiselle in the dining room. Mummy had hers carried upstairs. She had a special little table that was just the right height for when she was sitting on the chaise longue, so that all she had to do was swivel round and pop her feet into her slippers.'

'Who took her lunch up that day?'

'I believe mademoiselle did. To save the servants the extra work.'

'Then what happened?'

'We hadn't even finished our lunch when there was a commotion. We heard Mummy's bell ringing repeatedly – and although we could hear Martha charging up the stairs, mademoiselle and I went up too to see what on earth was going on. Poor Mummy had been violently sick. It was horrible – she just went on and on being ill. Mademoiselle and Martha tried to attend to her and I ran downstairs and rang for Doctor Owen, but his sister told me that he was out helping to deliver a baby. She asked if it was urgent and I said yes, I thought so, and she said she would get a message to him to come as soon as possible.

'Mummy carried on being horribly ill – I'm not sure how long it went on for, but it seemed like ages, and eventually she just sort of collapsed. Mademoiselle ran downstairs and telephoned Doctor Owen again, and when his sister said he still hadn't come home, mademoiselle asked where he was and then telephoned the Cannings' house, but I don't believe she managed to speak with the doctor himself. All we got was another message saying he'd be with us as soon as he could.'

'From what Doctor Owen has told us, I believe that Mrs Cannings' life was also in danger,' Fran put in quietly.

'Oh, yes, one doesn't blame Doctor Owen – and anyway, I don't think he could have saved Mummy by getting here any sooner.'

'I know it must be painful for you, but can you remember what happened after that?'

'Mademoiselle didn't want me to come back in the room. She

said she and Martha would tend to Mummy and I was to wait downstairs, watching for Doctor Owen so he could be let in as soon as possible. I knew mademoiselle was trying to protect me from seeing anything horrid and . . . and . . . it probably sounds dreadful of me, but I was quite glad to get out of the bedroom and wait downstairs. Oh, yes . . .' A new idea struck her. 'I was also supposed to be looking out for Reverend Pinder. Mademoiselle sent Binks to fetch him too – either just before or just after she phoned for Doctor Owen.'

'And did Reverend Pinder arrive quite quickly?'

'I think so. It's very hard to say how long things took. I wasn't looking at the clock the whole time.'

'Did Reverend Pinder arrive first, or Doctor Owen?'

'Does it really matter?' the girl asked crossly. 'I'm pretty sure the vicar came first and then the doctor. I took him upstairs and then I shut the door and waited out on the landing. The next thing was Martha came out of the room and she was crying. I asked her what was happening and she said, "The mistress is in a very poorly way, Miss Florence. I think you should prepare yourself for the worst". Then she gave me a hug. Martha has been with us for ages, so she's very close to the family.'

'And we understand that your mother died soon afterwards.'

'Yes. Mademoiselle came out and took me by the hand and told me.'

'Just a couple more details now,' said Tom. 'First of all, are you absolutely sure there were no visitors to the house that day?'

'Absolutely sure. And the other thing?'

'Did anyone suggest telephoning the bank to bring your father home?'

'Oh, yes,' the girl said. 'I forgot to say that when mademoiselle tried to get Doctor Owen and sent Binks for the vicar, she also telephoned the bank and asked to speak with my father, but I don't believe she spoke with him either. I remember her saying she'd had to leave a message for him too. Then after Mummy had actually died, I think it was Reverend Pinder who asked if anyone had broken the news to Daddy and mademoiselle said, "He is supposed to be on his way, but I will telephone the bank in case he is still there". And she did. I don't know what was said. I was with Martha and Annie in the kitchen at the time.

Poor Annie was trying to make tea for everyone, and having to stop and wipe her eyes on her apron every few minutes.'

Tea again, Fran thought. People always need tea at times like these.

'If that's everything,' Florence said, 'shall I send in mademoiselle next?'

'Before we talk with Mademoiselle Bertillon again,' Fran said, 'there is something else that might be helpful. Would it be possible to see the room where Mrs Ripley died?'

'Of course.' Florence rose at once. 'I will get mademoiselle to show you while I see about the arrangements for tea and go to sit with Miss Rose. It would be impolite to leave her all alone.'

TWENTY-SEVEN

'The room is much the same as when Mrs Ripley was alive,' Mademoiselle Bertillon said, as she swung open the bedroom door and stepped back, allowing Tom and Fran to precede her. 'Mrs Ripley's personal things have been removed, of course. I assisted Miss Florence with all of that. The wardrobes and drawers are still empty, as Mr Ripley continues to use his own room.'

'And where is that?'

'Through there.' Mademoiselle indicated a door in the wall beyond the double bed. 'It is a much smaller bedroom, next door to this one, and it has its own separate door on to the landing as well.'

'So Mrs Ripley used to lie on the chaise longue when she was feeling unwell?'

'She did. It has been pushed back against the wall now, but it used to stand so.' Mademoiselle indicated a more central position with a wave of her arm.

'And I think Miss Florence mentioned a little table that was used when Mrs Ripley was unwell.'

'This is it.' Mademoiselle walked across and tapped her hand on a low rectangular table, which had also been placed against the wall. 'Mrs Ripley would keep things to hand on there – her library book and the workbag where she kept her knitting and crochet – as well as using it for her meals.'

'How about Mrs Ripley's medicine? Was that kept on the table too?' asked Fran.

'Oh no. Mrs Ripley's medicines were kept in the cabinet on the wall, above the washbasin.'

They all looked across at the cupboard in question – an ordinary white wooden cabinet, of the kind found in many bathrooms.

'I suppose the cabinet has been cleared out too?' This from Tom.

'Yes, of course.'

'What happened to Mrs Ripley's medicine bottles?'

'They were all washed out and thrown away. There was no reason to keep them. They were prescribed only for Mrs Ripley, and there were no suspicions then about the way she had died.'

'Were there quite a lot of different medications in the cupboard?'

'Not very many. There was always a tin of Andrews Liver Salts. Some permanganate of potash. Cough syrup from the previous winter, and some Zam-Buk as Mrs Ripley was a martyr to her chilblains. I remember there was some tooth powder, and some oil of cloves for toothache. And of course a little tin of aspirins.'

'But so far as you know, she was not taking any of these things when she died, only the one lot of medicine prescribed by Doctor Owen?'

'Just that, yes.'

'And she had eaten the same as you had for lunch?'

'Yes.'

'What did everyone have to drink with their lunch that particular day?'

'Only water. Mrs Ripley would have taken a cup of weak tea after her lunch – she never drank coffee when she was under the weather – but she never got as far as the tea, because she was taken ill before it was made.'

'She was supposed to take her medicine at lunchtime, wasn't she?'

'Yes.'

'Did anyone see her take it?'

'No. I carried her tray upstairs and fetched the medicine from the cupboard for her myself and placed it on the table, but no one sat with Mrs Ripley while she ate her lunch that day. She was still fussing about with her slippers when I went downstairs to join Miss Florence in the dining room, so I did not see her take the medicine either.'

'I see the chaise longue is on casters,' Tom said. 'Will you just humour me a moment further, mademoiselle? I'd like to move the chaise longue back to where it was standing on the day Mrs Ripley died.'

Before anyone could question the suggestion, Tom swung into

action, wheeling the chaise longue across the polished wooden floorboards and then manoeuvring it on to the central rug before seeking directions from the governess in order to get the location just right. After that, he performed a similar operation with the small table and then asked Fran to sit with her feet up on the chaise longue.

'Sorry about this,' Tom said. 'I'm just trying to get a complete picture in my mind. Now then, Mademoiselle Bertillon, can you just go across and stand facing the washbasin, if you wouldn't mind?'

The governess, looking a little puzzled, complied.

'Can you open the cupboard, mademoiselle? Yes, that's right. Just stand there a moment longer, if you would be so kind.' Tom stepped behind the sofa and momentarily adopted a crouching position, which brought his line of vision pretty much on a par with Fran's. Then standing upright again, he said, 'Thank you ladies, that's most helpful. Don't worry, I will soon have everything back where it was before.'

When Tom had finished rearranging the furniture, they returned with mademoiselle to the study, where, just as they had done with Florence Ripley, they took her step by step through what she remembered about the last days of Mrs Ripley's life.

When it came to the question of summoning Mr Ripley, the doctor and the vicar, Mademoiselle Bertillon admitted that she was now confused as to the order in which the various calls had been made. 'I was . . . what is the expression? Outside myself with worry. To begin with, Martha and I were trying to calm and comfort poor Mrs Ripley. She kept on asking when the doctor would be there. She had great faith in Doctor Owen, you see, but then she collapsed and seemed to barely understand what we were saying, and it was then that I feared she might be dying and I thought of sending for the priest.'

'Reverend Pinder had not been to see her previously?' asked Fran.

'Oh, no. But now I wondered, do the Church of England administer the last rites in the way we in the Roman Catholic faith would do? I had never been engaged in a household where there had been a death before, so I took Martha aside and asked her, "Should we send for the priest?"'

'And what did Martha say?'

'She was no help. She said, "I don't rightly know". The servants, they are no use in situations like these. They are not used to making the decisions or thinking for themselves.'

'So you asked Miss Florence?' Tom suggested.

'No. Miss Florence was upset and frightened enough already by what she had seen. I was trying to keep her calm and find her things to do outside the sickroom. I decided for myself that it was best to send for the priest. I told Martha to go downstairs and send Binks.'

'Now you also decided to send for Mr Ripley,' Tom said. 'It was you who telephoned the bank, wasn't it?'

'It was. Normally I would never disturb Mr Ripley at the bank, but this was an emergency.'

'Who did you speak with?'

'I spoke with Miss Rose.'

'On both occasions?'

The governess looked startled, but she recovered herself quickly. 'Yes,' she said quietly. 'On both occasions.'

'When we first talked with you about this, I think you only mentioned telephoning once.' Tom spoke quietly.

'I must have forgotten to mention the first call. You must understand, Mr Dod, that there was great anxiety and confusion. I was upset for my mistress and trying to ease her suffering as much as possible, and at the same time trying not to distress Miss Florence. Martha was coming and going, there were calls to be made, and a hundred and one things seemed to be happening all at once. It is very hard now, all these months later, when I have tried to put those horrible things out of my head, to remember, did this thing happen first or was it that thing?'

'Of course, of course, we do understand how difficult it must be,' Tom said quickly. 'Thank you so much for your help. I think we should see Miss Rose next, don't you?'

TWENTY-EIGHT

There was a minor contretemps when Fran and Tom expressed their wish to talk with Miss Rose, for Florence Ripley had already instructed Martha to bring in the tea things and suggested they should all have their tea first. When Tom said rather firmly that it would only take a minute, as there was really very little to ask Miss Rose about, Fran noticed the way the girl's face immediately reddened in annoyance.

Miss Rose, however, was already getting to her feet. 'It's always better to get business out of the way before one starts on the refreshments,' she said, attempting to smile at Florence, but Florence moved to adjust the stack of dainty plates that Martha had placed alongside the cake stand and made no reply.

'We wanted to ask you first about a Mr Pascoe,' Tom said, once he and Fran were safely back in Mr Ripley's study with Miss Rose. 'I believe he had a falling out with Mr Ripley.'

'That was quite some time ago,' Miss Rose said. 'Mr Pascoe was a long-standing customer of the bank, but his business was in trouble and he kept on wanting to extend his credit. In the end Mr Ripley had to say "no". Mr Pascoe lost his business, and I believe he and his wife now live in somewhat reduced circumstances. It is very regrettable when such things happen, but the bank is not a charity and Mr Ripley does not have the authority to bail out lame ducks indefinitely.'

'Is it true that Mr Pascoe made threats against Mr Ripley?'

Miss Rose considered this for a moment. 'It is true,' she said, with a half-smile. 'But they were not the sort of threats that anyone would take seriously.'

'Why do you say that?' asked Fran.

'Mr Pascoe is a middle-aged windbag with an almighty chip on his shoulder. The sort of man who often says things like "I'll swing for you, Ripley" or "I'll see you in hell first".'

'Did you ever hear him say anything like that?'

'Oh, yes, several times. And not just at the bank, either.

He made similar remarks to Miss Simmonds at the post office when she refused to take his parcel because he hadn't put the correct amount of postage on it, and I remember hearing about another big altercation at the hardware store over something or other he'd bought there which he claimed had not been up to scratch.'

'But you did hear him threaten Mr Ripley?'

'Indeed, yes. In fact, on one occasion he also said he would swing for me. I expect there's hardly anyone in Durley Dean upon whom his wrath has not been vented at one time or another.'

'Why did he threaten you?'

'I refused to give him access to Mr Ripley's office. I am the gatekeeper, you see – or if you prefer, the dragon at the door. If Mr Ripley did not wish to see someone, it would be me they would have to deal with.'

'And Mr Ripley did not wish to see Mr Pascoe?'

'Not once he had given him the bank's final refusal, no.'

'Why not?'

'There would have been no point. Mr Ripley had already discussed matters fully with Mr Pascoe and made his decision. Unfortunately, Mr Pascoe is one of those men who won't take "no" for an answer. He presumably imagined that if he could have some more time with Mr Ripley then he might persuade him to change his mind, but Mr Ripley had no intention of changing his mind and so he asked me to tell Mr Pascoe he was unavailable.'

'One imagines this would not have pleased Mr Pascoe.'

'On one such occasion, Mr Pascoe became extremely offensive. He banged his hand on my desk and called me a liar, saying he knew perfectly well that Mr Ripley was in his office.'

'Goodness me,' said Fran. 'What did you do?'

'I told him very calmly and quietly that if he continued to behave in that manner, I would have no alternative but to send for Police Constable Godfrey and have him removed.'

'Was he right?' Tom asked. 'About Mr Ripley being in his office, I mean?'

'Oh, yes.'

'So in the course of your employment, you sometimes had to tell fibs for Mr Ripley?'

'Certainly not!' Miss Rose looked both shocked and annoyed.

'I never suggested to him that Mr Ripley was not in his office. I told him Mr Ripley was not available to see him, which is an entirely different thing. I agree that I sometimes had to adopt a tactful form of words, which may have conveyed a particular impression, but I always avoided telling an outright lie.'

When she saw that Fran was looking bemused, Miss Rose continued. 'For example, suppose Mr Pascoe asked me, "When will Mr Ripley be available to see me?" Although I knew the answer was probably "Never", I might use the words "I really cannot say", which would not be untruthful, you see.'

'Of course,' Tom said. 'It's no more than any good secretary would do. Now Mr Pascoe also mentioned some letters to us. Do you know anything about any letters between Mr Pascoe and the bank?'

'There would have been the usual letters warning him about his overdraft, that kind of thing.'

'He said that he'd been proved right,' Fran said. 'About what he had said in the letters.'

'I really can't think what he could have been talking about.' Miss Rose hesitated. 'Unless . . . Oh, the dreadful man! I wonder if it was Mr Pascoe who wrote those vile letters to the chief constable accusing Mr Ripley? What exactly did he say?'

'I think he said he wasn't sure when he wrote the letters, but now he had been proved right,' said Fran. 'He seemed to think you would attempt to somehow put the blame for Mrs Ripley's death on him. If it was Mr Pascoe who wrote the letters to the chief constable, suggesting that Mrs Ripley had been poisoned, what would have made him think that, do you suppose?'

'I don't for a moment imagine that he really did think Mrs Ripley had been poisoned,' Miss Rose said angrily. 'He would have written the letters out of pure spite, just hoping to stir up trouble.'

'Well, he has certainly managed to do that,' Fran said, before she could stop herself.

'One final thing Mrs Black and I are a bit confused about is what exactly happened at the bank on the afternoon of Mrs Ripley's death,' Tom said.

'I'm afraid I don't see what you mean.'

'When we first spoke to you, Miss Rose, you told us that

Mademoiselle Bertillon telephoned and told you Mrs Ripley had
died. You mentioned only one telephone call, which took place
when Mrs Ripley was already dead. Why did you lie to us about
that?'

Miss Rose's cheeks took on a shade associated with some of
the blooms after which she was named. 'I did not lie,' she said.

'But more than one witness has told us that mademoiselle
telephoned the bank as soon as it became obvious that Mrs Ripley
was seriously ill. When we taxed mademoiselle with this just
now, she admitted that it was you she spoke with during both
calls. So can you please explain, Miss Rose, why you tried to
give us the impression that Mr Ripley would have hurried home
the moment he heard his wife was unwell, when the truth is that
he had already been told about her illness but had not in fact set
off for home when the news arrived that Mrs Ripley had died?'

'I did not lie to you,' Miss Rose said. 'But nor did I tell you
the whole truth. I didn't think it mattered, but now I see that I
should have been more open. I would like you to understand that
I am entirely the person at fault here, and that Mademoiselle
Bertillon only assisted me because she thought it for the best.

'It is true that I took two telephone calls from Mr Ripley's
home that day. When Mr Ripley was busy with something and
had instructed our junior clerks that he was not to be disturbed,
anyone who telephoned the bank and asked for him would be
put through to myself in the first instance. That day he was
involved in the preparation of some quite complicated figures
which were needed for the annual audit. We were already behind,
as Mr Sanderson, one of our clerks, had been off work with a
septic foot. Poor Horace, he always worried a great deal over
such things, and when Mademoiselle Bertillon telephoned and
said he should come home immediately because Mrs Ripley was
ill . . . Well, I'm afraid I felt very cross with Mrs Ripley. She
was always so self-centred, you see. She never thought of her
husband's work, or how worried he would be if he had to leave
everything up in the air and come back to it the next day, when
time would be even shorter and the auditors all but breathing
down our necks. She was always crying wolf and making a fuss,
and I'm afraid I decided not to pass on the message immediately.
I thought that given another hour or so without interruptions,

Mr Ripley would be able to finish what he was doing and then go home and make the usual fuss of his wife.

'Then of course mademoiselle rang again, this time to say Mrs Ripley had died. I felt sick with remorse, and I was afraid of what Mr Ripley might think of me if he ever found out that I had denied him the chance to say goodbye to his wife while she was still alive. The next day I managed to speak with Mademoiselle Bertillon and told her that I had not passed on the first message. We talked about it and she agreed with me that there was nothing to be gained by telling anyone what had happened. It was most unlikely that Mr Ripley would have reached home in time, and both mademoiselle and I thought it could only create even more upset and that with everything happening so quickly the day before – people coming and going and so forth – no one in the family would ever need to know what I had done. Or rather, not done. Of course, we did not realize then that every little detail would be looked into. We never actually lied about it – we merely omitted to mention one of the two calls.'

'Do the police know there were two telephone calls?'

'Unlike you, the police do not appear to have asked the right questions in order to elicit this information.'

'And you have not volunteered it to them?' Tom asked, rather sternly.

'Do you think it would do Horace any good if I did?' Miss Rose exclaimed angrily. 'As it is, the police twist everything that is said about him. How would it look if they found out that he knew about his wife's illness but did not go home to be with her?'

'But you said that he didn't know . . .'

'As if the police are going to believe I kept it from him! Secretaries are not supposed to make decisions about what they tell and don't tell their boss. I imagine the whole idea would be ridiculed in court. It would be just one more thing to hold against him.'

'I'm sure—' Fran began, but Miss Rose cut across her.

'They're going to hang him, aren't they? People are already saying he's another Armstrong.' She burst into noisy sobs and rushed from the room.

'Oh my goodness,' said Fran, as she and Tom rose as one from their seats and followed Miss Rose out into the hall.

'Look here,' Tom said quickly. 'You try to hold the fort while I slip into the kitchen for a minute. There's something I need to check.'

At that moment, Florence and her governess appeared in the doorway of the drawing room.

'Whatever is going on?' Florence demanded. 'Why is Miss Rose so upset?'

'I'm afraid it may have been something that Mr Dod and I asked her, coupled with the awful predicament in which your father now finds himself.' Fran knew she sounded feeble.

'When Mademoiselle Bertillon and I invited you here it was not so that you would go about upsetting everyone,' Florence declared. 'You were supposed to be on our side – ours and Daddy's. Mademoiselle has just been telling me how the two of you started moving furniture about and you lay on the chaise longue, pretending to be Mummy on her deathbed, while mademoiselle had to pretend to be fetching her medicine from the cupboard, which is absolutely horrible. And what does Mr Dod think he's doing, going into the kitchen without even asking?'

Before Fran could manage to protest, Florence had marched off down the hall and through the baize door, and Mademoiselle Bertillon had hurried away in the opposite direction in order to comfort Miss Rose. After hesitating for only a second or two, Fran followed Florence Ripley into the kitchen, where Annie and Martha were watching events open-mouthed from their positions on either side of the scrubbed wooden table.

'What are you doing snooping around in the pantry?' Florence's voice was shrill and angry.

Tom emerged from one of the open doorways that led from the kitchen. 'Pardon me, Miss Ripley, but there was something I wanted to look at in the pantry.'

'In the pantry! No, Mr Dod, please don't say any more. I don't believe you have the slightest idea about what happened to my stepmother, do you? You are just playing at being detectives, going about upsetting everyone and snooping around my home.'

'But Miss Ripley,' Tom protested. 'You asked us to help you. And if you will only allow me to explain . . .'

'No!' For a moment, Fran half thought that Florence was about to stamp her foot like a petulant child. But instead she folded and then unfolded her arms as she said, 'It was a mistake to invite you to help. You haven't uncovered a single thing that's going to help Daddy. In fact, I think you are just playing some kind of game and that this whole thing will end up with you . . . oh, I don't know . . . selling stories about us to the papers or something.'

'Oh, Florence, we would never do something like that,' Fran protested, but the girl scarcely appeared to have heard her.

'I want you to go now,' Florence said. 'Please leave me and my family alone. If we need to help Daddy, then we may engage a firm of proper private detectives.'

'I think,' Tom said, as they climbed into his motor car a few minutes later, 'that we have just found out what it is like to be sacked.'

TWENTY-NINE

'**D**ear me, I'm sorry, but I can't help laughing,' Mo said. 'Just thinking about Tom being ticked off for lurking in the pantry by some slip of a girl.'

'I suppose it does have a funny side,' Fran said. 'Do look out, or you will spill that Martini.'

'Goodness, darling, that would never do.' Mo righted her tilting glass and took an appreciative sip. 'You really do make gorgeous Martinis. It's because you're not stingy with the gin. So come along, you must explain why Tom had gone fooling about in the pantry, and what on earth he was up to when he got you to lie on Mrs Ripley's couch.'

'He'd gone into the pantry to check on the ginger cordial. You see, Florence said her stepmother was very partial to it and that Mr Ripley bought some specially when she was first taken ill. It occurred to Tom that the ginger cordial would be a perfect medium for the poison, because, first of all, it was strong-tasting and would help mask the arsenic; and secondly, as no one else ever touched the stuff, the killer could add the poison and then bide his or her time, knowing that it would find its way into the victim's system eventually.'

'That's jolly smart thinking. And I suppose if the bottle was still sitting in the pantry, he could have got the contents analysed for arsenic.'

'Exactly. Except there was nothing doing with that theory, because he found the bottle on the top shelf, just where Florence had said it would be, and the seal hadn't even been broken.'

'Botheration! It was such a good idea.'

'Tom's never short on good ideas,' Fran said. 'The trouble is they're not the right ideas.'

'What about the business of getting you to lie on the couch?'

'Well, that did turn out to be a bit more useful, even if it was in slightly poor taste and helped to earn us the order of the boot. Tom explained it all to me afterwards, and I realized he was right. When Mademoiselle Bertillon went over and opened the door of the cupboard above the basin, it was absolutely impossible to see anything of the cupboard, or the little glass shelf just below it or the washbasin itself, because from where Mrs Ripley was lying on the couch all she could have seen was the governess's back. Mrs Ripley probably wasn't watching anyway – but even if she was, she would have been none the wiser if mademoiselle had uncorked her medicine bottle and slipped something into it. It wouldn't have taken a moment to do it, and of course Mrs Ripley couldn't see through her.'

'I didn't realize that the governess was a suspect,' Mo said.

'She has to be a suspect, as she's the last person who had access to Mrs Ripley's food and drink that day.'

'What about the other servants?'

'Well, yes, I suppose they're in the frame too, but they both appear to be absolutely harmless and, like Mademoiselle Bertillon, they don't have any motive. All three appear to have been genuinely fond of Mrs Ripley, for all her various foibles.'

'One of them may have had a secret motive,' Mo gestured vaguely with her glass, once more endangering its contents. 'Perhaps there was a love affair between the cook and Mr Ripley? Or maybe he bankrupted one of their brothers, as he did with Mr Pascoe? Mrs Ripley could have stolen an inheritance that was rightfully the governess's—'

'You obviously haven't seen their cook, and if you're going to be silly . . .'

'No, no, don't go all censorious on me. I will behave, I promise. Do tell on.'

'There isn't really much more to tell. We went back to Tom's aunt's house and told her what had happened, and then we packed our things and Tom brought me home.'

'You're not giving up, are you?' asked Mo. 'After all, it isn't as if the Ripleys were even paying you. I think that girl's got a damned cheek virtually throwing you out of the house when you were only trying to help. Besides which, didn't you originally set out to solve the case in order to put Tom's aunt's mind at rest?'

'We haven't exactly managed to do that,' Fran shook her head. 'In fact, Florence Ripley's right, really. We haven't managed to help anyone at all. There was certainly no point our staying on in Durley Dean. We'd already spoken to everyone who had any obvious connection with the case.'

'What about that poor old chap who got bonked on the head?'

'Mr Hargreaves? No, we haven't spoken to him, I agree. Word from Aunt Hetty is that they've found him a bed in the cottage hospital for a bit to help him recuperate. She goes there to read to patients and write letters for them sometimes, so she is going to have a chat with him and try to find out more about what he wanted to say to us, though Tom and I both think it's only that Mrs Smith has been claiming the three deaths are part of a pattern.'

'Yes, but what about the chap's so-called accident? I suppose the police aren't even investigating.'

'No. Doctor Owen virtually ridiculed the idea. He's convinced that it was just an ordinary fall.'

'You should be looking at the whole case in a different way,' Mo said.

'What sort of different way?'

'Why not consider each suspect in turn?'

'Half the trouble is that apart from Mr Ripley himself, we scarcely have any sensible suspects. Most of the evidence, for what it's worth, seems to point to Mr Ripley killing his wife in order to marry Miss Rose. Quite honestly, I've begun to think the real problem may be that because his daughter had asked us to help him, we didn't want to believe Mr Ripley was guilty, so we were trying to find evidence which pointed another way. As Tom said on the way home: instead of being open-minded, we'd become hired guns.'

'Gosh, that sounds exciting,' Mo said. 'Like those American gangsters one hears about. Time for a top-up, then we'll put our thinking caps on – or load up our unhired guns, or at any rate, whatever it is one should do to prepare the ground in such circumstances.'

'Well, getting blotto won't help.'

'Nonsense, darling. Lubrication is extremely good for oiling the mental wheels.'

'I say,' Fran said, when she had returned from the kitchen, bearing two replenished glasses. 'Would you mind awfully if

I borrowed that mustard-coloured hat you had made for your cousin Adela's wedding last year? It would go splendidly with my good brown coat, and I'm rather stuck for something to wear to this wedding on Saturday week.'

'Of course you may. I recommend plenty of layers if the weather doesn't buck up. Why on earth did they choose to be married in October?'

'Didn't want to wait until the spring, I suppose.'

'What sort of do is it going to be?'

'Church service, followed by a tea dance. Miss Spencely's family are Temperance, I believe, so there won't be any drink.'

'Goodness, how on earth will they toast the happy couple? Remind me again who these people are.'

'Richard Finney, the editor of the Robert Barnaby Society's journal, and Julia Spencely, who is also a member. They met through the society.'

'Hot bed of romance, isn't it, the Robert Barnaby Society? Well then,' Mo went on when Fran didn't answer. 'Let's get down to it. Who could have killed Mrs Ripley?'

'It's very difficult to see how it could be anyone outside the household,' Fran said. 'Mrs Ripley became ill immediately after her lunch. No one seems to be able to remember now exactly how much of the food she had actually eaten, but from what little the police have told Mr Gaffney – he's Mr Ripley's solicitor – it looks very much as if she took in a large quantity of poison and reacted to it very quickly. That means it was either in her lunch or in something else she took just before eating it, which of course leads us to the medicine.'

'Do you think she could have taken some other medicine – say an indigestion mixture – in addition to what the doctor had prescribed?'

'We asked Mademoiselle Bertillon about that,' Fran said. 'But she thinks that if Mrs Ripley had wanted to take anything else that was in the cabinet, she would have asked for it to be fetched at the same time as Mademoiselle Bertillon got the medicine out.'

'Hang on,' said Mo. 'Where would the servants or the governess have got arsenic from in the first place?'

'We thought about that too,' Fran said. 'The trouble is that the question of getting hold of the arsenic applies to just about everyone except Doctor Owen, who is sure to have had some in his dispensary.'

'And Doctor Owen didn't get there until she was dying. And if he'd put any arsenic in the bottle originally, Mrs Ripley would have shown signs of poisoning from when she first started taking it.'

'Exactly.'

'Same goes for the vicar.' Mo sighed, as if disappointed. 'I would have put my money on him but, just like the doctor, he arrives on the scene too late. I say, wasn't there a case where a poisoner made an arsenic solution by soaking flypapers?'

'I think so. The trouble is there are loads of ways of getting hold of arsenic. Weedkiller is the most obvious one. Or you can just go and buy some over the chemist's counter and sign the poisons register. They're supposed to dye it purple now when it's sold neat, but I'm not sure how long that's been going on, and you know what people are like for not throwing things away. I bet that bottle of ginger cordial will sit on the top shelf in the Ripleys' pantry for the next twenty years, just in case it comes in handy.'

'Does arsenic go off?'

'I've got no idea.'

'So it's just the servants, the governess and Mr Ripley himself?'

'And Florence.'

'And Florence,' Mo echoed.

'And the most likely scenario is that it was Mr Ripley himself. You see, on the morning of his wife's death, when he popped in to see her, just before going off to work, he could easily have pretended that he needed something from the cabinet or that he was putting the medicine bottle back after his wife had taken her breakfast-time dose. When he was standing in the corner, with his back to the chaise longue, he could have slipped the poison into the bottle and then gone to the bank as usual. He'd probably think it would look less suspicious if she died while he was out of the house. In fact, that might be why he didn't come home when Mademoiselle Bertillon first asked him to.'

'I thought the secretary said she didn't give him the message?'

'Well, she would say that, wouldn't she, if they were in

cahoots? If so, then it was rather clever of her to persuade mademoiselle to say nothing in front of the family about the first telephone call, supposedly in order to spare their feelings.'

'Very well then.' Mo took another slug from her glass. 'How would any of those people fit in with the death of Miss Shilling?'

'It's Miss Tilling, dear heart. And they don't have to. Not if Mrs Ripley was murdered and the others died by accident.'

'But if we are trying to see it from different angles,' said Mo, 'then perhaps we need to find a common denominator. Isn't that the way of it in geometry? Or am I thinking of algebra? Anyway, find your common denominator and you've found your murderer.'

'All right then.' Fran played along. 'We can be pretty sure that if someone killed Miss Tilling, it was someone she knew and would have admitted to the house. That rules out the Ripley servants, because they wouldn't have been among her circle of social acquaintances; and if they had called round on an errand or to see one of her own servants, she would have expected them to go to the back door.'

'The vicar, however, is well up the list of possibilities.'

'It's unfortunate that Mrs Smith went out that afternoon,' Fran observed. 'Her favourite seat is in prime position to see anyone going in or out of Miss Tilling's gate.'

'Is there only one gate?'

'Yes, just the one, and then callers can either take the path to the front door or the one that leads round the side to the tradesman's entrance.'

'So it was lucky for the killer but very unlucky for Miss Tilling that Mrs Smith happened to be out. Now your Miss Tilling would have let the doctor in too,' mused Mo. 'And probably also the governess, and most certainly Florence Ripley. And her father too, come to that.'

'The trouble is we don't know what any of these people were doing that afternoon.'

'But they are all possibilities,' said Mo.

'Which is all well and good,' Fran said, 'but what possible motive would any of those people have had for murdering Miss Tilling? The only one she's made an enemy of is Reverend Pinder, but we've already established that he can't possibly have murdered Mrs Ripley.'

'Which is particularly infuriating because when we get to Mr Vardy there's that really brilliant clue about the dog, which puts the vicar right on the spot,' Mo said. 'Whereas I can't see any of the others hanging about in a country lane at that time of night.'

'Florence certainly wouldn't be out on her own at that time in the evening,' Fran said. 'Nor would the Ripley servants, unless one or other of them was on their half-day. The same probably applies to Mademoiselle Bertillon, though I daresay Doctor Owen and Mr Ripley could easily excuse themselves and go out for an evening stroll if they wanted to. And here's another thing: how would they explain themselves when they arrived home soaked to the skin after wrestling with Mr Vardy in the pond?'

'The vicar lives alone!' Mo brandished the information triumphantly. 'He wouldn't have had to explain himself to anyone.'

'Whenever I've seen him – even when he's off-duty – he's always been wearing a heavy cassock. That wouldn't exactly have helped if he needed to wade into the pond and finish Mr Vardy off.'

Mo grimaced. 'That's another wretched complication. Is there anyone else who fits in with all three deaths?'

'Mr Pascoe is a rather nasty piece of work,' Fran said. 'But he doesn't appear to have a motive for killing anyone apart from Mr Ripley, and Mr Ripley isn't dead.'

'And there's no way he could have got at Mrs Ripley's medicine?'

'No.'

'There's still the point that he knew about the poison, which is why he wrote to the chief constable.'

'Miss Rose thinks that he didn't actually know Mrs Ripley had been poisoned, he just hoped to stir up trouble for Mr Ripley by writing something nasty to the chief constable. Tom says the police receive simply scads of letters from cranks and busybodies and people trying to make trouble for their neighbours – and although in the vast majority of cases they are full of nonsense, the law of averages suggests that if you throw enough darts, sooner or later one will hit the target.'

'So the general idea is that Mr Pascoe wrote his letters simply to stir up trouble with the police in order to get his own back on Mr Ripley, but by sheer luck he happened to hit on something which turned out to have some substance to it?'

'Mr Pascoe said as much himself.'

'What about his involvement in the trouble at the church?'

'According to Aunt Hetty, the Pascoes don't attend any church and appear to hold no strong religious convictions. In fact, none of the other parishioners seem particularly likely except Aunt Hetty's favourite, Mrs Smith, but she wasn't at the Ripleys' house, isn't likely to have been hanging around in the lane that leads to the Bird in Hand beerhouse and is just one of a very long list of people who might have been let into the house by Miss Tilling.'

'I suppose we have to consider who might have been able to attack Mr Hargreaves, too.' Mo sounded as if her enthusiasm for the common denominator theory was waning.

'Well, Mr Ripley was in custody, so we can rule him out – although we don't have any idea what his potential partner in crime, Miss Rose, was up to that afternoon. Mrs Smith and Reverend Pinder were both assisting at a wedding in the parish church, so they would have been within yards of Mr Hargreaves' cottage on their way to and from the service. The Ripleys' servants, Florence and Mademoiselle Bertillon can probably all vouch for one another. Doctor Owen was miles away at a football match, so he's probably got dozens of witnesses to his whereabouts. And if you really want to include him, we know that Mr Pascoe was out walking his dog not far away from the scene in the early part of the afternoon.'

'We're not getting anywhere, are we?' Mo sighed.

'Shall we have our supper?' asked Fran.

At that moment the telephone rang.

'I bet that's Tom with a new clue,' Mo said.

'Much more likely to be my mother checking up on me, or just wanting to spread the usual gloom and despondency.' Fran picked up the telephone. 'Hello, hello? Oh, yes – hello Tom.'

Fran turned her back to avoid Mo's triumphant, 'Told you so.'

'No, no. It's not a bad time. It's only Mo. We were trying to go through all our so-called evidence and getting absolutely nowhere with it. Mo has just predicted that you are calling with a fresh clue.'

'My compliments to Mo,' Tom said. 'She's almost right.'

'What do you mean – "almost"?'

'Well,' said Tom, 'this isn't so much a clue as another unexplained oddity which *might* turn out to be a clue, if we can work out what it means.'

'That sounds rather complicated.'

'Well, it is a bit complicated.' Tom took a breath. 'You know that Nottingham has two major football teams, Nottingham Forest and Notts County. One plays at the City Ground and the other at Meadow Lane, and like most cities where there are two clubs they play home and away games alternate weeks, so that when Forest are at home County are away and vice versa.'

'Yes, I suppose I knew that already.'

'Now if you remember, the first time we called at Dr Owen's house, the maid told us he had gone to Nottingham to watch Forest play.'

'Yes,' Fran agreed. 'I particularly remember her saying that because whenever anyone mentions Nottingham Forest, it always makes me think of Robin Hood.'

'Nottingham Forest were not playing at home last Saturday.'

'Oh.' Fran hesitated a moment, then said, 'I suppose the maid got confused about which match he was going to. He must have gone to watch Notts County, instead.'

'It's a possibility,' Tom said. 'Doctor Owen said the result was a draw – and as it happens, both Forest and County drew on Saturday. County drew three-each with Stoke, and Forest managed a one-all draw at Tottenham. Our maids use the old newspapers for laying the fires, but luckily they still had the Sunday sports pages, so I was able to check. The thing is that Doctor Owen was definitely talking about Nottingham Forest. He said something like "If *we're* not careful, *we* will be relegated". It's the way people talk about the team they support.'

'Perhaps he watches whichever team is playing at home?' suggested Fran.

'I doubt it very much. In the big cities, most people support either one team or the other, United or City, Rangers or Celtic, Villa or Blues. I think Doctor Owen told his sister and the servants that he was going to a football match in Nottingham that afternoon when in fact he was going elsewhere. Do you remember the way he appeared to relax when I said I wasn't much of a football man and hadn't seen the results? It meant he could bluff us, by saying he'd been to a match, and we would be none the wiser.'

'But it turns out that you are a bit of a football man after all.'

Tom laughed. 'Not really. Ever since the football pools took off, my bookkeeper, Miss Finnemore, has been in charge of organizing the office pools syndicate, and I gather from her that the syndicate has had a small win. Nothing that is going to lead to mass retirement of our staff, or anything like that, but amid all this talk of away wins and score draws and so forth, I suddenly remembered reading about how Nottingham Forest had been thrashed at home on the twenty-eighth of September, and it occurred to me that it was rather unlikely they would be playing at home again the very next week. So when I got home this evening, I got the newspapers out of the kindling box and checked.'

'But if he wasn't at the match, where was he? And why is he lying?'

'Jolly good questions. I only wish I knew.'

By now, Mo was all but bouncing up and down on the sofa with impatience. 'Come on, Fran,' she stage whispered. 'What is Tom saying? Do share.'

'Hold on a sec, Tom. Mo wants to know what's going on.' Fran moved the receiver away from her face and said, 'It's about a football match.'

'Oh.' Mo was disappointed. 'What on earth is there to say about a football match?'

THIRTY

Mo dropped her mustard-coloured hat off at Bee Hive Cottage a few days before the wedding. Fran tried it on with her brown coat and was initially relieved to find that the brown ribbon which adorned the hat was a perfect match, because she couldn't really afford to buy a new outfit on top of the cost of a wedding present. She had spent rather more than she'd intended on a pair of hand-embroidered pillow slips, but they were best-quality linen and she had fallen in love with the pretty design of pale-pink rosebuds entwined with forget-me-nots at each end. How romantic and luxurious to have pillow slips that weren't plain white. If she had been getting married herself, they would have been just the kind of gift she would have liked to receive.

The trouble was that after trying on the hat, she remembered that it also had to go with whatever dress she decided to wear, because the dress would be visible once the coat had come off and they sat down for the wedding breakfast. If the wedding had been earlier in the season, she could have risked her navy straw hat, which went with her blue dress and jacket, but it was far too cold for that now. She couldn't possibly wear a blue dress with a mustard-coloured hat, but that only left her brown dress with the polka dots, which was really too shabby for a wedding.

And it's the first time you'll be seen by Veronica, she thought. The Dods were not short of money, and Tom's wife was sure to be done up to the nines. If only she could think up a convincing excuse for not going: something which would work for Tom as well as for the bride and groom, because she could hardly explain to Tom that she did not want to meet his wife. On the other hand, she wanted to be there to support her friends, Mr Finney and Miss Spencely. In general, she liked weddings. There was going to be dancing and she hardly ever got to dance these days. Surely there would be some unattached men who would take pity on a wallflower and give her a turn or two around the room?

She wished she could bring herself to ask Tom how much he had told Veronica about their friendship, because as things stood she was unsure how to handle the occasion. Ought she to behave towards Tom as she normally would, in a natural, friendly way? Or would it be better to keep her distance? Tom had once confided that due to the unusual circumstances of their marriage, Veronica had told him she would have no objection if ever he discreetly strayed. Which was all very well, Fran thought, but surely Veronica could not help loving Tom enough to be a little bit jealous of any friendships with other women? Moreover, if Veronica had jumped to the conclusion that Tom was engaged in straying with Fran, then she would hardly think it discreet if Fran turned up at a wedding and insisted on sitting or conversing with Tom.

On the morning of the wedding, Fran was still dithering. Although she knew that she would have to wear the brown outfit, this did not prevent a desperate half hour in front of the bedroom mirror, putting on and taking off a whole series of completely unsuitable combinations of frocks, hats and jackets. In the end, she was barely ready when Freddy Dyson arrived in the village taxi to take her to the station. It was an expense, but she could not risk her good shoes and stockings by walking along the muddy lane to catch the bus.

In spite of some unsettled weather during the week, the day had dawned brightly and the clouds looked pale and high enough for the rain to hold off. Awful for the bride if it rained, of course. The train was running on time and Fran whiled away the journey by reflecting on events in Durley Dean. She wondered if Tom would want to talk about them today. Well, of course not. One didn't start ruminating about murders in a social situation. And anyway, there was no aspect of the case which they had not already fully explored.

They had now learned via Aunt Hetty that Mr Hargreaves had no clear recollection of what had happened to him in his garden a fortnight before. 'One minute I was walking down the path, looking at my winter cabbages and Brussels coming through, and the next I was waking up in bed, with Miss Francombe, the nurse, sitting alongside me.' Aunt Hetty had also established that Mr Hargreaves had only wanted to tell them that Mrs Smith had approached him in the village street to say that he too was in line for divine retribution. 'It seems foolish now,' Mr Hargreaves had told Aunt Hetty. 'At the time, it made me wonder if she knew who was doing these things. But I reckon she's just a touch daft, like her mother was before her.'

Aunt Hetty had also speculated to Tom about the possibility that Mr Hargreaves' fall had not been an accident. 'According to Aunt Het,' Tom said, 'Mr Hargreaves is getting a trifle deaf, and so he might not have heard if someone came up behind him.'

'It's definitely a possibility,' Fran had agreed. 'The front door was unlocked. Look at the way we just walked right in. But surely, if someone had hit him from behind, there would have been bruises – blood even?'

Tom, however, had demurred. 'It depends what they hit him with. Mr Hargreaves has got a reasonably good head of hair. Maybe no one looked for bruising at the back of his head. From what I remember at the time, Doctor Owen's main concern was with the wound at the front of his head, where he had hit himself on those coping stones at the side of the garden path. That and how desperately cold he was.'

Once the puzzle of the football fixtures had been explained to Mo, she had temporarily transferred the mantle of chief suspect from Reverend Pinder to Dr Owen. It was true, Fran thought, that Dr Owen appeared to have had more opportunity than most of the suspects. Now she came to think of it, the idea that Mr Vardy and Miss Tilling had died accidentally was principally based on Dr Owen's medical testimony. Dr Owen had lied about his whereabouts on the afternoon when someone might have attacked Mr Hargreaves. Dr Owen attended the parish church and the fact that he had not joined in very strongly when sides were being taken for or against the new vicar did not necessarily mean that he did not entertain strong views on these matters. Could it be Dr Owen who had been systematically removing Reverend Pinder's opponents? It all seemed to add up, except for his late arrival at the Ripley house. That was the piece of the puzzle which didn't fit.

At that moment the train began to slow. Fran collected up her handbag and the neat little parcel containing her wedding gift, automatically straightened her hat (though it needed no adjustment), and prepared to open the door and alight from the train.

There were two or three little groups of people dressed in their best and probably on their way to the wedding, but no one that Fran recognized, so she made the short walk along the main street to the church alone. As she reached the gate, she spotted Tom's Hudson parked a little way up the road. He and Veronica must already be inside the church.

Fran took a deep breath. Here goes, she thought, as she entered the building.

THIRTY-ONE

A nervous-looking young man came forward to hand her a hymn book. 'Bride's side or groom's?' he asked.

'Neither,' said Fran, scanning the half-filled pews ahead of her. 'I'm a friend of both parties.'

'In that case,' the young man said, 'you may as well sit wherever you like.'

Instead of continuing down the central aisle, Fran was momentarily rooted to the spot. She still hadn't decided whether she ought to go and sit next to Tom and his wife or not, but then she spotted Tom's distinctive broad back and was confused to note that he appeared to be alone. At that moment he turned his head and, seeing her, gave an unmistakable smile of welcome.

'Did you want me to show you to a seat?' the young man asked, clearly wondering why she had not moved on.

'No, no, thank you. I'm fine.'

Fran headed further into the church and slid sideways into the pew where Tom was waiting. 'Are you on your own?' she asked in the low voice one invariably adopted in church.

'Poor old Veronica went down with a horrid cold yesterday and didn't feel up to it,' Tom said. 'She insisted that I still come. As she said, Old Finney and Miss Spencely are my friends. Vee has never met either of them.'

'Gosh, what jolly bad luck,' Fran said, trying to eradicate every scrap of joy and relief from her voice. 'I do hope she gets well soon.'

'It's only a cold,' Tom said. 'Runny nose and all that. Nothing to fret about.'

Fran thought it was a lovely wedding. The bride wore a fashionable lace gown with a drop waist, and a mauve sash to match the Michaelmas daisies in her bouquet. Both parties made their vows in clear, confident voices, and Miss Spencely looked up so sweetly at Richard Finney when she promised to honour and obey that Fran almost needed to follow the example of the bride's mother and reach for a handkerchief from her bag.

Once the ceremony was over and the bride and groom had posed for photographs on the church steps and paid the obligatory ransom to a group of local schoolboys who had tied the church gates together in the North Country tradition, the entire party set off along the main street, with the newly-weds leading the way and passers-by stopping to cheer and applaud them all the way to the parish hall, where there was a sit-down lunch provided by professional caterers.

When Tom discovered that they had been seated at different tables, he swiftly exchanged Fran's handwritten place card for Veronica's, so that she could join him on a table about halfway down the room, between some cousins of the groom and an old school friend of the bride and her rather earnest husband, who looked as if he might turn out to be a bore until Tom diverted him on to the subject of cricket.

Another potentially awkward moment arose when the first course arrived and Fran saw that it was dressed crab, which she did not like. The very thought of it made her retch, but it would never have done to reject their hosts' hospitality and, desperate not to be impolite, Fran was vainly attempting to hide some of the crab meat under the garnish of shredded cucumber when Tom came to the rescue by offering a discreet exchange of plates and disposing of both portions of shellfish in double-quick time. There were fortunately no such problems with the Melton Mowbray pie and salad, or the strawberry ice that concluded the meal.

The speeches which followed were mercifully short, the bride's father inevitably saying that he was not losing a daughter but gaining a son, and the best man telling some frightfully lame jokes which were nevertheless greeted by uproarious laughter. After complimenting the bridesmaids, whose blushes clashed somewhat with their mauve satin, Richard Finney took the unusual step of asking everyone to toast not only the bridesmaids but also the late Robert Barnaby, 'without whom, I might never have met my fiancée . . . I mean, of course, my wife', which generated a polite ripple of laughter and more applause. The toasts were drunk in homemade lemonade, which was extremely refreshing, Fran thought, and much nicer than the beer and shandy which was occasionally offered at weddings where the family could not afford anything better.

Once the speeches were concluded, the ladies stood aside while the able-bodied men assisted in moving the tables and chairs in order to clear a space for dancing, and in next to no time a musical friend of the groom had tuned up and begun to play a waltz on his violin, which was the cue for the new Mr and Mrs Finney to take to the floor amid more applause from their assembled friends and relatives.

For the subsequent dancing, the fiddler was joined by a pianist and a chap on a double bass, and the trio cheerfully plugged away at waltzes and foxtrots, interspersed with an occasional livelier number for younger guests who were conversant with the Charleston and the Shimmy. In the meantime, while the bride and groom circulated, thanking everyone for their presents and receiving good wishes and congratulations in their turn, Fran and Tom were able to catch up with some old friends from the Barnaby Society, until eventually Tom noticed Fran's tapping foot and asked, 'Would you care for a dance?'

'I'm afraid my Charleston has never been seen in public. Mo taught me and we've only ever done it with the rugs rolled back at home.'

'High time it had a proper airing on the dance floor, then,' Tom said, taking her hand and guiding her to her feet before she could make any further protest. 'I should warn you, by the way, that I'm no Vernon Castle.'

Tom's rendition of the popular craze owed far more to enthusiasm than to skill, and his insistence on pulling faces to make her laugh ensured that Fran was absolutely breathless by the time they resumed their seats. It was the first time she had danced in public since parting from Michael, and she found it somehow liberating to have taken part in something which her mother had once described as 'a disgusting spectacle and completely unladylike', particularly when her old friend Miss Robertson, chairman of the Scottish chapter of the Barnaby Society, welcomed her back to her seat with the words 'Bravo, Mrs Black, a tremendous effort!'.

It crossed Fran's mind to wonder what Jean Robertson made of the fact that Tom's wife had stayed at home or the way she and Tom were talking and laughing together, and she was reminded sharply of the realities of obtaining a divorce and what it might mean in terms of giving up their friendship.

As the hour approached five o'clock and the caterers were clearing away the teacups and plates, which bore traces of dark, sticky wedding cake, the chap on the violin called for everyone's attention and announced that they would be playing one last waltz before it was time to wave Richard and Julia Finney off on their honeymoon. Turning to the dance floor, Fran saw that the new Mrs Finney must have slipped away to change, as she was taking to the floor in a dove-grey travelling dress, enhanced with a row of mother-of-pearl buttons.

'Come on,' Tom said. 'Last chance to cut a rug, as our American cousins would say.'

The slower dance meant more traditional positions. Tom's left hand in her right, his other arm encircling her waist. Without even thinking about it, there they were, bodies resting gently against one another, Tom leading in an easy, comfortable way. She looked up at him and understood perfectly the message in his eyes. She must stay in the moment and enjoy it, not think about the future or how impossible everything was.

'Thank you,' he said politely when the music had finally ended and he was escorting her back to her seat, his hand clasping hers just a little longer than was absolutely necessary. The words seemed to convey much more than the customary pleasantry.

They joined the crowd on the front steps of the parish hall, cheering and waving as the newlyweds drove off in Richard Finney's little Austin, accompanied by the clatter of the old tin cans tied to his rear bumper. The departure of the bride and groom signalled the conclusion of the celebrations, and Fran found herself swept up in thanking the bride's parents and bidding various Barnaby Society friends farewell.

'Safe journey home,' she found herself saying to Tom. 'I do hope Veronica gets over her cold soon.' Their brief moment was over, and everything had reverted to normal.

THIRTY-TWO

F ran was glad of her taxi ride back from the station, for it was dark and cold by the time she got off the train. Mrs Snegglington was gratifyingly pleased to see her – though this may have been something to do with her empty dishes on the kitchen floor – and it didn't take long to have the fire (expertly laid by Ada earlier in the day) blazing brightly in the sitting room. After she had fed the cat and made a pot of tea for herself, Fran switched on the wireless in order to dispel the lonely quiet. It had drifted off the station, as usual, and she spent some time fiddling with the knob which tuned it before the wireless finally stopped hissing at her and produced something intelligible.

'A new recording from across the Atlantic,' the announcer was saying. Everything new and exciting seemed to be coming from America these days, Fran thought. There had been a huge amount of fuss last year when Ulverston had seen the arrival of the first talking picture. She had not gone to see it herself, preferring the theatre to the flickers, but Ada had been full of it, and some of the men at the tennis club who liked to be thought of as in the swim of things had taken to saying 'You ain't seen nothing yet!', which Fran herself found rather vulgar, as no gentleman of her acquaintance had ever used the expression 'ain't'.

I'm getting out of date, she thought. Sitting here on the side-lines and most distinctly not in the swim of things. As if to mock her, the new recording turned out to be 'Ain't Misbehavin'.

'Chance would be a fine thing,' Fran said crossly, as she marched across to the wireless and switched it off in disgust.

At some point soon, she would have to tell her mother that she had decided to divorce Michael. She would also have to explain how things stood to Tom and the prospect of that seemed almost as bad. She had already written to Michael, telling him that she wished to discuss something important with him, using carefully neutral language so that the letter could not be open to any dangerous interpretation in the event that it ever came into the hands of the wretched King's Proctor. Michael had written back agreeing to meet her at the Grand Hotel in Grange-over-Sands for a conversation over a drink on Monday evening. In many ways it would have been easier to have him come to see her at Bee Hive Cottage, rather than going to the bother of getting the bus into Grange, but she did not want Michael in her home, wiping his feet on her mat, leaving his imprint on her sofa cushions, drinking out of her teacups, when she had just managed to successfully eliminate him from her personal life.

She picked up her library book, but it was no use. By the time she had read the conversation between Dr Aziz and Mr Mahmoud Ali on page eleven three times over without it sinking in, she knew that she needed something other than *A Passage to India* in which to immerse herself.

It would be awfully nice to telephone Tom . . . But that would have been extremely selfish after he had spent the whole afternoon with her while poor old Veronica nursed her cold at home. And anyway, she was going to have to get used to not talking with Tom all the time, besides which, she didn't really have anything to talk with him about. That was it – she would go through all her notes on the case. Not because it would give her a good reason to telephone Tom, but because time was running out for Mr Ripley, whose case had been listed for hearing at the next assizes. Although his daughter had rejected their efforts to help, Fran still felt as if they were bound by their promise to do so – and maybe, just maybe, Mr Ripley was innocent. After all, he could not possibly have hit Mr Hargreaves over the head a fort-night ago.

More than an hour later, when Fran rose to make herself a fresh pot of tea, she knew that her instinct had been right. The deaths in Durley Dean had retained her attention in a way that E.M. Forster had not.

There was no doubt, she thought, that Dr Owen's behaviour in pretending he had been at a football match was most peculiar. Was it connected to an attack on Mr Hargreaves? When one stopped to think about it, there would really have been no need to invent such an elaborate excuse. In order to have attacked Mr Hargreaves, the doctor could have merely concocted a story about a nearby house call – he didn't have to account for an entire afternoon. Then again, perhaps there genuinely had been some misunderstanding about which fixture he had attended. The simplest way to try and find out would be to call Dr Owen and ask him directly about it. Why not? Asking the question could not push them any further into the dark than they were already.

As she asked the exchange for Dr Owen's number, it did occur to her that the last time she had attempted to flush out information from a killer she had ended up imperilling her own life, but she reassured herself that Durley Dean was many miles away, and Dr Owen probably didn't even know where she lived.

It was the doctor himself who answered the telephone. When he discovered the identity of his caller, he made no attempt to conceal his surprise. 'Mrs Black, I wasn't expecting to hear from you again. Are you back in the neighbourhood? Not having any problems which require my professional services, I hope?'

'No, thank you, I'm perfectly well. I'm calling from home, actually. There's a little point that's rather puzzling me and I was wondering whether you could clear it up.'

'Well naturally, I will assist you if I can.'

'When you were kind enough to see Mr Dod and myself a couple of weeks ago, you told us that you had been to see Nottingham Forest play, but we realized afterwards that Nottingham Forest had not been playing at home that afternoon.' Fran paused, letting the unenunciated question hang in the air.

There was a pause, then Dr Owen said, 'I am just going to transfer you to the extension in my consulting room. Stay on the line, if you please.'

There was a click as if the line had gone dead and then silence until, just as Fran was wondering if they might have been cut off, another click preceded Dr Owen's return. 'Now look here, Mrs Black,' he began, and she noticed that the usual charm was wearing rather thin. 'You are quite correct in your deduction that I was not at a football match that afternoon. I have no idea why my whereabouts should be of any interest whatsoever to you and your friend, Mr Dod, but I would much prefer it if you would say nothing about this to my sister.'

'Of course,' Fran said. 'I don't see that there is any need at all for us to mention it to your sister, or indeed to anyone else.'

'Thank you.' The doctor sounded curt, rather than grateful.

'I wonder, though, if you were not at the football match, would you mind telling me where you did spend the afternoon?'

'Yes, I would. Frankly, I do not see what business it is of yours where I was.'

'No, of course not. It was just that . . . Well, when we were making enquiries, anything which seemed a bit out of place . . .'

'I understood that you were no longer making enquiries,' the doctor said crisply. 'Miss Ripley informed me that your commission on her behalf was at an end.'

'Yes. You see, I was just tidying up loose ends . . . for my own satisfaction, really.'

'I am not a loose end, Mrs Black. Good evening.'

'Good evening, Doctor Owen, and thank you very much for your time.'

After she had replaced the telephone receiver (she did love the sleek elegance of her modern handset, rather than the stumpy old candlestick model that so many people still had), Fran decided to check that all her doors were locked. It was silly to imagine that Dr Owen would realize he was suspected and come hotfooting across the country in the hope of silencing her, but once bitten twice shy.

She considered ringing Tom to tell him about the conversation, but then again it did not really amount to anything, being no more than confirmation of what they knew already.

THIRTY-THREE

F ran met her estranged husband in the lounge of the Grand Hotel, which was fashionably appointed with cane furniture and potted palms, but presently almost deserted. She was wearing the same brown coat and borrowed hat she had worn to the Finneys' wedding and, having left her coat with the cloakroom attendant, she was again conscious of the slight dowdiness of the brown polka-dot frock. Dancing with Tom had made her forget the frock. Looking down at it now reminded her of Tom dancing the Charleston and she smiled in spite of herself.

Michael was late, so she ordered a pink gin while she waited for him. One or two of the hotel guests passing through on their way to the dining room glanced at her a little curiously as they went by, and she also attracted a moderate degree of interest from the bellboy. It was unusual to see a woman sitting drinking alone. Where was her husband? Her friends? Fran stared at the reflection of the room, superimposed against the darkness in the glass of the hotel window, while she wished that Michael would hurry up.

She was just trying to decide whether, had it been daylight, the room would have enjoyed a view of Morecambe Bay or the golf course, when she saw his familiar figure appear in the reflection and turned her head as he approached.

'Hello, Fran, old girl.' His voice was falsely hearty. As he bent to kiss her cheek, she noted the paisley-patterned neck tie and caught a glimpse of some unfamiliar cufflinks. All chosen for him by Winnie-the-Ninny, no doubt. He had never worn anything so fancy when he had been living with her.

'Hello, Michael.'

A waiter appeared at their side before they had time to say anything more.

'I'll have what the lady's having,' Michael told him.

The lady! Fran saw the expression of curiosity on the man's face as he turned away. Why on earth couldn't Michael have dignified the situation by saying 'my wife'? Which was still technically correct and would at least have avoided the waiter tipping off the clerk on the reception desk that they were not a married couple, just in case they attempted to book a room.

'Now then, Fran, what can I do for you?'

'I think it is more a question of what I can do for you,' Fran said, trying to stay cool and not get cross. She lowered her voice, even though there was no one within earshot. 'I understand that Winnie is . . .' She hesitated, remembering her mother's unkind words about her own failure to produce a child. Somehow she could not bring herself to say the word 'baby'.

'That she is in an interesting condition,' she said, falling back on euphemism. 'And obviously you need to marry her if you are ever to give the child any financial security and indeed your name. I know I once said I would never give you a divorce, but under the circumstances I am prepared to do so.'

Michael did not bother to conceal his delight, unexpectedly grabbing her hand and pumping it up and down. 'Well, I must say that's splendid news, old girl. Win will be absolutely over the moon when I tell her.'

'I'm not doing it for her,' Fran said. 'And please don't call me that. I am not your "old girl".'

I can't believe I was ever in love with him, she thought. Why was I so blind? Could it have been because I was just desperate to escape from Mummy?

Michael was babbling on regardless and calling for a drink, just as if they had had a good win at the races or something. She cut in briskly, explaining the ins and outs of the matter just as Mr Long had explained it all to her, only pausing while the waiter delivered Michael's pink gin.

'You've changed, you know,' Michael said, once she had finished speaking and he had agreed that they should proceed as Mr Long suggested.

'Everything changes,' Fran said briskly. 'After all, you once promised to love and cherish me until death us do part – and that didn't last long, did it?'

THIRTY-FOUR

F ran had arranged to visit her mother the following day.
'Cook has managed to get a nice fresh piece of halibut,
knowing that it is your favourite,' her mother announced as
they sat down to lunch.

Fran decided it was not the right moment to tell her mother
that she did not particularly like halibut. It would probably never
be the right moment, she reflected.

Her mother rattled on, bringing her up to date about various
relatives and acquaintances, to say nothing of the campaign to
improve the farm cottages that were such an eyesore on the edge
of the village. Fran tried to concentrate, remembering to compli-
ment the wretched halibut while desperately wondering how on
earth she was going to raise the topic she had come about. At
this rate, she would be getting back on the bus with the thing
still unsaid.

Eventually her mother ran out of steam and asked if she had
any news.

Now or never. Fran took a deep breath. 'Yes, as it happens,
I do have something to tell you. It's about Michael.'

'You're getting back together!' her mother exclaimed. 'Oh, I
knew he would see the error of his ways eventually.'

'No Mummy, it's not that. You see . . .' Fran gulped. Her
mother's generation did not expect pregnancies to be casually
raised over the luncheon table, even when there were no men
present. 'The woman Michael has been living with is going to
have his child, so I have decided to give him a divorce.'

'No! Frances, no! I absolutely forbid it.'

'Mummy, please. I am twenty-eight years old.'

'And still my daughter. You cannot possibly consider it. A
divorce is out of the question. Divorce indeed!'

'It's for the sake of the child,' Fran appealed. 'Michael will
be able to marry the woman and give the child a father. Times
are changing and divorce is becoming quite normal now.

Lord and Lady Inverwood were divorced only last year.' Her mother was a sucker for the aristocracy.

'And are no longer received at court,' snapped her mother. 'Besides which, that is completely different. The aristocracy often have arranged marriages, and it is therefore entirely understandable if there are occasional incompatibilities. You married Michael of your own free will, making your marriage vows before God. You made your bed and now you must lie on it.'

'That is a very cruel thing to say.' Fran was finding it difficult to keep her temper in check. 'Michael left me. Do you seriously believe I should spend the rest of my life alone? Why should I be punished for a situation that was not of my making?'

'Don't overdramatize, Frances. You are not being punished, as you put it. If you had known the suffering of nursing a sick husband and losing both your sons as well, you might have something to complain about. As it is, you came into enough money to live independently and do not have to work for your living. There are plenty of good causes to which you could devote your time, if you only chose to do so.'

'Suppose the time came when I wanted to marry again and perhaps have children?'

'Don't be ridiculous,' her mother snapped. 'No respectable man would marry a divorcee. You cannot possibly contemplate remarriage.'

'Perhaps you would prefer me to live in sin with an unrespectable man?'

'Frances! Are you trying to give me a heart attack? That's it, isn't it? You would be glad to have me out of the way, I'm sure. You clearly care nothing about my feelings, springing this awful news on me like this. You were always a selfish girl. If Geoffrey and Cecil were still alive, they would not sit by and allow you to treat me like this. As for your poor father, he must be turning in his grave if he can hear you saying these things. Illegitimate babies and divorce! I never imagined such things would become topics of conversation in this house, let me tell you. Clearly you won't be satisfied until you have worried me into an early grave.'

THIRTY-FIVE

'So she didn't take the news very well,' Mo said.

'I think that's the understatement of the year.'

It was Friday evening and the two friends were having supper together at Fran's cottage.

'I tried to tell her that times were changing, but I'm afraid she just wouldn't listen. She kept going on and on about how I wouldn't care if she died of shame – as if anyone ever really did that – and then she started crying and said she couldn't eat her dessert. Oh, it was all just as horrible as I knew it would be.'

'Surely she can see that you are entitled to try and find happiness with someone else?'

'On the contrary, I think my mother feels I'd be far better off living like a nun and becoming some kind of saintly figure, doing good deeds in the parish.'

'Good Lord!'

'Not so much the Good Lord, but certainly getting on for Saint Agnes.'

Mo laughed. 'I bet you haven't told her anything about Tom Dod and the dastardly deeds in Durley Dean. Talking of which, what news on the case?'

'I spoke to Tom briefly on the telephone just before you got here, though actually we talked more about all this trouble in America. I wanted to know what he makes of it all. I really don't understand stocks and shares.'

'Oh, I leave all that sort of thing to Terence. I suppose it's rather like that grubby business involving that nasty fellow Hatry, who was up to no good on the London Stock Exchange.'

'This sounds far worse,' Fran said. 'People have been ruined overnight. Some have even jumped off bridges and thrown themselves under railway trains, according to the newspapers.'

'Dear me,' Mo said. 'One doesn't usually associate that kind of hysteria with Americans. Sounds more like the Italians or the French.'

'Tom says it is going to cause a lot more uncertainty and hardship.'

'Well, yes,' said Mo, who never liked dwelling on anything unpleasant for long and had taken no particular interest in the so-called Wall Street Crash. 'But what did Tom have to say, if anything, about the mysterious demises in Durley Dean?'

'Nothing very much,' Fran said. 'There's nothing new from Aunt Hetty, and Tom is no wiser than we are about why Doctor Owen would pretend to be at a football match when he wasn't there.'

'Well, he was obviously up to no good!' Mo was emphatic. 'I know I had previously made the vicar odds-on favourite, but that was before evidence started stacking up against the doctor.'

'I've been thinking some more about the doctor,' Fran said. 'He is sort of on the spot in every case. Though I can't really see a motive . . .'

'The man's a homicidal maniac. He doesn't need a motive.'

'Setting aside the question of motive, I started thinking about Mrs Ripley's medicine. Suppose when Doctor Owen visited the day before she died he gave her something else to take, which she didn't mention to anyone else?'

'That's a good idea. I wonder what it could have been.'

'It would be odd, though, that she didn't take it until lunchtime the next day.'

'Maybe she was just following his instructions.'

'Well, yes, perhaps,' Fran said. 'But then I sort of dismissed the idea, because Doctor Owen wouldn't have been able to guarantee that Mrs Ripley wouldn't mention this new medication to anyone else – and if she had, then when she became ill after lunch suspicion would naturally have fallen on the new medicine. The other thing is that in the normal scheme of things she would have kept it in the cabinet over the washbasin with all her other medicines and asked Mademoiselle Bertillon to fetch it for her when she fetched the stuff she was already taking.'

'You're right, of course.' Mo sounded somewhat disappointed.

'Hold on a minute.'

'What? Where are you going?'

'I'm just going to fetch my notebook. I want to see exactly what was said about the original medicine.'

Fran returned a moment later, turning the pages of her notebook as she spoke. 'Goodness, this is scratty handwriting. It's really difficult, trying to make notes while people are talking. Ah, yes, here it is . . . When we went to see Doctor Owen, he told us that on his first visit to Mrs Ripley he prescribed her a couple of days' supply of the mixture of powdered rhubarb, soda and bismuth, and then when he went back on the third day of her illness he prescribed her some more. That's two lots of medicine, but no one else ever mentions this second bottle.'

Mo considered the problem for a moment. 'If he said "prescribed" rather than "gave" then presumably he wouldn't have had an additional bottle with him. It would need to have been made up when he got back to his surgery, and he would probably have dropped it off when he visited next day.'

'By which time Mrs Ripley was already dead.'

'On the other hand, if she didn't have very much of the stuff to start with, she might have been running out, in which case he would have either dropped it off or sent it round sooner. Let me think . . . those little bottles generally hold about a dozen teaspoonfuls. How often did Mrs Ripley have to take her medicine?'

'Four times a day, one dose at each mealtime and one with a milky drink before bed.'

'So if Mrs Ripley took a dose on the afternoon that Doctor Owen first saw her and then one with her supper and another at bedtime, that's three doses. She would have taken four each day on the next two days, so the breakfast time dose on the day she died would have finished off the bottle and she would have needed to start the new bottle of medicine at lunchtime.'

'Oh my goodness!' Fran said. 'I think we may be on to something here.'

'Did the French governess mention anything about it being a new bottle of medicine?'

'No, but of course she may have forgotten. Remember no one appreciated the potential significance of details like that at the time, because they all assumed Mrs Ripley had died of natural causes.'

'Look out,' Mo said. 'Something's fallen out of your notebook.'

Fran bent to retrieve the sheet of paper. 'It's nothing much,' she said, glancing at it. 'Just a few points I jotted down last Saturday evening when I tried to undertake a review of the evidence. A lot of good that did. I never even noticed the point about the medicine.'

'Better look through them again now, in case anything else ties the doctor in,' Mo suggested.

'Very well then.' Fran shoved another log on to the fire, then resumed her place in the armchair and began to read from her sheet of paper. *'Mr Vardy disliked Reverend Pinder so much that he had a different clergyman conduct his funeral.'*

'I don't see there's anything much in that,' Mo said. 'Move on.'

'Miss Rose says things in such a way that she misleads people without actually lying to them.'

'The diplomatic lie. Well, we all do that.' Mo affected a regretful tone. 'So-o-o-o sorry I can't make it, darling, but I have something else on.'

'Doctor Owen was not at the football match on Saturday afternoon.'

'We're still no wiser on that score, though we suspect he was bashing that poor old chap over the head.'

'Mrs Smith claimed that she tried to call on Mrs Ripley during her last illness, but Mrs Ripley wasn't well enough to see her.'

'That's the diplomatic lie again, surely? Mrs Ripley wouldn't have wanted to see Mrs Smith because the woman's such a frightful idiot. What's odd about that?'

'Only that no one else mentioned her calling.'

'Probably thought it didn't matter. You and Tom were only asking about people who actually got into the sick room, where they would have had a chance to get at Mrs Ripley's food and medicine. Mrs Smith didn't gain access to the house, so that puts her out of it completely.'

'Oh my goodness,' Fran repeated. She reached for her notebook again and began to rifle through it.

'Darling, whatever is the matter? You look as though you've seen a ghost and it's still almost a week to Hallowe'en.'

'Here it is.' Fran was as breathless as if she'd been running a race. *'Mrs Smith told us that when her brother was busy she used to help him out by answering the telephone and that sort of thing, and also that she had even helped out in the dispensary on a few occasions when he was very tied up.* We know that Doctor Owen was extremely busy on the first day of Mrs Ripley's illness and also on the day that Mrs Ripley died. He told us his sister dropped off the first lot of medicine for him. Suppose it was Mrs Smith, rather than her brother, who dispensed the second lot of medicine and took it round to the house?'

'But hold on—' Mo began.

Fran had sprung to her feet again. 'I'm just fetching my address book,' she said. 'I need to make a couple of urgent telephone calls.'

THIRTY-SIX

'Hello? Is that Tom? Mrs Dod? Oh, I see, well, I'm so sorry to trouble you at such a late hour, but I wonder if I might speak with Tom . . . Yes, that's right. It's Frances Black here.'

At that moment it no longer seemed to matter what the woman with the pleasant voice at the other end of the telephone line might think about a female friend of her husband telephoning so late. Fran was far too excited and full of news to consider the risk that Veronica Dod might be the sort of spiteful woman who would tip off the King's Proctor to the effect that would-be divorcee Mrs Frances Black was having frequent telephone conversations with a man friend.

She waited for a moment or two while Veronica fetched her husband. She could hear very faint music in the background – presumably a wireless or a gramophone record – and then Tom's voice came on the line.

'Hello? Fran? Is everything all right?'

'Yes, it's me. Sorry to ring so late, but I think we may have solved the case.'

'We?'

'Mo and I. We've been through the evidence and tied up one or two loose ends, and we're pretty convinced we've got the solution.'

'Well, come on then, don't keep a fellow in suspense.'

'It's Dulcie Smith,' Fran said. 'Aunt Hetty's instincts were right all along.'

'But I thought we agreed that Mrs Smith didn't have access to Mrs Ripley, which ruled her out completely?'

'She didn't need to have direct access to Mrs Ripley. She only needed access to the medicine. Don't you remember how she told us that she occasionally helped with dispensing when her brother was busy? When Doctor Owen initially visited Mrs Ripley, he only prescribed enough medicine for twelve doses, so on his third visit, knowing that Mrs Ripley would run out after her breakfast dose the next day, he must have asked his sister to make up a bottle of rhubarb and whatever it was and drop it in. He did mention that he had prescribed a second dose, but he didn't think to mention that his sister had been the one who made it up and dropped it in, because that was a fairly routine occurrence whenever he had a lot of work on.'

'And no one in the Ripley household remembered that Mrs Smith had called,' Tom said.

'Actually,' Fran said, 'someone did. We just didn't ask the right person. I telephoned them tonight and spoke to Mademoiselle Bertillon. I explained our thinking and she went round to ask the one person who was at the house that day who we didn't bother to interview.'

'What? Who on earth . . .?'

'Binks,' Fran said triumphantly. 'Binks was working out in the garden as usual when Mrs Smith arrived and he distinctly remembers her calling him across to the garden gate, handing the bottle to him, and asking him to take it into the house. He in turn handed it over to Martha at the kitchen door and Martha took it straight upstairs, where Mrs Ripley told her to put it into the cupboard where the medicines were always kept. In all the excitement that followed, Martha had completely forgotten the transaction – but even if she had remembered, she probably wouldn't have thought anything of it.'

'Crumbs!' said Tom. 'It feels as if it was done under our very noses without us noticing.'

'When I explained the situation to Mademoiselle Bertillon, she put on her hat and coat and went straight round to Mr Binks's cottage, and she was back to me within half an hour, confirming what Binks and Martha had said. Mademoiselle also volunteered the information that while she couldn't remember when the first bottle of medicine ran out, she did remember that when she and Martha were clearing out the medicine cabinet, about a week after Mrs Ripley had died, she particularly noticed that the bottle of medicine prescribed by Doctor Owen was virtually full, because Martha commented on it and said rather sadly that the medicine had not done Mrs Ripley any good.'

'This is absolutely amazing,' Tom said. 'And I suspect there is more to come.'

'There is. It was mostly Mo who worked out the truth about the medicine,' Fran said modestly. 'But when we looked at some of the questions that had struck me during a previous review of the evidence, a few other things jumped out. Do you remember Miss Rose explaining how at the bank she used to phrase things so that she did not actually tell lies and yet managed to conceal the truth? Well, Mrs Smith does the same thing. Remember the eighth commandment? "Thou shalt not bear false witness".'

'There's also a commandment "Thou shalt not kill",' Tom pointed out.

'Mo and I reckon that Dulcie Smith is so dotty that she doesn't realize that what she is doing is wrong. At some stage she became so brainwashed about what she perceives as Reverend Pinder's mission that she imagines she is furthering God's work by smiting the people who are standing against the vicar. Remember the way she claimed that Mr Vardy and Miss Tilling had not died by accident, but by the Lord's hand? And also that she was always out doing the Lord's work?'

'I do,' Tom admitted. 'But there's still a lot here that doesn't fit.'

'Bear with me. The first death was Mr Vardy. Mrs Smith sat in her drawing room and described his death to us just as if she had been a witness to it. "He walked too close to the edge of the pond, slipped in the mud and fell in." I'm pretty sure those were her exact words.'

'Well, anyone might have surmised as much.' Tom's tone was doubtful.

'But when you are surmising, you say things like "I suppose" or "I expect". Mrs Smith spoke as if she knew. She said that his heavy coat and working boots hampered him from getting out of the water. How did Mrs Smith know he was still wearing his working boots?'

'Perhaps her brother mentioned it to her, after he'd been called in to look at the body.'

'*Unless you were standing in the lane, you couldn't hear him shout.* That's what Mrs Smith said, but how did she know he shouted out if no one could hear him unless they were standing in the lane? As she herself pointed out, no one heard anything at the Bird in Hand beerhouse.'

'I see what you're getting at, but how on earth can you prove that Mrs Smith was standing in the lane? In fact, why on earth would she be standing in the lane?'

'Mademoiselle Bertillon isn't the only person I've spoken with this evening. You remember the Brayshaws mentioned that their old vicar came back to take Mr Vardy's funeral service? Well, at one point I commented that Mr Vardy must have really loathed Reverend Pinder if he arranged for another clergyman to take his funeral service, but Mo laughed and pointed out that most people don't get to organize their own funeral and, anyway, although Mr Vardy had been cross about a lot of the things Reverend Pinder was doing, he'd still been taking communion from him – which set me wondering why his funeral service was taken by someone else. I couldn't ring Reverend Pinder himself, because there is no telephone at the vicarage, but I rang your Aunt Hetty instead and luckily she knew the answer.'

'Which is?'

'Reverend Pinder was on his annual holiday when Mr Vardy was buried, so naturally it was necessary to call in someone else.'

'And Mr Vardy would have been buried within a few days of his death . . .' Tom prompted.

'Precisely. Reverend Pinder was away from the parish for Mr Vardy's funeral *and* when he died. It's our own fault again, I'm afraid, for not asking the right questions. If we'd asked the vicar what he remembered about Mr Vardy's death, he would have told us that he wasn't around when it happened. But instead, we asked him whether he agreed with Dulcie Smith that the deaths were all part of a pattern.'

'So what about Saul, the dog?'

'According to Aunt Hetty, whenever Reverend Pinder goes away, his dog is looked after by Mrs Smith.'

'Crumbs,' Tom said.

'Mo and I think that what happened, broadly speaking, is that Mrs Smith was looking after the dog and took it for its last walk of the day, along the lane where the beerhouse is. Mr Vardy happened to leave the Bird in Hand beerhouse just as she was passing, and of course he recognized the dog and said hello to it. Mrs Smith probably continued a few yards further up the lane and then turned back for home – by which time Mr Vardy would have been walking, perhaps a little bit unsteadily, a few yards ahead of her. He would have turned off into the field, climbed over the same stile that we did, and walked towards the pond. Perhaps Mrs Smith paused to watch him crossing the field, or maybe the dog stopped to sniff something in the hedge, or perhaps Mr Vardy fell in at just the moment she was passing the stile, and his shouts and splashing alerted her that something was happening. But anyway, one way or another Mrs Smith became aware of the accident from the lane.

'Remember that she was full of condemnation for this man. He had been drinking and he'd stood up against the vicar, and been generally behaving badly so far as she was concerned. So instead of doing anything to fetch help, she stood and watched him drown, believing that it was no accident and that God wanted him to die.'

'That's a rather chilling picture you paint,' Tom said. 'But having seen and heard Mrs Smith, I have to admit that I can see it happening just as you say.'

'We think that while she wouldn't have wanted to broadcast to the world that she had stood by and watched Mr Vardy drown when she might easily have tried to get help, at the same time she regarded it as the Lord's work. She may even have believed that being in the right place to witness Mr Vardy's death was some sort of sign.'

'A sign that this was the kind of thing which ought to be happening to anyone who stood in the vicar's way,' Tom said.

'Exactly. Then there's Miss Tilling. In a way, we managed to ask the wrong question about her too.'

'Go on,' said Tom.

'As I said before, Mrs Smith tends to answer questions truthfully, so when we asked her whether she had seen anyone *going in* to Miss Tilling's house, she told us she hadn't. However, if we'd asked her whether she saw anyone *coming out* of the house that afternoon, she might have had much more of a struggle with her conscience.'

'Spit it out,' Tom said. 'I'm afraid you're far too clever for me this evening.'

'From where she was sitting, nosing out of the window as usual, Dulcie Smith would have seen first Clara, the cook, going out of the gate on her half-day, and then a little bit later she would have seen Alice, the maid, going off with a parcel under her arm. At that point she would have known that Miss Tilling was alone in the house, which offered a small interval for some mischief.

'We know that Miss Tilling would have let Mrs Smith in, and we can surmise that Mrs Smith would have been a prime candidate to take an interest in Miss Tilling's father's religious library. As they started going back downstairs, she could easily have used the figure from the shelf as a cosh, then sent the rest of the china raining down on top of poor Miss Tilling as she lay at the bottom of the stairs. After that, all she had to do was let herself out of the front door and pop back across the road.'

'And when the police asked a question implying that she had spent the entire afternoon goosegogging out of the window, she told them that, on the contrary, she had been out doing the Lord's work when Miss Tilling died,' Tom finished for her. 'Which seen through her lunatic's blinkers was no more than the truth. You have the method for Mrs Ripley's murder sorted out – and as for the attack on Mr Hargreaves, she must have sneaked through his cottage and out into his garden on her way either to or from handing out hymn books at the wedding. The question is, how do we prove all this?'

'Mo and I have a theory about that, too,' Fran said.

THIRTY-SEVEN

'I can't believe so much has happened in just a fortnight,' Mo said. 'I suppose you saw the papers this morning? It was all over the front pages about Horace Ripley's release. "Dramatic new evidence", the police superintendent said. Not a word about you, me or Tom, of course. Still, at least Mr Ripley has sent you this hamper from Fortnum and Mason. Jolly small price to pay for getting off the hook. How long have you had that bottle of champagne chilling?'

'It's been standing in a bucket of water outside the kitchen door for absolutely ages. I'll go and get it in a minute.'

'Very sporting of Tom to tell old Ripley to send it up here.'

'Tom said you and I deserve all the credit, but of course he did a lot of the spadework. And if his father hadn't turned out to know someone who is a friend of the chief constable of Nottinghamshire, it might have been a lot harder to persuade the police to listen to us.'

'The thing that I still can't get over,' Mo went on, 'is how well your idea about Mrs Smith worked. Who would have imagined that all one would have to do would be to get Reverend Pinder to go along with a senior policeman and simply ask her to tell the whole truth about what she had been up to? The woman must be an utter fruitcake.'

'I don't think there's any doubt about that.'

'And the doctor brother didn't have a clue about it? Of course, we never did find out what he was up to when he was supposed to have been at the football match.'

'Oh, but Tom did,' Fran said quickly. 'As you know, Tom went down to talk with the chief constable personally and he was there at the police station when they brought Dulcie Smith in.'

'Goodness! What sort of state was she in?'

'Strangely serene, Tom said. Still convinced that what she had done was not wrong, I suppose. There will never be a trial. She will have to be put away somewhere.'

'But what about Doctor Owen and the football match?'

'I was getting to that. Doctor Owen had come with his sister to the police station, and after she had been taken off by one of those police matrons, Tom went over and commiserated with him. Apparently, Owen feels terribly responsible for not really noticing that his sister was getting odder and odder. He confided in Tom that he has been very preoccupied lately. You see, he has met someone and fallen in love with her, but the lady in question is not only much younger than him but is also a Unitarian, so he felt sure that his sister, with her strong religious convictions, would be implacably opposed to their marrying. The fact that his sister had made her home with him for the best part of ten years was obviously an added complication. For weeks now, Doctor Owen has been pretending to attend various sporting fixtures every Saturday, when in reality he has been gallivanting about with his lady love. He didn't want to tell us where he had been – not because he had been up to no good, but because he was worried about his sister finding out what he had been up to before he'd figured out a way of telling her about this woman himself.'

'Aren't families a menace?' asked Mo. 'Terence has written asking me to go out and stay with him again, and his mother is pestering me to agree. She knows that Terence and I are perfectly happy with arrangements as they are and don't really crave each other's company, but she suggests I go for a short stay, just for form's sake.'

'You would enjoy the voyage,' Fran ventured. 'Getting away for part of the winter would be nice.'

'Oh, good heavens, don't you start! I've already had the conversation about sea air being so terribly good for one and the delights of strolling along the promenade deck under the tropical stars.'

'There is always bridge and dancing and deck tennis,' Fran said mischievously.

'And often a lot of frightfully boring people who want to tell you their life story over dinner every night. Of course,' Mo brightened slightly, 'there are usually some splendid young officers, too.'

'By the way,' said Fran, 'there's more news from Durley Dean about Reverend Pinder. According to Aunt Hetty, the bishop has

been belatedly enquiring into the problems within Reverend
Pinder's flock and rumour has it that, although the vicar cannot
possibly be blamed for the dreadful things which have happened,
in the opinion of the archdeacon the situation has not been handled
terribly well. It has therefore been decided that in the best interests of all concerned Reverend Pinder will be moving to another
parish very soon.'

'Let's hope they will appoint a man who can heal the
divisions,' Mo said.

'I went to church myself last Sunday,' Fran said. 'It was a special
service for All Souls' Day. I felt much better afterwards.'

'Better about what?'

'About what had happened in Durley Dean. The thought of
all that hurt and upset being caused in the name of the Church
had unsettled me, I suppose.'

She did not add that it was not only the events at Durley Dean
that had upset and unsettled her. Tom had come up for a sort of
celebratory lunch on the day after Dulcie Smith's arrest and she
had told him of her decision regarding the divorce and explained
that, as a consequence, she would no longer be able to see him,
just in case someone snitched to the King's Proctor about their
friendship and it was assumed that they were having an affair.
His face had clouded immediately and he had been silent for a
while.

'I'm most terribly sorry,' she had said. 'You know that I enjoy
your company tremendously, but one simply cannot afford to
jeopardize the proceedings. You only get one go at this, and if I
put a foot wrong I will be shackled to Michael for the rest of
my life.'

'Of course, of course. I completely understand – and for what
it's worth, I think it's very brave of you and absolutely the right
thing to do in the circumstances.'

'Thank you.' Her voice had almost broken as she said it. 'I
knew you would understand.'

'I shall miss seeing you, that goes without saying. We've had
a lot of fun these past few months, but what you say is absolutely
right and one must take it on the chin.'

They had said no more about it just then, but later he had
driven her back to Bee Hive Cottage and, starting as she knew

they must continue, she had not invited him inside, but instead said goodbye and thanked him for lunch as they sat in the car. After that, he had come round to her side of the car to hold the door open for her, and just as she had her hand on the garden gate he had said, 'You do know that if things had been different, I would have asked you to marry me once you are free?'

She had only been able to nod, and all but stumble up the path before standing on the step and waving him away blindly, determined not to reach for her handkerchief until he had gone out of sight.

Mo brought her back to the present, saying, almost as if she had read Fran's thoughts, 'You know, I don't think we ought to drink that champagne after all. Let's just have our usual Martinis, and save the champagne until Tom can share it too. After all, it was his investigation, not mine.'

'Thanks to my forthcoming divorce proceedings, I may not be seeing Tom for a very long time. Perhaps never, in fact.'

'Rubbish,' said Mo. 'I bet he manages to think up some excuse to contact you within the week.'

'I told you,' Fran said, 'any contact with Tom is too risky. We have both agreed to suspend all communications.'

All the same, she went to the back door, fished out the champagne – which felt icy to the touch after spending the better part of a November day out of doors – dried off the bottle and put it at the back of the pantry, before mixing their usual Martinis.

THIRTY-EIGHT

11 November 1929

My dear Fran,

Mindful of your instructions, I have not telephoned you, just in case the evil King's Proctor is already listening in on your telephone line, though this seems unlikely as your petition is still in the preliminary stages. You will note that I have also taken the precaution of marking the envelope PRIVATE, *in case the KP is in league with the local post-master. However, just to be on the safe side, I suggest that you burn this letter when you have read it, in order to prevent it falling into the wrong hands.*

I am breaching your embargo on communication between us because word of your cleverness over the Durley Dean case has come to the ears of a family in Devon via the Chief Constable of Nottinghamshire, and the family are desirous of our services in connection with another mystery.

It is no use my attempting to take on an investigation alone – you and Mo really must take all the credit for the Durley Dean affair, I was nowhere near reaching the correct solution. If you can think of any way at all in which we might be able to work on another case without jeopardizing your situation, please write to me and let me know. If you put your answer into a postbox under cover of darkness, I am sure you will get away with sending me just one letter. Once I have read the contents, I will, if necessary, eat the whole thing, envelope, stamp and all, in order to protect your reputation.

Yours sincerely,
Tom

Mo must have second sight, thought Fran. It had only taken three days for her to be proved right. She read the letter through again then carried it across to the fireplace, where she hesitated before the flames. From her position on the chair nearest the fire, Mrs Snegglington exhibited mild curiosity as Fran turned abruptly on her heel, fetched her correspondence box from the room across the passage, where there was no fire to take the chill off the room, and sat down to write a reply.